VISIONS OF THE DEAD
A ZOMBIE STORY

OTHER LIVING DEAD PRESS BOOKS

MONSTER PARTY
THE TURNING: A STORY OF THE LIVING DEAD
THE DEAD OF SPACE BOOK 1 AND 2
PLAYING GOD: A ZOMBIE NOVEL * THE JUNKYARD
PLANET OF THE DEAD * THE HAUNTED THEATRE
ZOMBIES IN OUR HOMETOWN
NIGHT OF THE WOLF: A WEREWOLF ANTHOLOGY
JUST BEFORE NIGHT: A ZOMBIE ANTHOLOGY
THE BOOK OF HORROR* KNIGHT SYNDROME
THE WAR AGAINST THEM: A ZOMBIE NOVEL
CHILDREN OF THE VOID * DARK DREAMS
BLOOD RAGE & DEAD RAGE (BOOK 1& 2 OF THE RAGE VIRUS SERIES)
DEAD MOURNING: A ZOMBIE HORROR STORY
BOOK OF THE DEAD: A ZOMBIE ANTHOLOGY VOLUME 1-6
LOVE IS DEAD: A ZOMBIE ANTHOLOGY
ETERNAL NIGHT: A VAMPIRE ANTHOLOGY
END OF DAYS: AN APOCALYPTIC ANTHOLOGY VOLUME 1-5
DEAD HOUSE: A ZOMBIE GHOST STORY
THE ZOMBIE IN THE BASEMENT (FOR ALL AGES)
THE LAZARUS CULTURE: A ZOMBIE NOVEL
DEAD WORLDS: UNDEAD STORIES VOLUMES 1-7
FAMILY OF THE DEAD, REVOLUTION OF THE DEAD
RANDY AND WALTER: PORTRAIT OF TWO KILLERS
KINGDOM OF THE DEAD * DEAD HISTORY
THE MONSTER UNDER THE BED * DEAD THINGS
DEAD TALES: SHORT STORIES TO DIE FOR
ROAD KILL: A ZOMBIE TALE * DEADFREEZE * DEADFALL
SOUL EATER * THE DARK * RISE OF THE DEAD
DEAD END: A ZOMBIE NOVEL * MISADVENTURES OF THE DEAD
THE CHRONICLES OF JACK PRIMUS
INSIDE THE PERIMETER: SCAVENGERS OF THE DEAD
BOOK OF CANNIBALS VOLUME 2 * CHRISTMAS IS DEAD…AGAIN
EMAILS OF THE DEAD * CHILDREN OF THE DEAD
REVIEWS OF THE DEAD
THE GORE SCORE VOLUME 1
ZOMBIE EROTIC
SEX IN THE TIME OF ZOMBIES

THE DEADWATER SERIES

DEADWATER * DEADWATER: Expanded Edition
DEADRAIN * DEADCITY * DEADWAVE * DEAD HARVEST
DEAD UNION * DEAD VALLEY * DEAD TOWN * DEAD GRAVE
DEAD SALVATION * DEAD ARMY (Deadwater series book 10)

VISIONS OF THE DEAD
A ZOMBIE STORY

JOSEPH GIANGREGORIO
ANTHONY GIANGREGORIO

ACKNOWLEGEMENTS

First and foremost, I would like to thank my father, because without him, this book wouldn't be as great as it is now. I would also like to thank my Mom, who has supported me throughout the process of writing this book.

And last but not least, I would like to thank some of my friends who have supported me and were thrilled that I was writing my first book.

J.A.G.

* * *

Visit Anthony Giangregorio's website at www.undeadpress.com

Chapter 1

Present Day (Halloween 2009)

"Dammit, we're surrounded!" Jake Roberts yelled while he and his friend, Bill Monroe, were being forced back by hordes of bloodthirsty zombies. The hatchback they were riding in up to five minutes ago was now wrecked and useless two blocks behind them, the two men ending up on foot.

And that was never a good thing in a world where the dead walked and were everywhere, waiting to attack and feed on you.

The only thing Jake had to defend himself with was his two katanas, which had always saved his butt since the zombie outbreak began. Despite the present fate of the world, filled with loss and despair, Jake still had hope.

He was still filled with the hope and determination that his fiancée, Melissa, was still alive somewhere out there and he would search every inch of the country until he found her again. These were the things he held onto, the reasons he got up every morning.

Glancing over his shoulder, he could still see the large smoke cloud drifting into the sky where the pillars of gray and black were tugged apart by the wind. The fire and carnage that created the smoke had taken everything he had left in this slowly dying world. A massive funeral pyre of his former life.

At the moment, all he had left of his past was Bill Monroe.

And the only thing Bill had left in this dead world was his M-16, the clothes on his back, and Jake.

Jake slashed his katanas from side to side, the blades spinning so fast they could barely be seen as he chopped off head after decayed head. Many of the heads began to bounce about as the ghouls caught them and tossed them away. It got so bad it started to look like a concert with one to many beach balls blown up.

With gritted teeth, Bill was riddling the ghouls with holes, the corpses dancing a jig of death as pieces of flesh were shot away to slap the ground.

Even though he was battling for his life, Jake couldn't help but remember how they had ended up in this terrible situation, and he wondered if this would be the day he died, and out of all the days for it to happen, Halloween, his favorite day of the year.

He had lost everyone he had ever known or loved. His brother, mother, father, and all his friends except for Bill had been taken by the zombies he called pusbags thanks to the damn bacteria from the garbage plant all those years ago.

"Pull it together, Jake, or we're done for!" Bill yelled, shoving the barrel of his M-16 into the mouth of a ghoul and firing. A large hole appeared at the top of the ghoul's head, brain matter spraying everywhere as pieces of bone flew off to strike other bodies like shrapnel.

Jake snapped out of it and continued to fight on, slicing through another head, just like he had done, time and time before.

Weird, he thought, all this started over contaminated vegetables, tomatoes mostly, but as soon as he thought this, a couple of female ghouls flanked him from behind. His peripheral vision picked them up and he realized they were both not bad looking in an undead kind of way. Even though half their faces were missing, which looked like someone had taken an electric sander and shaved their skin to the bone, their bodies were still intact. One full-sized breast was showing on one of the dead women, the brown nipple standing at attention in death. Both female ghouls were wearing cocktail dresses for going out on the town. Jake thought they looked sexy, the dresses showing too much leg.

"Damn it, I always hate to do this when they're kind of cute," he said while slicing his katana through one of the necks, blood dripping out of the jagged hole, and then slicing the other dead woman in half. To make sure the ghoul that was cut in half was truly dead, he jammed his katana through her left eye, blood and brains geysering out of the small hole as the tip of the blade appeared out of the rear of her skull.

"We can't fight them forever, Jake!" Bill called. "I'm running low on ammo, we need to get out of here," he said while trying to survive the mosh pit of zombies he was in.

"I know, I'm thinking about it!" Jake yelled

"Then think faster!" Bill screamed, slapping in a fresh magazine. That was the second to last one left.

Jake was now looking around desperately, and out of pure luck he saw an electrical post with a four foot wide platform near the top, and an idea came to him. This might be the chance he and Bill were looking for. If they could get up the pole, they could take a breather. Years ago, electrical posts had platforms added because a hapless worker on the job had lost his life.

"Bill, up there! We can go up that electrical post!" Jake called, gesturing with the bloody tip of one of his katanas after slicing through another zombie's head.

"You're a genius," Bill laughed, then sprayed four ghouls with hot lead before they could reach him. As their bodies fell to the ground, there was an opening in the crowd.

"I made an opening, run for it!" Bill yelled, charging through the opening and shouldering ghouls out of the way like he was a linebacker for the Patriots.

Jake also saw the opening and he followed, not taking any chances when battling hordes of rotting ghouls. When they were running past them, trying to get to the post, Jake was cutting heads in half, slicing one zombie's head clean off at the mouth, and if it had been seen from overhead, a viewer would have witnessed the bottom of the brain just pour out of the severed head when the ghoul dropped to the ground.

Bill was also shooting heads, and when he hit his targets, the zombies' heads would usually snap back from the impacts, their skulls exploding like a frog with a firecracker shoved up its ass.

Finally, they got to the electrical post, so Jake put his two katanas back in their sheaths, cringing at the gore that would now become lodged inside, and began climbing.

Bill swung his rifle over his shoulder by the strap and began climbing as well, both moving as if their life depended on it, and it did. As soon as they got to the top, they slumped to the platform, exhausted. Their limbs felt like lead weights, the battle taking its toll on their bodies. Both men were covered in gore and Bill moaned as he tried to move away from the edge, not wanting to roll off.

If he had the energy he would have called out, "I've fallen and I can't get up," remembering that old commercial, but Jake wouldn't understand and no one else alive was in earshot to hear him.

Jake was exhausted, too, and as he sucked in another heavy breath, the memories of when the world died began to filter back to him all at once.

Three months ago (July, 3, 2009)

"Hey, old timer, stop daydreaming, and start helping me load these tomato boxes into the truck," Jake said while whipping a tomato at his friend's head. "I want to get on the road so I'll be home on time tomorrow for my family's annual cookout."

"Ah! Dammit, knock it off, Jake, that could have hit my eye. And I keep telling you, I'm Bill, not *old timer*. And another thing, don't waste tomatoes," he said while picking up the tomato and putting it back into one of the boxes after inspecting it to make sure it was still okay. Other than a small dent, it was fine.

"What the hell were you looking at that was so interesting any-way?" Jake asked while walking towards Bill.

"I was just looking at the abandoned garbage plant over there, and I still wonder why they put a tomato farm next to it," he said with a disgusted look on his face.

"Why'd you just say that with that look?" Jake inquired.

"You see, son, forty years ago that same garbage plant outside this city of Pittsfield, Mass., was the biggest thing that ever hit this town since sliced bread. This plant brought in new people from all over New England and that's where mostly everybody worked, even me, back when I was still young. I was twenty and my best friends, Peter and Fred, worked there with me. But one day some-thing terrible happened that reeked havoc on our little town." He paused for a little bit.

"Well, what the hell was it?" Jake asked trying to get an answer out of Bill.

"You see, there were these scientists stationed at the plant. They had this idea about some kind of chemical or bacteria that would eat at the garbage, but nobody had ever heard about it before, it was totally experimental. So, one day a scientist got a little too careless and dropped one of the containers that held the bacteria or whatever. At least that's what I heard. The stuff got out and he breathed it in or got it on his skin or something like that. So he screamed for help and the people around him did try to help him, but it was too late, they said he turned into a zombie, of all things."

"A *zombie*, seriously? What a load of bullshit. Look, old timer, if you think I'm so young as to actually believe what you're..."

Bill shoved his hand in Jake's face, stopping the young man from finishing so he could continue the story.

"So, anyways," Bill said, "the scientist went crazy and he ended up attacking Peter's father who worked there too. The guy ripped his throat out with his teeth, it was unbelievable. And then get this, Peter's dad came back from the dead, he actually opened his eyes and began running around, though half his throat was torn out. They had to shoot him and the scientist when they found out they couldn't save them, so they shot 'em in the head, which is the only way to kill a zombie, you know, by killing the brain. Then they decided to terminate the project. Everybody was saying someone dumped the bacteria into the town's water supply, but that was proven incorrect. Peter was never the same after that. After the funeral he moved out of state and though I tried to stay in touch, he never replied to my letters. In fact, your grandfather, Fred Roberts, was actually the one who killed the scientist and Peter's dad. Then he filled me in on everything later that night over a few shots of whiskey, he was pretty shaken up, I tell you."

"Wow! Great story, I almost believed you there for a second. So if you're done with your trip down memory lane, could we finish getting these boxes into the truck so we can get to Boston 'cause I want to get home for the Fourth of July. And another thing, my grandfather never killed anybody when he was young because my dad would've told me about it, so I'm gonna forget you said that right now."

"Hey, the story was all true," Bill said with a nasty tone that could make anyone cringe.

"Hey, aren't you assholes out of here yet!" came a deep voice from across the lot. Both Jake and Bill turned to see the foreman heading towards them.

"Oh, great, not this guy," Jake breathed.

"You," the foreman said to Bill. "Are you finished loading those tomatoes or what? I swear, you're so damn slow. Shit, I could get three men younger than you in here for what I'm paying you."

"Hey," Jake said, "leave the old guy alone."

The foreman turned to Jake. "Oh, you want some, too? Fine, tell you what, you're on my shit list, too, just for sticking up for this old fart. Now both of you, get going, if these tomatoes aren't delivered on time then don't bother coming back 'cause you're both fired!" Without waiting for a reply, he spun and left.

Bill's face was a mask of dejection as he watched the foreman moving away. Jake felt for the old guy and he walked up next to him, placing a consoling hand on his shoulder.

"That guy is such a tool, don't let him bother you. You know what, Bill? How 'bout we stop at Burger King on the way back, my treat."

"Fine, but I'm driving," Bill said, trying to feel a little more joyful about the situation and his tenuous job.

"Fair enough," Jake said as he moved around the side of the truck and tossed in the last few boxes.

"Don't forget to lock the tailgate," Bill said from inside of the cab.

"I did, I'm not stupid," Jake said, hopping into the passenger seat.

But what he didn't realize was that though he did lock it, it wasn't latched properly.

Five minutes later, they were driving away from the tomato farm and out to the road. The reservoir, connected by a river, ran through the town parallel to the road Bill and Jake were on.

First, they went to Burger King, and after filling up on carbs, fries, and diet Cokes, they continued on to the Mass Turnpike leading to Boston.

The road meandered along the reservoir. The tree branches bent overhead like they were going through a tunnel, the sun high in the sky.

While the two men were occupied chatting inside the cab, Jake, who was in the passenger's seat, was yelling about something to Bill and the older man yelled back, for the moment not watching the road.

At that precise moment a little rabbit came up from its burrow to greet the day. To get the food he needed for his family, he had to cross the road. As soon as the rabbit hopped out into the middle of the asphalt, he was startled by the screeching of tires, and that was when he decided to run back to his burrow. After a couple of minutes, he peeked out to see a truck on the side of the road, the front left tire touching the river's edge, and he saw tomatoes scattered everywhere, the tailgate down which had allowed the boxes to spill out. They were in the river and on the ground, little red orbs coloring the green grass scarlet.

"What the hell, Bill, you should've ran that rabbit's furry ass over. Now we're in the damn river," Jake snapped while looking out his window to see their shipment scattered everywhere.

"Damn, my head, I whacked it on the steering wheel," Bill said while rubbing the bump on his forehead. "Okay, don't get nervous, we can fix this. You go outside and try to salvage as many tomatoes as you can while I back up the truck," Bill told him while he put the truck in gear. "If we can't get enough salvaged then we're both gonna need to find new jobs tomorrow."

"Okay, fine, but don't take too long, I'm gonna need your help, too," Jake said as he slid out of the cab and into the ankle high grass. Jake went to the rear tires and removed any boxes that had fallen near them out of the way, then he waved to Bill, letting him know it was clear to try and back up

After several minutes of tires spinning, flying grass and mud, the truck was finally out of the river's edge and back on the pavement. As soon as Bill got the truck out, Jake finished collecting the tomatoes, most of them coming from the river where a few boxes had fallen in. The boxes were wasted, wet and soggy, but the tomatoes were fine. He made a small pile on the edge of the road while Bill was freeing the truck.

"Wow! That was fast. You're done collecting them already?" Bill asked in a surprised tone.

"Bill, it's been like a half an hour of you trying to back the truck up, yeah, I'm finished."

"Oh, okay, then let's start loading them back up so we can get going again," Bill said. "We're already running behind schedule."

When all the tomatoes were loaded again, dozens now without boxes, they were finally ready to get back on the road.

As they both hopped into the front cab, Jake decided to ask Bill a question about his story from earlier that day.

"Hey, Bill, do you think scientists could have dumped the bacteria into the river or the lake? You know, like they were trying to get rid of the evidence or something?"

"No, I don't think so. I think they took the stuff back with them to where ever the hell they came from, and hopefully they disposed of it properly or put it in a freezer or something. Hell, I don't know, Jake, I'm not a goddamn scientist. And another thing, I thought you locked the tailgate properly," Bill said, while getting comfortable behind the wheel.

"I did, it must've come loose somehow," Jake said, closing his door.

With both of them in the truck and the engine running, they were off.

However, there was some truth behind Bill's story.

What Bill could have never known was that though the scientists didn't put the bacteria in the town's reservoir, they couldn't take it back with them as it was an *off the books* experiment.

So they decided to dump the bacteria into the river of the town instead. The scientists thought the running water would dilute it to the point it would be harmless, but they were wrong, dead wrong.

Instead, the bacteria thrived in the water, multiplying exponentially. When the tomatoes, which they were taking to the market, were irrigated, the farmers used the very same water from the lake, which the river had fed for many years. So as the bacteria grew over the countless years, it began to accumulate in the soil of the crops, and then the tomato plants soaked up the water with the bacteria included. For all these years the bacteria was still harmless, the amount so minor to do no harm, but this first new crop of tomatoes had accumulated a deadly dose of the bacteria, so much so that it was deadly to humans.

The only way to kill the bacteria inside the vegetables was to cook them at a high temperature. But if one of the tomatoes infected by the bacteria was consumed raw, then it will take the host anywhere from an hour to minutes to transform into a blood thirsty, ravenous zombie. The time depended on the constitution and size of the host.

And unknown to Jake and Bill, they were bringing the deadly vegetables to market.

Chapter 2

Now

Jake and Bill were just stirring from their restless slumber, hearing the moans and the calls of the undead from below, realizing they had slept for the past four hours or so.

Deciding to stand on shaky legs, Bill wanted to check their surroundings for any vehicles they could steal. That made him snicker. Like there was anyone left who was going to notice them stealing one. Peering over the heads of the ghouls below, there was nothing in sight, except for the hundreds of zombies milling around the utility post. The only other relevant structure was a large building two hundred feet away.

Jake also stood up, wiping sleep from his eyes and immediately felt pressure on his bladder. Great, he needed to use the bathroom really, really bad. It took all of three seconds to decide what to do, as there wasn't much of a choice.

Making sure his katanas were safe, not wanting to knock one off the platform, he unzipped his pants and began to urinate.

"Hey, you like that, you fuckin' pusbags!" he yelled as he urinated on the upturned faces. "Drink up, 'cause this is the only thing you're gonna get out of me!" Jake croaked as he continued to spray the ghouls below. In retrospective, the ghouls didn't seem to mind it, and Jake became more disgusted with them because of it. They showed no emotion, no cries of outrage. They just moaned and wailed the same as ever.

"Jake, stop playing around and look around for a car or something we can use to get out of here," Bill said, still desperately looking for something to drive.

"You're wasting your time, old timer. We're dead whether you like it or not," Jake said, zipping up his pants.

His stomach began growling and he realized he hadn't eaten anything for a little over twelve hours, so if he wanted to survive, he and Bill needed to get off the platform and soon or they would end up joining the decayed carcasses below sooner or later.

But with no plan of escape before him, Jake sat down, staring at the ghouls below.

Nothing happened for the next three hours, no help came, no plan to escape presented itself, and Jake thought to himself that this had to be the end of Jake Roberts.

Bill was sitting on the other side of him, cleaning his M-16 and checking how much ammo he had left.

"Hey, Bill, do you think we'll ever get down from here?" Jake said quietly, his bravado gone.

"Maybe we will, maybe we won't," was all Bill had to say.

"It'll be a miracle if someone came driving by, got surrounded by those pusbags, and while they were gettin' eaten by the hundreds of those fuckers below, we could just take their car, and escape."

"It could happen," Bill remarked as he slapped in the last magazine into his rifle.

But it didn't happen and the next two hours went by slower than the others.

And then over the wails of the undead, came the distinctive sound of an engine, a car engine. Somebody was actually trying to get through the rotting zombies. From his position, Jake could see it looked like an old Honda. There was a woman in the driver's seat, and her car was quickly being surrounded.

At the sound of her car, more than half the ghouls turned and began stumbling towards the vehicle.

"Bill, hey, Bill, look over here, quick! I think our prayers have been answered," Jake said, pointing to the besieged car. Bill spun around to see what Jake was talking about and his jaw dropped.

"Well I'll be damned, that's sure as hell convenient," Bill said upon seeing the car.

Jake shrugged. "Hey, shit happens sometimes, this time it's good for a change, that's all."

Seconds later, the car was completely surrounded by rotting bodies. That was when Jake saw the front windshield shatter, the smash filtering up to him, and he spotted the woman driver being dragged out of her seat by the hundreds of ghouls trying to get at least one piece of her flesh. The woman was kicking and screaming, but there was nobody to help her, expect for Jake and Bill, who were a hundred feet away and trapped themselves.

The ghouls dragging her out of the car were the first to get a few bloody chunks out of her. Her clothes were torn from her body and then dead hands ripped and tore into her mid-section. The ghouls were soon tearing out slimy, stringy intestines and chewing merrily on them. One particular zombie was taking chunks of muscle and skin from the body and throwing the bloody gobbets to the undead crowd behind it. One ghoul ripped out one of the woman's breast implants and started chewing on it. When the ghoul decided it didn't like the taste of silicone, it threw the implant to the ground, spitting silicone out of its mouth.

Miraculously, the woman was still alive, but as she gasped her last breath, one ghoul reached deep into her throat and pulled out her esophagus, then began chewing on it like it was a Twizzler. The woman's ribcage was then cracked wide open and there was nothing left inside, except for her heart, which was soon ripped out as it beat for the last time in the ghoul's pale hand.

Jake and Bill saw all this from afar and Jake looked up to the sky and said, "Thank you, God."

Bill slapped him on the back of the head with his hand and looked down at him like a disappointed father would to his son. He knew it was terrible for another person to die, just so they could save their own asses, but this was the law of the jungle, if somebody had to die so they could live, then so be it. Jake just didn't have to be so happy about it.

But even with the car so close, they were thinking about how they were going to go from where they were to the car which was a hundred feet away. Then Jake smiled widely as an idea came to him.

"I got it, we could climb down, and since the ghouls are so close together, we could run over their heads or on their shoulders as far as we could and then we can just cut and shoot our way through the rest. It's brilliant," he said, his mood turning from grim to joyful.

"Are you kidding me? That's the worst idea I've ever heard," Bill remarked, spitting into the undead crowd below.

"It's the only one we got right now, so let's go for it. If we don't make it, then you can haunt me for all eternity," Jake smirked.

Bill said nothing at first, but as he gazed over to the Honda he saw it was still running. Small puffs of smoke from a worn cylinder were causing the car to burn oil. That meant that sooner or later it would run out of gas and their chance of escape would disappear like the smoke from the exhaust into the wind.

"Fine. If we do die, then I'm gonna haunt your ass good in Hell," Bill said.

Jake strapped his katanas to his back and began to climb down the metal rungs of the pole, with Bill following close behind, his M-16 around his shoulder. When they were at least halfway down, the zombies turned their heads upwards, wanting the two figures coming near them. They shuffled close to the post, so close there was barely enough room to slide a ruler through.

"All right, this is working out better than I expected," Jake said, trying to psych himself up.

"Oh, yeah, this is working out wonderfully," Bill said sarcastically.

When they were almost in reach of the ghouls' gripping hands, he made a leap of faith and began running over the heads of the zombies, Bill doing the same thing, though not with as much dexterity. But this only worked for a good ten feet. Then they ran out of running room and they found themselves six feet off the ground, in mid-air, with both of them about to land on a trio of ghouls each. While Jake was in mid-air, he pulled out his katanas, stretched his arms out – katanas facing down – and forced them into two skulls of the zombies, his katanas going through the heads of the ghouls like a warm knife through butter. Bill was also about to land on a body, but he landed on the walking corpse with such force that all of his body weight caved in the ghoul's ribcage.

"This is it, run!" Jake yelled, dashing to the car as he sliced the head off the last zombie before him. But there were many more behind and they were out for his blood.

As he made his way to the car, Jake started slicing and dicing heads and bodies. Bill heard him and also began running, blowing heads off ghouls that opposed him. Jake was spinning and doing leaps, trying to stay out of reach of pale hands, and Bill was doing the same, albeit more slowly, thanks to his older years.

When the two men were only a few feet away from the idling car, there was a wall of undead bodies blocking them, and with lightning quick reflexes, Jake cut down the ghouls that were in front of them, slicing the zombies in half, dark blood squirting everywhere as he stepped on one of the bottom halves of a bifurcated corpse that was still wallowing on the ground. Bill did the same thing, following closely behind, his M-16 spitting death the entire time.

When they reached the car, they jumped onto the hood, Jake's foot landing on the slaughtered carcass of the dead woman, and leaped through the broken windshield. Bill then leaped in too, the barrel of the M-16 still hot from discharging round after round.

As Jake was squirming to get into the driver's seat, trying to get away, the engine still running, the first couple of ghouls tried to get inside the car. When Bill realized this, he took his rifle and shoved the barrel into the closest one's mouth, putrid skin burning against the hot metal, and pulled the trigger. Bullets demolished the first ghoul's head and then continued into the next zombie, then right into the one behind it. The ghouls fell off the hood, taking a couple of the zombies down with them, as well as the corpse of the woman.

"Great thinking," Jake said, putting the car in drive, with most of the walking corpses down on the ground in front of him. Jake floored the gas pedal and they started moving forward, too slow for his liking.

Moving little by little, inch by inch, the car ran over bodies, the rotting heads, torsos, and legs crushed underneath the weight of the vehicle. When Jake was finally near the end of the crowd of zombies and freedom, he found that the car couldn't move because there were so many ghouls in front of him, they were choking the wheels. He had to think of something or he knew this time it would most definitely be the end of Jake Roberts and Bill Monroe.

Bill glanced into the back seat, seeing if there was anything there he could use to help the situation, and saw a small box with a glass bottle full of liquid and a small cloth sticking out of the top spout.

Immediately he knew what it was. It was a Molotov cocktail and he wondered why the woman hadn't use it when she'd first found herself trapped by the zombies. Without hesitation, he reached over grabbed the bottle and lit the cloth with a cigarette lighter from his pocket.

"Fire in the hole, Jake!" Bill called out as he rolled down his window and forced the bottle out and away from the car as undead hands tried to grab him.

The bottle fell a few feet away, smashing on the pavement, the flammable liquid dousing the closest legs of the ghouls. Dead and decayed from months of walking around as the undead, they went up like matchsticks.

A couple seconds later, all the ghouls in front of them and on the right were immolated in flames and the smell of burnt meat penetrated their olfactory senses to the point Jake was about to throw up. But he kept it down long enough to get through the burnt corpses that were on the ground twitching, and hopefully dead for good.

"Go, Jake! You have your chance!" Bill yelled, slapping the dashboard.

Now free from the crowd of zombies in front of them, their smoking carcasses sizzling in the sun, he began rolling again, the blackened bodies collapsing under the weight of the Honda. In less than a minute they were back on the road and the area was free of walking corpses.

"Jesus Christ, Jake, I can't believe we made it out of there alive," Bill said.

"Huh, never doubted it for a second," Jake laughed, inside himself knowing it was the farthest thing from the truth. There had been a few hairy seconds there when he thought his time was up.

"Well, maybe so, but now that we're free, where should we go?" Bill asked, relieved to be safe once again, at least till the next time.

Jake's stomach rumbled, and he realized now that his adrenalin rush was wearing off, how hungry he was.

He knew he would need to set off for New Hampshire sooner or later in hopes of finding Melissa, but he also knew he wasn't ready yet. There was no way of knowing what dangers were waiting for him along the way.

But they had to go somewhere for now and try to rest up and though he hadn't been there in quite a while, he knew of one familiar place nearby, though up till now he'd had no reason to go there.

If it hadn't been ransacked by looters then it would be as good as any other place to hole up for a day or two. If it was untouched, then he knew there would probably be canned food in the cupboards, so he took a right at the next intersection that would lead him onto Route 1A.

"How about my home?" Jake suggested. "It's only a few miles from here."

Bill nodded and then looked out the window.

As soon as Jake said the word *home*, memories began flooding back to him, to that fateful day months ago, when his family was torn away from him by the initial outbreak.

Chapter 3

(July 4th 2009)

"Mom, Dad, I'm home! Bill just dropped me off in front of the house and he let me take some tomatoes, too," Jake called out, trying to figure out where his parents could be. "Mom, Dad, where are you guys?"

For some reason his parents weren't home which was odd. At this time of day, his father would usually be in the kitchen or doing work on his computer, and mom would be upstairs or in the living room.

"Wait a minute, upstairs, that's where they are," Jake said under his breath while snapping his fingers, wondering why he didn't think of that before.

He put the box of tomatoes on the kitchen table and went up the stairs. The first room he came to was his parents' bedroom and for some reason they weren't there either.

While he was searching through the rest of the floor, he heard a noise coming from the bathroom. Opening the door, he stepped into the bathroom and slid the shower curtains to one side, but no one was there, and that was when his thirteen year old brother Andrew came up from behind him and yelled, "Hi, Jake!"

"Holy shit!" Jake yelled, as he jumped and landed in the bathtub. "You little bastard, what the hell did you do that for? And where's Mom and Dad?"

Andrew furrowed his brow as he gathered his thoughts. "Well, first, they went to the supermarket to get the things for the cookout this afternoon and the second thing is I'm gonna tell them you said, *hell, shit, bastard* and *bitch*," Andrew said, pleased he was getting a rise out of his brother.

"Well then go downstairs and call them and tell them we already have tomatoes and then throw them in the fridge for me, will ya. And I didn't say bitch," Jake said.

"Now you did," Andrew said with a grin and ran off to call their parents. Jake went into his room to take a nap, his younger brother irritating him to the point he wanted to scream.

He shook his head as he thought about Andrew. Even though he had a runt for a brother, he still loved him, though he would never tell him that. Andrew was about to turn fourteen and puberty was hitting him hard.

He was now almost as tall as Jake, who was twenty, thanks to a growth spurt he'd had when Jake left to work in Pittsfield for a few months. His father, Matt Roberts, was a research consultant, so he was always on his computer. He'd just bought himself a fancy new sports car, which his mom said was probably a mid-life crisis thing in his life. His mom, Meg, was a secretary for the CEO of some big company in Boston.

As for Jake, he was just a twenty year old tomato farmer trying to make a living, but he still lived with his parents because houses were just way to expensive these days, and he didn't have anyone he trusted enough to try and get an apartment with. So he kept saving his money until he had enough for a house.

Sure he could have gone to college, even the community one, and tried to become a big shot lawyer or CEO, too, but he wasn't in to that whole suit and tie world. No, he was just a blue color shlub.

While he was thinking about what his future could have been if he'd actually applied himself more, he drifted off to sleep.

An hour later, Jake was startled awake by the doorbell. He lay in bed, waiting for someone to get the door, and when it chimed again he realized he would have to answer it himself. But when he descended the stairs he saw Andrew had beaten him to it.

"Hey, Jake, our grandparents are here and everybody else is just pulling up and Mom and Dad just pulled into the driveway, too!" Andrew yelled, when Jake was obviously right behind him.

"Oh, great," Jake muttered, "now I have to listen to my grandfather try to get me to become a doctor or a lawyer." He and his grandfather didn't really see eye to eye on how Jake wanted his life to go.

"Hey, Jake," his father said as he entered the house with his wife right behind him. "Snap out of it, will ya? Stop daydreaming and help me get these burgers on the grill. Oh, and it looks like your fiancée's here," his father said, trying to make him lend a hand. There was a lot to do and he could use all the help he could get.

"What? Oh, sorry, but I have to go out and see Melissa right now. Get Andrew to help you, please, Dad."

"Let him be, Matt, he's in love," Meg said as she smiled at Jake.

Jake's father merely frowned, but he let Jake be.

Jake's girlfriend, Melissa Jacobs, was the best thing to ever happen to him since learning about sex. She was a year younger than him at nineteen, but the one year difference meant nothing in their relationship.

She had a slender body and curves any man would die to wrap their arms around, with brown hair and big blue eyes that could make any guy melt in seconds. Today was their two year anniversary together, and even after an entire twenty-four months as a couple, he still didn't know how he'd managed to get her to become his girlfriend first and later his fiancée.

In his eyes, she was still way out of his league, but he knew better than to say anything.

So with his parents and grandparents talking happily as they headed out to the backyard, Jake plastered a wide smile on his face and headed out to see Melissa, only now with an extra spring to his step.

The cook-out had been going on for a few hours and everyone was having a blast, talking, eating, and playing games.

"Hey, Meg, we need some more tomatoes cut," Matt said, holding the empty plate in the air.

"Okay, I'll go in right now," Meg said, grabbing the dish and walking into the kitchen.

When she opened the fridge, she saw the box of tomatoes Jake had brought home. Up till now they had been eating tomatoes already in the house, but now she reached and grabbed three of the new ones. Unbeknownst to her, these tomatoes were contaminated with the bacteria from the farm, the same crop that had been delivered to the market and was now on its way to dozens upon dozens of other homes.

Setting them on the counter, she picked up her favorite knife and began cutting them in neat slices. When somebody outside in the yard called out her name, she wasn't paying attention and sliced her finger. Some of the juice of the tomato seeped into the fresh cut, the bacteria immediately beginning to infect her.

"Shit," she snapped upon realizing she'd cut herself, then looked around to make sure no one heard her curse. She took pride in not swearing, even when she was mad, but sometimes she would slip up, such as now.

Matt was entering the kitchen to grab some more bottles of soda when he heard her cry out.

"What happened?" Matt asked as he moved up next to her.

"Nothing, I just cut my finger, that's all."

"Okay, listen, you go into the bathroom and get cleaned up and I'll finish cutting the tomatoes," he said, consoling her. She nodded and after applying a loving kiss to his cheek, she headed off. Unfortunately there was nothing Meg could do to stop the bacteria already flowing through her system, attaching to her blood, no matter how much she cleaned the wound.

While Meg went to get cleaned up, Matt finished slicing the tomatoes. Then he carried the dish outside and the instant he set it down, everyone dug in, laying them on burgers or dropping them onto their salads. The only three people who didn't eat them were Jake, Melissa and Matt, all three disliking the taste of fresh tomatoes.

"Hey, Jake, how come you don't like raw tomatoes? If you don't like 'em raw, then you're not a real Italian," his grandfather said, giving him a hard time.

"I just don't, okay?" Jake remarked. "I just don't like how they taste, but I do like 'em when they're cooked."

That was when his grandfather teased him by putting a tainted, sliced tomato into his mouth for kicks. His grandfather was from his mother's side of the family, and he always liked to tease him. He was always pressuring him to get a well paying job so he could take care of Melissa when they were married.

"Mmmm, that's good," his grandfather said as he swallowed the tomato slice with a wide smile.

A little less than an hour later, just as the cook-out was ending, everybody began to feel a little weird.

"Matt, I think I'm going to go upstairs and lie down," Meg said, feeling feverish.

"You, too? Damn, seems everyone's feeling under the weather," Matt said. "Your father, my brother, his wife and some of our friends," he added, concerned for everyone's welfare. "Maybe some of the meat I got from the supermarket was spoiled or something. Oh, shit, you don't think it could be food poisoning?"

"It's possible, dear. Since everyone's leaving, I'm going to take some aspirin and lie down. Can you clean up without me?" Meg asked.

"Sure, I'm fine, honey, you go rest," Matt said while waving Jake over.

"Yeah, Dad?"

"Jake, your mother's not feeling well and is going to go lie down for bit. Can you take your brother up to his room; he doesn't look good either."

"Sure, Dad, but listen, everyone's left and most of them looked a little pale, do you think it was something they ate? 'Cause you and me seem fine and so did Melissa before she left."

Matt tried to think what he hadn't eaten that the others had, and at least he would have an idea if it was the food, but then what else could it be?

"I don't know, son, but you take your brother upstairs. I'll go turn on the news and see if there's anything on about spoiled meat or something. Hell, maybe it was the lettuce, it happened before," Matt said.

"Okay, Dad," Jake nodded and went to go bring his brother upstairs. Andrew looked so pale it was like his skin had pancake make-up on it, his eyes seeming glazed over like he was drunk.

Jake half-walked, half-carried his brother upstairs and laid him on his bed, then covered him up. Andrew's breathing was labored, a dry wheezing coming from his throat, and Jake couldn't help but get scared. Sure, Andrew was a pain in the ass, but he was blood, family. He may have wished him dead a thousand times but those were just idle thoughts when he was angry. He loved his little brother.

Deciding this must be a horrible case of food poisoning, and it would pass in time, he left the room. As he passed by his parents' bedroom, he could hear his mother wheezing in much the same way as Andrew.

"What the hell is going on around here?" Jake asked himself.

His father's voice floated up the stairs and Jake spun, hearing the concern in his tone.

"Jake, you better get down here and hear what's on the news!" Matt called.

Jake ran down the stairs two at a time and dashed into the living room to join his father, wanting to see what was on the news. Jake didn't watch the news normally, only if something was happening in his own city or right in his backyard. When Jake got into the living room, Matt just pointed at the television and said, "Look, son."

On the television, there was a special broadcast coming live from a hospital in Boston, and behind the reporter there were people running about, some lying on the ground. That wasn't what was so strange, however. What was strange was that these people appeared to be attacking other people and actually eating them. As Jake stared in shock, he saw a woman knock a man to the ground and sink her teeth into his neck, tearing out a thick chunk of flesh and muscle. Blood shot from the wound to splatter on the sidewalk like scarlet rain and the woman went in for more. The entire time the man screamed for help to no avail.

"Hello, I'm Michael Rourke, Seven News. I'm live at Boston Medical Center and behind me is what looks to be some kind of mass hysteria. For some unknown reason, patients of this hospital who were admitted earlier today with symptoms of food poisoning are now attacking innocent people. Nobody knows why this is happening, but it's...holy shit!" Mike gasped as a person being chased got between him and his cameraman then ran on. The reporter continued. "I've gotten word from the Boston Police Department and they say to stay out of this section of the city until they've contained everyone who appears to be under this strange influence of violence. There have been reports of people who were attacked actually coming back from what appears to be the dead, and then, they too, are joining their killers to attack others. But that can't be right, it's medically impossible."

As soon as he finished his sentence, a woman in her mid-thirties behind him rose up from the ground with half her face missing. She looked left and right and then spotted the reporter. With a guttural snarl she began stumbling towards him in a half-walk, half-jog.

The cameraman's voice called out to the reporter.

"Uhm, Mike, there's a woman behind you and she looks pissed. And half her face is fucking missing," the cameraman said, and then the camera was dropped to the ground with both the reporter and the cameraman screaming bloody murder outside of the frame as they were attacked from all sides.

"Oh my God, holy shit, get this bitch off me!" Michael Rourke screamed out of view of the camera, and then he dropped to the ground, his face striking the sidewalk as he appeared in front of the camera once again.

But to say he needed the make-up department to touch him up would have been an understatement.

Where his nose once was there was now nothing but a gaping maw filled with blood and mucus. Dark red plasma spit out of the exposed nasal cavity, his mouth gaping open in a rictus of death.

Then the picture went dark and a second later the news desk appeared.

A frazzled man with perfect hair and wearing too much make-up cleared his throat and tried to maintain his cool.

"Uhm, it appears we lost the feed and our apologies for the graphic scenes of violence. We'll get you more footage of this story shortly. As you can see on the bottom of your screen, there are phone numbers you can call if you feel you need…"

That was when the screen turned completely black and for some reason it didn't come back on. Before either Jake or Matt could do or say anything, the lights and television began to flicker and then went out all together.

"What the hell is going on?" Jake asked as he looked around stupidly.

"I don't know, son. Guess the power's out for some reason. Go get some candles and I'll see if I can find a flashlight."

Suddenly, a loud bang sounded from above them, which was the location of Matt's bedroom. Immediately, Matt figured his wife must have fallen out of bed or collapsed while trying to get up.

"That sounds like your mother," Matt said and went to the stairs leading to the second floor. "Meg! Are you all right, Meg?" Matt called up the stairs, taking the steps two at a time as he charged up them.

Jake was left in the living room, alone to think about what he'd seen on television.

This morning everything had been completely normal and then Boston had gone completely crazy, all in what seemed like a few hours; that just wasn't right.

He was about to go back outside and check on who was left in the yard when he heard his father screaming.

Running up the stairs, he reached the door, now closed, and when he pushed it open, his mouth fell open in horror as he stared at the most shocking thing he'd ever seen in his twenty years of life.

Now

That was when Jake was pulled from his daydream thanks to Bill's voice yelling at him.

"Hey, Jake, snap out of it, damn it! You're heading right for that tr…" Bill screamed, but it was too late.

Jake realized he'd drifted off into one of his daydreams and hadn't paid attention to the road. Maybe it was exhaustion or maybe he just wanted to finally end it all once and for all, but either way he was now staring at the large trunk of an oak tree.

There was no time to swerve out of the way. Before he could hit the brakes and slow their forty miles an hour speed, the front bumper of the Honda wrapped around the trunk of the tree, like it was hugging it in a lover's embrace.

The sound of crashing metal and breaking glass attracted every zombie in the surrounding area.

On stiff legs they began moving towards the crashed car.

They were hungry. This area had been picked clean of living humans, but now they had a chance to feed once more.

And those people were Jake and Bill.

Chapter 4

Now

Inside the wrecked Honda there was no sign of life, both Jake and Bill unmoving. All around the car, rotting, flesh-eating ghouls were pouring out of the nearby houses and they quickly began to swarm around the smashed vehicle. They wanted the bodies that were in the dismantled mess called a car because these ghouls hadn't eaten for more than a month.

While all of this was happening, only a few houses away from the crash, there was a natural gas leak in one of the homes. The entire home was filled with flammable gas from more than week of seepage, and one small spark would be all it would take to ignite it. While this house filled with gas, across the street another home smoldered as flames licked out the windows after the sun had been magnified through the pane of one of the glass windows, causing a pile of debris and paper inside the home to smoke and then burst into flames, the process similar to when an evil child roasts an ant with a magnifying glass.

The flames quickly spread through the house, devouring everything worth burning, including three desiccated corpses sprawled on the living room floor, most of their insides and flesh missing, as well as their brains.

With Jake and Bill still a few blocks from where they wanted to be, and a large crowd of ghouls surrounding the car, the situation was looking pretty grim.

Back at the burning house, a small ember caught on the wind after escaping from a shattered window. This piece of ember, floating on the wind, was taken from one house to the other one filled with natural gas. The basement window of the house in which the gas was leaking was wide open. The ember was carried right through the window, and with the gas filling the cellar, that single glowing piece ignited the gas and the house blew up in a huge fireball of orange and yellows, the walls and roof disintegrating and thrown a block or more in all directions. The house explosion shook the entire area, knocking ghouls off their feet and throwing a few wandering the streets into the air like they were nothing more than dried leaves.

Debris scattered everywhere, as far as five hundred feet, and more ghouls were taken down as wood and cement crashed back to the earth.

While the neighborhood shook from the explosion, inside the Honda both Jake and Bill were stirring. Jake was the first one awake and he glanced around, not understanding why he'd just heard what sounded like the world exploding.

"Oh, my damn neck," Jake groaned. "Hey, Bill, you okay?" he asked this while trying to wake up Bill.

After trying to see if he broke any bones by moving his arms and legs, he was pleased to see all he'd suffered for his effort and poor driving was a few cuts and bruises, plus a lump on his forehead where his skull had connected with the steering wheel before the air bag went off. Next to him, the deflated air bag sagged in front of Bill like a spent balloon. If it hadn't been for the air bags, he had no doubt they would both be dead.

"What the hell happened?" Bill muttered. "It feels like someone's playing the drums in my head," he grunted, still dazed from the crash. Finally regaining some of his composure, his eyes quickly looked outside to see almost a score of zombies surrounding them, most of them still picking themselves off the ground after the explosion knocked them down.

"Oh my God," Bill said upon seeing the approaching ghouls. "We have to get out of here, now," he added while pushing open his door.

Jake saw what Bill was looking at and he used all his weight to force open the dented driver's door, and after three tries it finally opened with a creak of ruined metal. As the door popped open,

Jake slid out of the Honda to land heavily on the ground, while Bill did the same on his side.

With both Jake and Bill sprawled on the pavement, still shaken from the crash, the zombies around them began to swarm in.

Neither Jake nor Bill had the energy for a fight, so they both decided to head to Jake's house on foot, hoping they could lose the ghouls in one of the backyards. All they would have to do is climb a picket fence or two and the ghouls would be left behind.

After Jake grabbed his katanas, Bill doing the same with his M-16, the two men hobbled away, the dead beginning a slow pursuit.

Twenty minutes later, after cutting through three yards overgrown with grass and weeds and a swimming pool filled with scummy water, the two companions were finally at Jake's house. Both of them couldn't remember the last time they had been so hungry and tired.

Jake thought he would collapse any minute from exhaustion and he was almost dragging himself to the back door of his house

"Oh, shit, I just thought of something," Jake said as they approached the rear door.

"Yeah, what's that?" Bill inquired.

"Well, I don't have a key to get inside."

Bill chuckled then. "Shit, Jake, we'll just kick the damn door in if we have to and then barricade it shut."

"No, we won't, this is my house, for Christ's sake, we're not gonna destroy it," Jake said defensively as he stopped at the door.

Bill frowned and looked at the door over Jake's shoulder. "Tell you what, smart guy, before we go and argue about it, why don't you just see if it's unlocked."

Jake shook his head. "That's crazy, why the hell would it be unlocked?"

"I don't know, but just try it, please."

With a sigh, Jake turned and reached for the doorknob, and when he turned it, his eyes went wide with surprise to see the door was indeed unlocked.

"Damn, someone must've forgot to lock it," Jake said with a slight grin on his face.

Bill said nothing in reply, but pushed Jake inside.

When Jake stepped into the house, memories flooded back and he forced them down. They were too painful right now to deal with.

"Looks clear," Jake said as they stepped into the kitchen which was right off the back door. "How about you check the basement and I'll check this floor. Here, take this last box of cookies on your way." He handed Bill a crushed box of Oreos while he pointed to the door leading to the basement.

"Thanks, okay, watch yourself up here," Bill said and walked to the door with the cookies in hand. It wasn't long before he was shoving them into his mouth, three at a time.

With Bill's footsteps stomping down the stairs, Jake decided to check the rest of the kitchen for food. That was when he tore open the cabinets to see if anything was still edible. At first all he found were mouse droppings and empty boxes with stale crumbs. The little rodents had been busy, it seemed.

But at the last cabinet he opened, he found a box of cherry Pop-Tarts with half of them still inside, the wrapping still intact.

He took one out, ripped open the silver covering, and began chowing down, the stale pastry tasting like heaven. After he was finished, his mouth was so dry his tongue felt like sandpaper and he searched some of the lower cabinets to see if he could find anything to drink. Even if it was warm, he didn't care; a drink was a drink. At first he had no luck and for the hell of it he tried the kitchen tap, but all he got was air. He sighed, knowing that would happen, but still hoping he'd be wrong.

Then he got lucky yet again, finding a couple of loose apple juice boxes in the back of one of the lower cabinets. They had been placed there to be put in his brother's lunches, but now they were up for grabs and then some.

Drinking greedily from one of them after dealing with the little straw and the tiny hole on the container, he set the other one on the counter for Bill.

Though he would have loved to drink it himself, he wanted to give his friend one, too. With a somewhat satiated stomach, he began to explore the rest of the floor.

The second room he encountered was the family room and the first thing he saw was the set of keys hanging on the wall near the front door. He recognized them immediately. They were for his father's old but mint 1969 Chevrolet Camaro. He hadn't thought about it but chances were the car was still sitting under the dust cover in the garage; perfect as the day his father restored it.

Wondering if the car would run, he pocketed the keys so he and Bill could check later and when he turned, he spotted a family portrait hanging on the far wall.

Memories of his family flooded back in force and he remembered what had happened to them back at the Fourth of July cookout

And worse yet was the fate they'd suffered by his hands.

The Past (The cookout)

After Jake watched the news report with his father, Matt ran upstairs to check on his mother, then Jake heard Matt scream. So he ran up to see what was wrong.

When he reached the second floor, he was horrified at what he found.

"Mom, what the hell are you doing?" Jake yelled while trying to get his mother off his prone father.

She was on top of Matt, her face deep inside his abdomen. Matt's eyes were wide and filled with pain and disbelief, his mouth opening and closing in shock. Bloody spittle dripped out of the corner of his mouth and he gagged, spewing a red froth onto Meg's back.

Jake pulled her off Matt and tossed her to the floor. She was thirty pounds lighter than him and this wasn't too difficult. It was when she fell to the floor that Jake got a good look at her face and what was clenched between her teeth, hanging there like a dead eel.

His father's large intestine was hanging out of her mouth, blood dripping to the floor to stain the carpet.

"Oh my G..." Jake began to stutter and then promptly threw up all over the bedroom floor, bits of what he'd eaten at the barbeque now mashed together into a bitter gruel. After he was done emptying his stomach, with spittle still coming out of his mouth, he turned at the sound of a creaking floorboard to see his brother standing at the bedroom door.

"Andrew, run, go get help!" Jake yelled, trying to get Andrew to do what he was told for a change.

Behind him, Meg was getting back up and moving for him, and at the same time Andrew growled deep in his throat and ran at Jake.

Andrew was now the same as his mother, a blood thirsty zombie from Hell. That was when Andrew lunged at Jake, trying to tear a piece out of him with his teeth. Jake sidestepped him and Andrew ran right into Meg, both of them landing on the bed, limbs tangling together.

Jake stared in amazement as his family rolled on the bed while his father moaned with his insides torn out; he felt himself going faint.

What the hell was going on? It was like a bad horror movie come to life only the make-up effects here were way cooler.

Though faced with an unbelievable scenario, Jake had always been one to accept things at face value. Where many people would have shook their head, not wanting to believe their eyes, Jake merely nodded and accepted this as his new reality.

"All right, goddammit, whatever the hell is going on here, I'm gonna end it right fucking now!" he screamed at his family. "Wait a minute..." That was when Jake remembered what Bill had told him, of what happened to the zombie scientist all those years ago at the plant. "You have to kill the brain," Jake whispered as he reached behind him for one of his dad's priceless katanas sitting on display in the corner of the room on a walnut shelf.

"At least these'll be good for something. I'm sorry for what I've gotta do to you guys, I really am, but I have no choice."

With tears in his eyes, as Meg began climbing off the bed to charge at him, Jake swung the katana and cut his mother's head clean off. It flipped in the air, her hair splaying out like a halo, and then dropped to the floor like a fumbled football. Blood geysered from the jagged stump of the neck as the body began to bounce off a bureau, then the walls, and then the television stand in the bedroom. Then the TV, already unstable thanks to a bad leg, slipped from its perch to flatten the decapitated body to the floor, while blood still seeped out of the neck wound to soak into the carpet.

Jake wasn't thinking about what he was doing. He couldn't focus on the fact he'd just cut his mother's head off. Who could? Instead, he reached behind him and picked up the second matching katana to the one in his hand from its display stand, went over to Andrew, and sliced at his brother's head, taking off an inch of his skull like he'd peeled a banana. Pink brains could be seen glistening in the light of the room, but the boy was still very active.

With a yell, Jake sliced downward at his brother's shoulder blades with the sword in his right hand. The blade was razor sharp and it slid into flesh and bone easily, only getting hung up on the clavicle for a brief instant, then the blade slid through and came out the other side. The other blade was now coming down and it did the same from the opposite side, slicing through muscle and tendon to come out covered in dark gore.

Jake then ripped the katanas apart, so there were now four separate chunks of Andrew. The boy's innards oozed out of his body to splash on the floor, the blood still fresh, the entrails sliding and moving like living snakes dipped in blood.

"Now that is what you call some *Highlander* shit right there," he gasped, breathing heavily as his brother's body slumped to the floor resembling butcher shop leftovers. Despite this, the head was still alive, the eyes and teeth moving like a marionette's, but as the brains slid out of the top of the skull, the face became immobile.

"Now what the hell am I going to do with these things?" Jake muttered in awe of what he'd just done. He could see Matt's face and his father's eyes were still. He was dead, the wounds inflicted on him by his wife certainly killing him.

Not knowing what to do, he decided to put the bodies in the bathtub for now. Then he could try to make sense of what happened and what he should do next.

Totally emotionless, not wanting to feel for his lost family, he grabbed the chunks of his brother's body and carried them to the bathroom, trying not to heave at the disgusting remains. When he was there, he chucked them into the tub.

After a few minutes of lugging the pieces and getting blood all over himself, Jake picked up his mother's body and dragged it into the bathroom, as well. He put the headless body in the tub on top of Andrew.

He leaned against the doorframe and cried, not too long, just for a minute or so, as he tried to deal with his shock and loss.

When he'd gathered his wits again and returned to the bedroom to get his mother's head, he couldn't find it anywhere.

"Now where the hell did it...holy crap!" he gasped.

Jake found the head, but the mouth and eyes were still moving.

How can this be? Jake thought. Instead of picking it up, he was so freaked out when his mother's eyes swiveled towards him and her mouth curled up into a death grin, that he panicked and kicked the head like a place kicker going for the field goal.

The head crashed through the window, bounced across the front lawn, and rolled into the street.

After kicking the head, he needed a break to take in what he'd seen, so he left his dead father on the floor and went to the bathroom to wash up, to splash some water on his face. He pulled the shower curtain closed so he didn't have to look at the dismembered bodies.

When he went back to the bedroom to take care of his father, the body was gone, only a dark red stain remaining where he'd bled out.

"Shit, where'd he go?" Jake mumbled to himself curious as to how he could be missing. He'd seen his dad's face; the poor guy was definitely dead.

Floorboards creaked behind him from the other side of the door, and as Jake reached for the edge and pushed the door closed, he was greeted by the vacant eyes of his father looking back at him.

With a groan and a wail of hunger, Matt lunged for him, but Jake realized what was happening and backed away. He picked up one of the katanas he'd set on the bed so he could dispose of the bodies and thrust the blade into his dad's heart. With the blade poking out of Matt's back, the tip jutting out of the center of his shoulder blades, Jake push him out of the bedroom, across the hall, and into the bathroom tub so he could join the rest of the family.

Like he'd seen on TV when he would watch samurai movies, he twisted the sword, shredding his father's heart, then pulled the sword free. But Matt was still very active, so Jake backed up, slammed the bathroom door closed, and quickly locked it.

He could still hear Matt behind the bathroom door, scratching and banging, low moans of what sounded like despair filtering through the wood.

Jake was shaken by what he'd done, but he forced himself to stay calm. He wondered how he was supposed to explain all this to the police. After all, how does someone tell the authorities that his family turned into blood thirsty zombies and had to be killed?

Going to his bedroom, he stripped, wiped as much blood from his face and arms as he could and then changed into new clothes.

Okay, I think it's time I got out of here, Jake thought while running downstairs to collect what he needed. He grabbed his backpack and started filling it up with all of the essentials, from water bottles, food that didn't need to be refrigerated, magazines, Twinkies—everyone's favorite apocalypse snack—and so on. He also took the katanas with him and their sheaths, because unlike guns, they didn't need to be reloaded. All packed and ready to go, he took the keys to his dad's Cadillac. He considered taking the Camaro, his father's sports car, but decided the newer car would be better. The Camaro was always getting tinkered with and he didn't want it to break down when he needed it the most.

There was a slight grin on his face at finally being able to drive his father's luxury pride and joy; next to the 1969 Camaro in the garage, the Caddy was his dad's favorite piece of property. It was a 2008 V-8 Cadillac and his father had joked he loved it more than he loved his family. The Cadillac was a symbol, it was proof he'd made it out of the projects of East Boston to make something of himself.

Stepping through the front door of the house and closing the door behind him, Jake gazed out onto the street, and what he saw blew his mind.

It was utter carnage outside the house. There were fires in the distance while emergency sirens and screams for help carried on the wind like a symphony of destruction. And there were people on the street, too, but they didn't look very healthy. In fact, they looked a lot like how his family had looked.

Good God, they are zombies! Jake thought.

It was when a zombie with a missing eye spotted him that he dashed to the garage, unlocked the door with the alarm button on the key ring and jumped into the driver's seat.

He only had thoughts for his fiancée, for Melissa

Melissa had gone home when everyone had been sick and when the news had reported the tragedy at the hospital she wanted to see to her family.

Was she okay? His dad's cell phone was on the seat next to him, left there when Matt went to the grocery store. He did that all the time, running around the house yelling, "Where the hell is my damn cell phone!" But then Meg would call it with hers and he would run around searching for the ring.

As he dialed Melissa, all he got was a busy signal. He tried another number, a friend of his, but he received the same for his trouble.

That meant whatever was happening was growing.

The zombie that spotted him was almost upon him so Jake started the Cadillac. Melissa's house was only a few streets away so it should be easy to drive over there and see if she was okay.

Once he found her, they could gather her and her family and travel north to her family's cabin in the New Hampshire Mountains. She loved it up there and would talk about the place whenever the subject came up.

Placing the car in drive, Jake pulled out of the garage, the front bumper knocking the zombie to the driveway like a hit and run at midnight on an empty street.

Feeling better about having a destination, he tried to keep the images of what he'd done to his family, the people he loved most in the world, out of his mind and focused on the here and now, of survival.

The Cadillac rolled onward into a very changed world.

Chapter 5

While Jake was searching the first floor of his house, Bill was in the basement. While investigating, he munched on his Oreo cookies, crumbs slipping from his mouth to fall on the floor like he was leaving breadcrumbs to find his way back upstairs. When he reached the middle of the basement, he caught the scent of decayed meat. Searching where the smell could be emanating from, he realized one of the windows was open to the outside.

Upon walking to the window to close it, he found himself tackled to the floor by a rotting, skinny zombie, the body sliding through the window like a snake. Bill landed on the floor with a loud thud, the ghoul on top of him, fetid teeth trying to bite his face off.

He could smell the putrid breath of the ghoul as cold air blew into his face and it made his stomach spew forth the cookies he'd eaten only seconds ago. The vomit left his mouth like Old Faithful and shot up into the zombie's face, then rebounded back down onto his own. With vomit covering his face, and the smell of the ghoul mixing with it, he felt his senses becoming overwhelmed. The entire time the ghoul never ceased its attack, fingernails constantly trying to rip his eyes out as teeth clacked on empty air.

That was when he remembered the M-16 which had been on his shoulder and was now lying on the dusty cellar floor beside him. With one arm holding off the zombie, he reached out and wrapped his hand around the rifle. The safety was off, it was always off. Raising the weapon up to the snapping head, he shoved the muzzle under the ghoul's chin, and without hesitation, he squeezed off a shot.

The 5.56 mm round went straight up and through the zombie's brain, blowing its skull into a hundred pieces. Dark blood shot out in all directions, mixed with a generous portion of yellow and brown pus.

Viscous fluid sprayed onto Bill's face, mixing with the vomit and spit dripping from the ghoul's mouth. With the zombie truly dead, Bill pushed the body away from him and to the side, then sat up.

Spitting out the foul tasting gruel, he tried not to think too hard about it, and when he was ready, he climbed to his feet. While wiping his face clean with paper towel found on a nearby work-bench, he stared down at the corpse of the ghoul that almost got him.

Looking up, he heard Jake's footsteps as the young man ran across the kitchen to the basement door and he decided to go greet him, wanting to let Jake know he was all right, all the while still wiping his face.

Jake snapped back to reality, shoving the horrible vision he'd witnessed about his family back down deep into his mind, and though he tried to be strong, it still brought tears to his eyes. That was the first time he'd ever killed another human being and to top it off, it had been his own family, his flesh and blood.

No sooner did he set the photo down, then he heard a muffled gunshot coming from downstairs. He recognized Bill's M-16 in an instant and bolted for the basement door, his katanas ready for a fight.

But when he got there, he was greeted by Bill and an odor so bad he didn't want to know what had made it.

"I heard a shot, old timer, what the hell happened? Jesus, look at you. You look like shit. And what's that disgusting smell?" Jake asked, covering his nose, with his shirt sleeve.

"Oh, just a little bit of everything, from puke to spit to zombie blood," Bill said casually while smiling sarcastically.

"A pusbag, but how did...?" Jake stopped upon hearing a crash from upstairs.

Bill followed Jake's gaze when, he too, heard the pounding.

"Sounds like you got company up there. You know who it is?" Bill inquired.

Jake shook his head no. "No idea."

After deciding the first floor was clear, both men headed back up to the second floor. When Jake approached the top of the stairs, he heard more scratching and pounding, and realized it was coming from the bathroom.

Looking back to Bill, he made a small statement with a smile.

"Oh, shit, I don't believe it, but that's my dad," Jake said, surprised as he stepped onto the second floor hallway with Bill following, his rifle ready to shoot anything that jumped out at them.

"Funny how he didn't make any noise when I was up here before."

"Maybe he heard the gunshot," Bill growled, not liking where this was going.

When Jake reached the bathroom door, his father began to moan and growl louder, wanting to break free of his solitary confinement and Jake thought: *How could he have survived for this long?*

Moments later, Jake heard scratching again, but it wasn't coming from the bathroom this time. Instead it was coming from his bedroom.

"It's coming from the room down the hall," Bill said as he stretched out his neck, gesturing with his chin.

"Yeah, I heard it, too. That's my room," Jake whispered.

Jake took a few steps towards his room and reached out to grasp the doorknob of the closed door. *Funny, I don't remember closing it the last time I was here,* he thought.

The scratching was now louder than ever, and he turned to Bill, then glanced at the older man's gun, wanting to have it ready.

"Okay, on three," Jake whispered. "One, two...three," he said and opened the door as the word *three* left his mouth.

As the door swung inward, something he couldn't see, thanks to the shadows in the room, lunged at him. He tried to get out of the way so Bill could shoot the shape, but he only managed to trip over his own two feet, causing Bill to lose his aim.

And to top it off, his arms were stuck to his sides as he was now in the doorway and couldn't get his katanas up, so he wasn't able to defend himself.

Bill was still trying to get a shot, desperately trying to get a lock on the dark form before it could attack Jake.

Jake had time for only one thought. *Oh shit, here comes the pain.*

Two hours earlier

"Oh, yeah, woo-hoo! Get that one, Danny, get that one over there!" Lucky yelled, encouraging his friend to drive over another zombie. Former Sergeant Danny Wilson was driving a 2007 Dodge Ram and it could run over anything on two legs whether it was living or dead, so he ran over the hapless ghoul that wandered into his sights with pleasure. The walking corpse was hit head on, the head snapping off the torso as the legs went one way and the arms another. It was like a rag doll with poor stitching had exploded. The large front tire drove over the legs, the sound of crunching floating up to the two men, which was quickly followed by the pelvis becoming nothing but bone chips draped in rotting meat. Blood splattered onto the windshield, so Danny turned on the wipers to wash it away.

"That's another twenty points, man, we're good!" Danny shouted with glee. "Hey, Lucky, check on Duke, how's he doin'?" he asked, concerned for his pitbull in the back of the truck.

"He's doin' fine, Sarge," Lucky said but didn't turn around to actually check on the pitbull in the rear bed.

"I said not to call me Sarge anymore, Lucky. We're out of the damn Army for good. And turn your damn head around and see if my dog's okay!" he snapped.

Lucky glanced through the small back window. "Just like I said, he's fine. Keep on hittin' those piles of shit. Hey, soon we're gonna need to find somewhere to stay for the night." Lucky's face creased in thought which wasn't a pretty sight. "Hey, Danny, do you think Roberts is one of them now?" Lucky asked, referring to Jake being a ghoul. "I bet he's a zombie right now or dead," he chuckled. "I never liked him ya know. Duke seemed to like him, though. I wonder if that's why he's been depressed lately; because of what we did to him and the old guy," Lucky said.

"Fuck him. I should've put a bullet in his head the second he arrived and ended it the instant I knew that guy was gonna give me trouble. He deserved what he got."

"Still, sucks about the plane, and all the guys. I miss Ricky and Johnson. Shit, Mark was cool, too."

Danny waved his words away. "Doesn't matter now. All that does is that we're still alive."

"Yeah, guess so." Lucky glanced up at the sun, seeing it would be dark in a few hours. "We're gonna need to find someplace to stay for the night," he repeated. "And maybe this time Duke can sleep in the truck. The dog farts all night, it's terrible."

"Fuck you, Lucky. Duke's my dog and nobody's gonna take him away from me, ever," Danny said in an angry tone as he struck another zombie a glancing blow with the front bumper, this time sending the body flying off into the gutter, where it flopped around like a short circuiting robot.

Danny and Lucky were a couple of white trash, trailer park hicks who had joined the Army to escape their shitty lives. They didn't care about anyone but themselves though Danny cared for his dog, Duke. They'd met in Iraq during the war, and had been friends ever since. Danny was in his late twenties, though already balding on top. He was a little husky, about two hundred and fifty pounds with his clothes off, and had a thing for plaid shirts with the sleeves torn off.

Lucky's original name was David Wietzel, but everyone began calling him Lucky because though he'd lost an arm, an ear, and two of his front teeth in the war when his troop transport ran over a hidden mine, he was still alive. Even before the war, the man had gotten so many stitches when he was younger that he now looked a lot like Chucky, the psycho doll from the movies. He was in his late-thirties and was really scrawny.

With their military experience, the men were well armed, knowing only their guns would keep them alive to see the rising of the sun each day.

They had military grade M-16s, hand grenades, two sniper rifles with night scopes, and a few other neat toys tossed in for the hell of it. All the gear had been salvaged from the destroyed camp that had been set up at Logan Airport.

"Hey, Danny, take a look at that house over there. It doesn't look wasted like the rest."

"Yeah, you're right, all the windows are still intact and the front door looks solid. If the back looks the same we're golden," Danny mused.

It was true. All the other homes on the street had blasted out windows, more than one showing fire damage. But this one house looked pristine, as if the owners had left for a few hours to do some shopping.

"We could stay there for a while," Danny considered while taking the turn to the street the house was on.

"Holy shit. Look at this place, it does look good. Wonder why no one went inside yet?" Lucky asked, stepping out of the truck, happy to find a suitable house for the night. There were a few zombies on the street but they could be taken care of quickly. Once they were put down, the two men could hide in the house for the night. But if just one zombie saw them, they would wake up with the house being surrounded by the undead.

"Who the fuck cares?" Danny snapped. "Listen, I'm gonna bring Duke inside the house first so he can search it, then I'll go in through the back door to see if there's any tools we can use. You go park on the street behind us so if we have to get out fast, all we have to do is hop a fence or two and we're gone. Plus, if anyone comes by they won't know we're in here," Danny said barking orders.

Until recently he was the lead man running the camp at the airport, but that was all in the past now.

"Why can't we just check out the garage and put the truck in there?" Lucky asked.

"'Cause it's too fucking big, the truck won't fit. Now just do what I say, will ya?"

"Got it, boss," Lucky nodded, doing what he was told. He then rounded the Dodge, jumped into the driver's seat and backed out of the driveway.

Danny brought Duke to the front door and told him what to do, like the dog understood.

"Duke, you hear me? Right now, you damn mutt. You're gonna go inside and kill anything that's in there so it's clear for us, okay? I'll be back in fifteen minutes or so to get you." Duke's tail was waving back and forth, the dog excited to hear his name. At that moment, Danny turned the doorknob, surprised it was unlocked; glad he wouldn't have to kick it in and then have to figure out how to re-secure it.

It happened more times than not. Many people just abandoned their homes for the rescue stations, not caring whether it was locked or not. Many families knew they would never be back.

He shoved the dog in and closed the door behind Duke, then went to see what he could find in the backyard.

Duke was just happy to finally be free to explore someplace new. He was free to run around the house, except he had to stay in the confines of the four walls which was kind of a downer. He wanted to run in a park or on the beach. Duke was going into every room as fast as he could, sniffing everything and leaving his mark. After he was done checking out the first floor, he climbed the stairs to the second floor.

As soon as Duke was on the top step, he heard scratching coming from the other side of the bathroom door. Duke gave his fiercest bark and menacing growl, but when he realized the door wasn't opening, he moved on to another room, his eyes constantly watching the bathroom door. He could smell the decay and rotten meat inside the bathroom and it made him nervous.

Outside on the street, Lucky was having fun running over the ghouls wandering around like drunks at last call. But he was a little too cocky and when he revved the engine to run down an old woman with half a face, he lost control of the vehicle and the left tire struck a smaller car.

The tire rode up the bumper and onto the trunk, the Dodge flipping over and rolling onto its side. Lucky was thrown around inside the cab and he cracked his head, falling into unconsciousness.

No sooner did the truck come to rest then the walking dead turned and moved towards the truck and the now unconscious driver. Perhaps Lucky should have read the sign nailed to the large oak tree on the edge of the sidewalk.

Think Twice, Save a Life, SPEED KILLS.

Danny Wilson entered the garage through a side door. It was locked, but he was easily able to jiggle the latch with a six inch pocket knife he carried for just such an occasion

After stepping into the shadows and making sure the coast was clear, he closed the door and looked around the garage, his eyes adjusting to the dim light.

A car with a dust cover on it was in the middle and he went to it and pulled it off, waving away the floating dust.

What he found made him smile from ear to ear.

Sitting silently in front of him was a blue, 1969 Chevrolet Camaro with chrome rims and custom exhaust.

"Shit, now this is what I call a car," Danny said with eyebrows raised in astonishment. Man was he excited. This was the kind of car someone like him could only dream of owning. It had to be worth twenty grand easy. Though the car's finish was covered in dust, the paint still managed to pick up whatever ambient light was in the garage and reflect it like a polished mirror.

As he went to inspect the car, he realized there were no keys for it.

"Shit," he muttered. He didn't want to hotwire such a sweet ride, and ruin it. Not feeling this excited in along time, he quickly began moving around the garage, trying to find the keys, or if he had no choice, the tools he would need to hotwire it.

It was as he ran around the rear bumper—his eyes spotting some wire cutters hanging on a peg on the wall—that his when his left foot slipped on a small pool of oil. The garage floor was painted and the oil made it like ice. Before Danny realized what was happening, he was falling. He dropped so fast he never managed to get his hands between himself and the cement floor.

His temple smacked the cold cement, and like a light switch being flicked, Danny was plunged into darkness, now lost in a void of unconsciousness.

Duke continued sniffing around the second floor of the house.

Upon entering what was once a master bedroom, he immediately smelled the stale stench of death. The blood on the walls and carpet were old, pieces of brains and gobbets of flesh long dried to the consistency of beef jerky.

Still, the dog sniffed a small piece and wolfed it down greedily. He'd learned not to be fussy of what he put in his stomach.

After leaving the room behind, he went to another room, one with a twin bed. Using his snout to open the door, he padded inside, but the door was uneven, and as the door opened halfway it then stopped and began to close again.

Duke, seeing the door closing, spun and ran back to it, but he miscalculated and ended up using his paw to push the door closed. With a soft click the door locked, trapping the dog inside.

He scratched at the door for twenty minutes but when no one came to let him out, he gave up.

So after inspecting his new home for another five minutes, he curled up in the shadows in the far corner of the bedroom and lowered his head to sleep.

He wasn't going anywhere until a human came to let him out.

Chapter 6

Jake prepared to feel the agonizing sharpness of pain as teeth sank into his warm flesh. He could see Bill wasn't going to be able to shoot the dark shape lunging for him.

So it came as quite a surprise, when instead of feeling yellow teeth chewing at his face, he instead felt a cold, wet nose press against his forehead and then the zombie began licking him.

Licking him?

Hold on, this can't be right. What gives? Jake thought while trying to focus on the shape on top of him. When he could see more clearly, after being dazed from the attack, he realized it was Duke, the dog from back at the rescue station set up at the airport.

"Holy...Duke? What the hell are you doing here?" Jake said, pushing the dog off him, though now more gently.

Bill, who had been about to shoot after finally acquiring a target, now lowered the rifle, happy to see it wasn't a ghoul.

"Well, I'll be, how the hell did he get here?" Bill asked as he leaned down and scratched Duke behind the ears.

Jake joined him, the dog wagging his small tail happily. Both men were glad to have another living companion back. Then Jake realized Danny and Lucky must be around, too, because they took Duke everywhere they went. Danny loved the dog more than any human, and there was no way Duke would be here without him, that is, unless Danny was dead.

Jake could only hope. He owed that asshole big time for what he'd done to Bill and himself.

"Shit, Wilson must be here, too," Jake said with a scowl. "I can't wait to get payback on that son-of-a-bitch for what he did to us back at the airport."

"Now hold on there, hotshot, we don't know that for sure, but right now let's look around the perimeter of the house," Bill said, moving to the door.

Climbing to his feet, Jake nodded. "I just want to know how they found us."

Bill shrugged. "Who knows, maybe they just picked this house at random. After all, next to the rest of this block yours was the only one that looked intact. Shit, even if I didn't know this was your house I would've chosen it."

"Well, maybe, but it still seems like a big coincidence," Jake replied as he hefted his katanas. "If this was a movie, the audience would be pretty pissed off right about now."

Bill shrugged. "If it was I'd tell them to get over it. Sometimes life's like that. You can bitch about it or go with the flow. I choose the latter."

"Fair enough, old timer, fair enough," Jake grinned.

The sound of a door harshly opening and hitting the wall filtered in from outside. Both men looked at one another and Jake dashed into his bedroom, going to the window.

The window looked out over the garage, and when he gazed down, his jaw dropped open when he saw Sergeant Danny Wilson exiting through the doorway. The man was rubbing his head and had a pained expression on his face.

"Bill, come here, it's him. Wilson's here," Jake said as he watched the man stumble around like a drunk. If Danny was here, then where the hell was Lucky? The skinny prick was Danny's sidekick in every sense of the word.

When Bill reached the window, Duke was following happily with a hanging tongue. The dog hopped up on his rear legs, his front paws now on the window frame. As the dog looked outside, he immediately recognized his master.

Before Jake or Bill could stop him, Duke began barking excitedly. Danny turned at the sound, knowing his dog's bark, and his eyes went wide as he looked up and locked gazes with both Bill and Jake.

"That cocksucker's still not dead?" Danny hissed with fury in his eyes. "Well, he's gonna be dead when I get through with him." He unslung his rifle, turned, and charged for the front door.

"Shit, he's coming, and he's got a rifle like you have," Jake said to Bill.

Bill looked around the room. "There's no place to really defend ourselves up here, Jake. The bullets in these guns will cut through the walls of your house like paper. Shit, he could just go downstairs and shoot through the damn floor; sooner or later he's gonna hit us. And if we try to get away, he's only gonna shoot us in the back."

"You're right, we need a way to distract him," Jake said, remembering his father was still trapped in the bathroom. "Okay, here, take the keys to my dad's Camaro and wait for me outside. Just climb through the window. I'll bring Duke with me," Jake said as he ran to the bathroom door, ready to open it.

That was when he heard the front door splinter as it was kicked in.

Bill opened the bedroom window and pushed out the screen with the barrel of his rifle. He turned around to tell Duke to stay put, but the dog was already gone, having followed Jake.

"Oh, Jake, Daddy's home! Time to die, you little fuck!" Danny called out as he strode into the house. He showed no fear. Going to the stairs, he climbed them with stomping footsteps.

He was filled with rage, wanting to finish what he should have started months ago, and that was to kill Jake and the old fart traveling with him.

At the top of the stairs, Jake could hear Danny coming for him and knew he had only seconds.

Swallowing the knot in his throat, he unlocked the bathroom door, swung it open, and jumped out of the way. His zombified father stumbled out of the bathroom, emaciated beyond belief. After feeding on the sliced and carved meat of his family left in the bathtub, he'd had nothing to feed on for months.

Jake didn't wait to see what would happen next, but dashed back to his bedroom, Duke following like a love sick puppy. The two had hit it off immediately when Jake met the pooch at the camp, and Duke actually liked him more than Danny.

At the open window Bill had climbed through seconds before, Jake paused as he crawled over the sill to hear Danny and his father fighting. The sound of bodies falling down the stairs, then a few gunshots, filled the house and Jake knew Danny was more than just a little occupied.

"Thanks, Dad," Jake said fondly as he thought of his father saving him even in death.

Not caring if Danny was alive or dead, Jake climbed out onto the small roof below his window, then he waved Duke to follow. At first the dog didn't want to go, but when Jake coerced the animal, Duke jumped up and scurried through, his rear legs scratching the wall below the sill as he scooted over the frame.

Now on the small roof, Jake was able to see Bill trying to enter the garage door. The door was locked. Danny, in his dazed state had locked it behind himself as he'd exited the garage. Bill could have shot the lock, but that would alert any undead in the area, a definite no-no these days.

Dropping his katanas off the roof and to the side to aim for the grass, he then followed them, hopping off the roof. He let his knees bend, went into a roll and came to his feet. The roof wasn't too high and the grass helped to cushion his fall.

"Come on, Duke, come on, I'll catch you," Jake called to the dog who was nervously moving back and forth on the edge. Duke whined a few times, but when Jake called again, clapping his hands, the dog leapt into the air. Jake was below, waiting for him, and he caught the dog like a mother would a falling baby. Both dog and man fell to the grass and Duke hopped away, Jake chuckling.

Rolling back to his feet, he headed towards the garage door to join Bill.

"So where the hell is the key?" Bill asked, irritated.

"I have no idea, here, let me try something," Jake said and used one of the katanas, wedging the tip between the door and frame right where the lock was. The sword was of superior metal, not some tin-plated junk found on one of those TV shopping networks, and the door popped open with a dull clack.

Stepping into the gloom of the garage, Jake breathed a sigh of relief upon seeing the Camaro still safe and sound. After seeing

Danny come out of the garage, he had visions of flat tires and busted windows.

"I'll drive," Bill said as he went to the driver's door. Jake was okay with that, not feeling like he had to be the driver. Yes, it was his father's car, but for now it was just a vehicle that would get them to safety.

"Fine," Jake remarked as he opened the passenger door, Duke climbing into the back seat and curling up on the leather.

"God I hope this car still works," Jake said to himself, remembering what his father always said about the car never working. Not to mention it had been sitting for months and the battery hadn't exactly been new to begin with. Though the car was mint, there was always something wrong with it, usually small, but his father was always tinkering with something.

Bill put the key in the ignition and turned it while pumping the gas pedal. The engine whined and sputtered a little, but wouldn't start. Frowning, he tried again, the engine turning over as he muttered words of encouragement.

Jake was doing the same thing as he rubbed the dashboard with his hand, muttering *it's okay* and *I love you, now start for me, please.*

After a couple more tries, just as the battery was about to die, Bill finally got the car started and Jake was thrilled as the engine roared to life, blowing out thick, black noxious fumes of oily smoke out the exhaust.

"Get the garage door, will ya, Jake? I really don't want to crash through it like in the movies," Bill said as he looked at Jake.

"Huh? Oh, yeah, right, sorry," Jake said and hopped out, rolled up the door and climbed back inside just as Bill began moving.

But as the car rolled out of the garage, Danny appeared from the side and stepped in front of the car. Bill stopped, the engine purring, the smoke from the exhaust clearing somewhat as the oil lubricated the engine.

Danny looked like he'd gone ten rounds with the Devil himself and Jake grinned, glad his dad had given Danny a workout.

Danny grinned as he raised his rifle and prepared to blow both Jake and Bill away, but when he squeezed the trigger, all he got was a dry click. The magazine was empty.

Cursing, Danny tossed it to the ground and drew a large machete strapped to his waist. The blade was covered in dried blood and there were many nicks on the edge, most of them from hacking at human bone.

"Stay here and watch Duke, Bill. This is gonna end here and now," Jake said, exiting the car and stepping out onto the warm pavement.

"So, Roberts. Thought you could pull a fast one on me, huh?" Danny said with fury in his eyes. "I don't need a gun to take you out," he said while waving his machete in the air.

"Neither do I, Sergeant. And I'm glad I now have the chance to thank you for leaving Bill's and my ass out at the airport," Jake said, acting sarcastically. "So how'd you get away from my dad?"

"That zombie in there was your dad, huh. Well, he almost got the upper hand on me till I pulled out my little friend," Danny said, waving the blade like a magic wand. "You see, we both fell down the stairs and when we were on the first floor, he ended up on top of me. So I just took my baby here out, and with my other hand holding his head back, I jammed the tip right into his left eye. And that's what I'm gonna do to you, too," Danny snarled.

"We'll see about that, *Sergeant Wilson.*" Jake said the name with contempt.

Danny shook his head. "Forget the Sergeant crap, Roberts, there's no more Army for me or Lucky, no thanks to you."

"Me? I didn't do anything, *Danny*," Jake said the name as if it was something foul in his mouth.

Then, before Jake realized the man was through chatting, Danny was charging at him, trying to get the upper hand by attacking when Jake wasn't ready.

The machete came at his head and Jake moved out of the way at the last second, the large blade missing his face by less than an inch. With a howl of rage at missing, Danny spun and continued the attack, wanting to draw first blood.

But Jake was quick, the younger man dodging and weaving, deftly avoiding being cut.

Jake managed to move a few feet away as Danny overreached a blow. Jake pulled his katanas from their sheaths, the whisper of steel loud in the quiet driveway.

But not quiet enough, and as the two men fought, a few ghouls spotted them, hearing Danny's yells of anger. Slowly, they turned and began moving towards the battling men, their teeth clacking incessantly.

"That was a cheap shot, not waiting for me to draw my swords, should've expected that from you," Jake hissed as he held the bare blades in front of him. "Now we'll see how you do against an armed man."

"Not a chance. I'm military trained and can handle any situation," Danny said with confidence. As far as he was concerned there was no doubt he would win.

Bill got out of the Camaro, his M-16 up. He'd decided this was going on for far too long and wanted to put a bullet in Danny's back, but Jake stopped him.

"No, Bill, I want to do this with honor," Jake hissed.

"Fine, Jake, whatever," Bill said while rolling his eyes at the ridiculous statement, but he was already prepared to shoot Danny if it looked like Jake was in trouble. Honor my ass, what did the young man think this was, a samurai movie? Duke was still in the Camaro, but he was barking furiously. Danny thought the dog was cheering him on, as did Jake. No one spoke canine so there was no way to know for sure.

With a growl from deep in his throat, Danny charged at Jake, but he was prepared, and with katanas stretched out, he was already seeing himself slicing Danny in two, only that wasn't what happened. Jake made the mistake of underestimating his opponent.

Danny was a trained fighter and just before he reached Jake, he slid on the ground and rolled past the katanas, coming up behind a stunned Jake.

Spinning around, Jake tried to counterattack, but Danny had kicked out with his right leg in a swinging kick, knocking both katanas out of his hands like a judo master. As Danny's foot landed, he jumped up again and his left foot snap-kicked Jake in the chest, sending the man falling to the driveway. Before Jake could recover, Danny was on top of him, the machete held high for a killing blow, the tip angling to penetrate Jake's left eye.

"No one knows I tried to get you killed at the airport, I kept that little nugget to myself, and when you're dead for good, that'll stay my little secret," Danny smirked, his eyes twinkling with venom.

Bill raised his M-16, realizing if he didn't do something immediately, Jake was dead, when he was knocked to the side by Duke as the dog charged out of the Camaro. The door hadn't been latched and the dog forced it open, causing Bill to lose target acquisition.

Before Bill could shoot, Duke was out of the car and running directly at Danny. The dog was like a missile, crossing the distance between the car and Danny in less than two seconds. Leaping into the air, Duke opened his jaws wide and latched onto Danny's arm, the one holding the machete.

"What the fuck? You're my dog, goddammit; get the hell off a me!"

Duke ignored his former master's cry, squeezing his jaws tighter.

With a growl to match the dog's, Danny punched Duke in the forehead with his free hand. The first blow did nothing, but by the third punch Duke gave up and let go, taking a chunk of Danny's arm with him.

As sharp teeth let go, Danny kicked out with his right foot, sending Duke sprawling across the driveway. The dog let out a rather human screech of pain as he rolled on the pavement, but soon he was up and ready for another attack.

"Fuckin' mutt. You'll pay for that," Danny snapped, not paying attention to Jake for a few precious seconds.

Jake took the chance to attack, not wasting the opportunity Duke had given him. Rolling to the left, he reached out and picked up one of the katanas and came to his feet, all in one fluid motion.

Danny, realizing Jake was coming for him, shifted his attention away from the dog, but he was too slow to stop what was happening. His face went wide with terror as Jake brought the katana down in a sweeping motion.

The blade flashed in the sunlight as it sliced through muscle and bone like it was made of paper.

Danny's right arm was sliced off at the elbow, the severed limb falling to the driveway, the fingers still twitching. The machete fell from the spasming hand to clatter on the ground. Jake grinned as he brought the katana back, and with his entire body weight behind it, sliced horizontally at Danny's neck.

Danny had time for one high-pitched squeak of pain as he stared at the gushing stump that had been his arm, when the blade sank deep into his throat, slicing it in twain, the head popping off to roll onto the driveway, landing on its side. The eyes seemed to blink, as if Danny didn't understand how he'd gotten on the ground, especially as he could see his body to the left of him. Then the eyes glazed over in the severed head as the decapitated body fell over, blood shooting from the neck stump to bathe the ground a dark crimson.

Breathing heavily, Jake looked down to see Duke gnawing on the severed arm and disgust crossed his face. "No, boy, that's gross, leave that alone," he snapped, but Duke only growled, happy to have a meaty chew toy.

A low moan caught Jake's attention and he turned to see that the zombies approaching him had finally reached the end of the driveway. There was no time to try and run to the car, so Jake picked up his other katana and went to work, slashing torsos open, slicing heads from shoulders, and carving flesh like it was Thanksgiving and they were turkeys. Rotten entrails splashed onto the driveway, bile pooling in the sun, and each body toppled over to spasm like it was being electrocuted. But there were more coming, and after getting rid of the first ones in line, Jake turned and sprinted for the Camaro, calling for Duke to follow him.

The dog picked up the severed arm and trotted after him, his head turning to see the ghouls behind. But Duke was only interested in his new toy and didn't want to deal with zombies at the moment, or share his new toy.

Reaching the car, Jake stopped Duke. "No, boy, not in my car, drop it, now!" he said in a commanding tone. The dog lowered his head, and when Jake pointed at the ground, the dog reluctantly complied, Duke's muzzle now covered in blood.

While Jake dealt with Duke, Bill started the car again, the engine rumbling with power. The 350 engine was eager to please and Bill was ready to leave.

Climbing in after Duke, Jake slammed his door and slapped the dashboard. "Go, Bill! Go, man, go!"

"Shit, you don't have to tell me twice," Bill replied as he floored the gas pedal.

The car shot forward, the left front tire driving over Danny's torso with a dull crack as the ribcage was crushed. Blood shot out of the open neck like a stepped on ketchup packet and the rear tire did much the same as the front.

Bill continued on, striking ghouls with the front bumper as he made his way down the street. Some of the zombies ignored the car, instead moving to Danny's cooling corpse. In seconds, they were tearing apart the crushed body, feeding on the still warm meat.

Bill turned at the next intersection and slowed when he saw an overturned pickup truck, a Dodge if he was correct. There was a large crowd of zombies around the overturned truck and when Bill slowed the car, he saw one ghoul turn away from the others and walk away with a prize in its hands. Both Jake and Bill's mouths fell open when they realized it was the severed head of the former Private Lucky.

"Well," Jake said. "I guess we just found out what happened to Lucky."

"Naw! That can't be Lucky, he's military trained, just like Danny," Bill cracked with a smile, remembering Danny's tough talk.

"No, that's him, you can see the scar tissue where his ear should be."

"Yeah, no shit," Bill remarked. "Guess you're right. Poor bastard, no one deserves to go out like that."

A dozen ghouls took an interest in the Camaro, breaking off from the main horde to try and reach the car, so Bill swerved further away and stepped on the gas. The engine roared and the car shot forward, leaving the visceral scene of carnage and death behind.

"Hey, that was some shit back there with Danny," Bill said as he maneuvered around a wrecked station wagon. "You know I had your back if you got into trouble, right?"

Jake nodded, his right hand on the dash and his left on one of his katanas, the other leaning against the seat. "Yeah, Bill, I kinda figured as much. Thanks."

"Not a problem, just wanted you to know that," Bill grinned.

A corpse was lying in the road, its body nothing but skin and bones so Bill didn't bother swerving around it, the Camaro rolling over it. One of the tires found the head and squished the skull into a gooey pulp, a dull *crack* filling the air for a second.

"Listen, Bill. If we're in the area anyway, let's go check on my girlfriend's house. I want to see it."

"Sure, why not, just tell me where to go. Hopefully it'll be better than your place was."

Jake glanced to Bill but didn't reply. He knew what the older man meant. As far as a homecoming, his had been the worst in history. Hopefully, Melissa's house would be better.

With a surge of power the two men felt through the floorboards, the Camaro turned another corner and was lost from sight, the ghouls still feeding on poor Lucky's corpse like they were a fat man and he was a blue plate special at the local diner.

Ten minutes ago

Ten minutes ago, Lucky was still very much alive. But he was out cold after whacking his head on the steering wheel. The airbag hadn't gone off and now he had a large welt on his temple the size of an egg.

As he lay immobile, a score of undead bodies were slowly surrounding the truck. Seeing Lucky's body, they immediately dove into the open and shattered windows, pulling the still form of the man onto the street.

Lucky came to when the first set of brown teeth sank an inch deep into his leg, tearing out a large chunk of his flesh, his blood shooting high into the air thanks to a torn artery.

His gun was still in the cab, and with nothing but his hands for defense, he was quickly incapacitated and torn limb from bloody limb as he screamed for the pain to end.

He got his wish soon enough.

One ghoul put its hand where Lucky's arm was amputated and began tearing at the stump, while others tore into his mid-section and ripped out his insides.

Another ghoul twisted Lucky's head around and around until the skin ripped like old leather, the head popping off to trail a bit of spinal column

Lucky's eyes and mouth were still moving for a few seconds as the head was dragged away by the happy ghoul. Seconds later the orbs stopped moving and the face went slack, the lower jaw sagging, the mouth hanging open.

The zombie holding the severed head wandered away to eat in peace, while its brethren continued devouring the corpse.

A Camaro drove down the road, quickly speeding up when the occupants saw the carnage, but the ghouls paid it no mind, instead feasting on the warm innards of the man called Lucky.

In hindsight, maybe he wasn't so *lucky* after all.

Chapter 7

Now

Bill swerved around a wrecked car in the middle of the street as he drove deeper into the war torn neighborhood. Next to him in the passenger seat, Jake was solemn, his eyes glossy.

He seemed to be thinking of something else other than their destination.

Bill assumed Jake was torn up about having to kill Danny, but that was the farthest thing from his mind.

Now, with Danny gone, Jake knew he could focus on his true mission, the reason he continued to fight though the odds were stacked against him.

He was still searching for Melissa.

In the back seat of the Camaro, Duke barked softly, wanting some attention, but with Bill focused on driving and Jake lost in reverie, the dog went unattended.

"We gotta go somewhere soon, Jake. Night's coming," Bill said as he drove over the desiccated corpse of a zombie lying prone in the street. The tires cracked and crunched as the dried muscle and sinew of the body was flattened into dust.

"Yeah, I was thinking the same thing," Jake replied. In truth, he was thinking very heavily about it. Melissa's house was only a few blocks away and he desperately wanted to go back there, to at least see what was left of her home.

Her clothes were still there, the pictures on the walls; it would be something if he couldn't have her with him now.

But then he remembered what had happened so many nights ago at her house and he shuddered, not wanting to recall those images but knowing he was helpless to stop them from invading his mind.

The Past (July, 4th 2009)

Jake had a rough time getting from his house to Melissa's. It would've normally taken a mere fifteen minutes or less, but instead, it took him three hours. Nearly every street was cluttered with overturned cars, houses on fire and zombies walking everywhere, attacking anything that was dumb enough to enter their danger zone.

It was obvious something had happened to this neighborhood. People were already beginning to panic as the dead attacked the living. Screams could be heard coming from somewhere nearby and the constant sound of emergency sirens filled the air, a symphony of the world collapsing in on itself.

After taking the long way around, Jake was finally turning onto Melissa's street, but when he approached her house, he spotted at least twenty zombies moving in and out of the open front door to her home.

Parking the car in what for the moment was a clear area, though that would change as the zombies spotted the car, Jake jumped out of the Cadillac and began cutting bodies down left and right.

He wasn't going to let these, these *creatures*, desecrate his fiancée's home.

"You bastards are gonna pay," he snarled as he charged towards the first zombie, an old woman with hair curlers and sporting a blue sweater knitted from scratch before her arthritis had been too much and she'd had to stop. Of course, that was all before she'd died and come back as a walking corpse after a nice garden salad layered with store bought tomatoes from Jake's farm.

When the old woman wasn't looking, Jake took one of his katanas and punctured a hole through the back of her skull, so the end of the katana shot out the front-left eye socket. Sliding it out with a coating of gore and brains, he chopped another body into three big chunks.

Another came at him and he cut at the neck and waist line, the legs still moving while the rest of the body was dissected. The legs didn't stop twitching till they hit the ground.

The head fell free and rolled away like an off balance basketball, blood seeping from the open wound.

With the head lying on the ground, Jake jammed the tip of one of his katanas into the top of the skull, spearing the cranium, the blade sliding into the brain. Hefting his sword, the head was now on the tip like a mounted trophy from an ancient cannibal tribe, and he began hitting the remaining ones with the severed head, cracking their skulls with his makeshift mace.

He did this until there was only one more ghoul in his way. With only one more left in his sights, he threw the head away, raised his arms in the air, so that the katanas made an 'x', and brought them down across the ghoul, completely slicing through the body, blood shooting out to bathe the ground in red gore.

Heaving from the fight, the battle finally won, he was covered from head to toe in blood and viscera. Without hesitation, he spun on his heels and ran inside the house to see if anyone was there.

There were seven more zombies inside the home on the first floor, but he took each one out before the others knew he was among them, slashing them to the floor in bloody pieces.

Finally, he was alone in the house, only the incessant droning of thousands of flies to keep him company, and he began looking for Melissa or her family.

After a couple minutes of endless searching, he found no sign of her and the only occupants were the two corpses on the living room floor. Putting two and two together, he had to say those were probably the bodies of Melissa's parents.

They were a mass of blood, bone and entrails, with faces torn off, an arm over there, a leg on the other side of the room, and their skulls cracked open like egg shells, the brains scooped out and long gone.

In their present condition, they were unrecognizable.

With a heavy heart. or one filled with hope, depending on how he looked at the situation, he prepared to leave. After all, if Melissa's body wasn't here, then she must have left before the zombies had attacked.

It was as he was leaving that he heard soft weeping coming from a closet at the end of the hallway. Walking slowly to the closet, stepping over some of the fallen bodies of the dead ghouls on his way, he raised his katanas, not knowing what to expect.

Upon reaching the closet door, he slowly turned the doorknob and swung it open. To his surprise, it was Melissa's little sisters, Cara and Jessica.

Cara was the youngest at twelve. Jessica was fourteen, and everyone called her Jess for short. Cara was just beginning to wear make-up, though now her mascara was running from her tears. She didn't do very well in school and always caused trouble for her teachers, but inside she was just like every other young girl who was trying to make an identity for herself.

Jess was a straight A student and was the complete opposite of Cara. She was popular and had many friends, all who loved her. She'd also had a thing for Jake ever since Melissa had brought him over to meet the family for the first time.

"Cara, Jess, thank God. Are you guys okay?" Jake asked in surprise as he stared at the two girls.

"Jake?" they said, simultaneously.

They charged out of the closet, plowing into him, pushing him to the blood-covered floor.

"What happened here? Where's Melissa?" Jake asked, wanting answers.

"Oh, Jake, it was horrible," Cara said, sniffling constantly. "They started coming into the house before we knew what was happening. They attacked Mom and Dad and they *ate* them." Fresh tears were on her cheeks.

"So, we hid in the closet, thinking they wouldn't find us in there," Jess said, who was also crying though more reserved.

"That was smart, if you hadn't done that, you'd probably both be dead now, too. But where's Melissa?" Jake asked, worried for his girlfriend.

That was when both girls took a step away from him.

"What're you two not telling me?" Jake asked, concerned with the look on their faces.

"Melissa never came home," Cara said. "You see, she did call that she was coming home on her cell phone after the barbeque at your house, but while she was talking, she suddenly stopped and screamed for some reason. Then we were disconnected."

Jake turned around and his eyes creased in thought. Walking back and forth with a worried face, he wondered if the dropped call could mean Melissa was dead. His stomach rolled inside him at the thought of her being dead.

His eyes took in the room full of bodies as if for the first time. Blood splattered the walls like a madman with a brush had painted it, and before he could stop himself, he threw up, hot liquid splashing onto the floor as he purged his insides.

The tragedy of the day had finally caught up to him. The images of his family and how he'd killed them, his father now locked in the bathroom, it all came rushing back to him in a seething flood, and he felt so sick he could barely see straight.

He'd just killed his entire family! How could he do that?

His legs felt weak and the world began to spin, and before he knew what was happening, he pitched forward, striking his head on the steel radiator against the wall.

Falling into unconsciousness with a gash on the side of his temple, he could hear the two girls calling out to him, but by then his eyelids fluttered and he heard no more.

Now

Jake snapped back to reality when Bill pulled up to Melissa's house.

After a quick discussion, Bill agreed that if they had to go somewhere, then Melissa's house was as good a place as any other at the moment.

Bill pulled the Camaro into the driveway and then backed it up so he could leave in a hurry if necessary, the front bumper now facing the street, the rear bumper facing the house.

The area around the house was empty for the moment, no one around either living or dead. Many homes had been evacuated over the past few months.

Jake climbed out of the car with Duke following behind him, the dog pausing to pee on the light post on the front lawn, while

Bill did the same on the opposite side of the car. Finished peeing, Duke padded back to Jake, growled softly, and was about to bark until Jake raised his hand to stop him.

"No, Duke, quiet," Jake hissed. "We don't know how many pus-bags are in any of these houses."

Duke lowered his head with his ears slanted back, the tone of Jake's voice enough to silence him.

"That's what I'm afraid of, so come on and let's get inside before any of them sees us," Bill said, moving to the front door.

Both Jake and Duke followed him, the dog trotting with his tongue hanging out and small tail wagging. As soon as they stepped into the foyer, the redolence of decayed meat penetrated their olfactory senses.

Flies were everywhere, buzzing about as they tried to escape the prison they had been birthed into. Bill was trying to figure out where the flies were coming from when he saw the desiccated husks of Melissa's parents still lying on the living room floor, as well as the multiple dead zombies and body parts Jake had chopped down a few months ago.

"What the hell is this?" Bill asked as he covered his nose and began breathing through his mouth to cut down on the stench.

"Yeah, I kind of forgot about them," Jake said, holding Duke back.

Maggots were here and there, crawling up and down the remains, constantly feeding off what was left of the corpses, but after months their numbers had dwindled immensely.

Jake tried desperately to cover his nose with his shirt sleeve, but it barely worked. Even in the miasma of decay and rot, he could detect the subtle hint of vomit, left over from when he'd puked.

Right now, Bill just wanted to get to the kitchen, find something to eat and drink for both him, Jake and Duke, and then leave this place of death.

He only hoped the second floor was better. With the doors closed and the windows wide open to let in fresh air, the second floor could work for the night.

"Come on, let's see if there's anything left to eat and drink in the kitchen and then we can head upstairs," Bill said while moving to the rear of the house where he assumed the kitchen was.

Upon entering the kitchen, Bill and Jake began ransacking the place to see if there was anything salvageable, Duke sniffing the corners of the room. Taking a chance, Jake checked in the fridge and spotted a case of beer. Even though it was warm, it was still drinkable.

Holding his breath to keep out the stink of rotting food, he grabbed the beer and slammed the fridge closed, then rubbed his nose to get out the stench that hung there like month old cheese.

After months of no electrical power, the items in the fridge were now so degraded and rotted that the putrid contents would make a zombie smell and look appealing.

"Hey, Bill, want a beer?" Jake asked, waving the can in the air.

"Sure, throw it here," Bill said, catching it when Jake sent one across the kitchen.

After taking a sip, Bill checked the cabinets and found saltines, Ritz crackers, two boxes of cereal, and three cans of sardines. It looked like others had been here before him looking for food, but hadn't done a thorough job, which was a good thing for Jake and Bill.

Deciding this would have to do for now, they took their meager supplies and went upstairs to see if the rooms could be used for the night. They were in luck and everything was still in order. Dusty, but still in order.

Evidently the ghouls had remained on the first floor.

Bill took Melissa's parents' bedroom, not wanting to go near Jess or Cara's bedrooms, the guilt over what happened to them still too fresh in his conscience.

The parents' bedroom faced the front of the house and let him keep an eye on the street to make sure there was no trouble. With a wave goodnight, the older man entered one of the bedrooms, Jake and Duke doing the same.

Jake picked Melissa's bedroom, also staying away from Jess and Cara's rooms, a pang of loss filling him as he read the small signs identifying the girls' rooms. As he entered Melissa's room, he sighed at all the familiar objects, having many fond memories with her on the bed.

It wasn't like they did anything serious, mind you, just heavy make-out sessions and spooning. They'd both agreed to wait until they were married to have sex, and though he was still a virgin, he'd already made a solemn vow that no matter what happened to him in this dead world he now lived in, he would have sex before he died.

First he opened the window to let in some fresh air, then tossed his share of the food and beer onto the bed. He put his katanas on the floor, knowing he would need to clean them soon. He cracked open another can of beer, placed a soup bowl taken from the kitchen onto the floor, and poured out half the can for Duke, who greedily lapped it up.

As the dog drank, he scanned the room with a weary heart.

Bill was across the hall and he peered into the room to check on Jake.

"Hey, hotshot, listen up, I think I'm going to bed, so wake me if there's any trouble," Bill said.

"Sure, fine, I will," Jake said, taking a sip from his beer. Though warm, it still tasted wonderful.

Duke finished his bowl of beer and looked up at Jake, seeing his new owner drinking from the can, and began to whine.

"What, you want some more? You lush. Okay, fine, here, but so help me if you get drunk. You strike me as a mean drunk, too."

Duke ignored his words and lapped up the beer, and when he was through, he made a large belch that would make any man jealous.

"You know, that's all you're gonna get," Jake said, looking down at Duke, who was begging for more.

Getting up, he walked around the room some more and then found a photo album of him and Melissa on a bookshelf. Jumping onto the bed while eating some crackers, he opened the album to the first page, and admired all the pictures he'd taken with her.

He saw the album was filled from front to back with photos of both of them and it brought a tear to his eye. To see all the memories he'd made with her ever since they began going out, and she'd kept them all.

Duke jumped on the bed and lay on Jake's lap, snuffing happily now that he'd drank his fill. Jake handed the dog a cracker and the animal consumed it hungrily, almost taking Jake's fingers with it.

Chuckling, he scratched Duke's head.

Soon, Jake felt the beer making him drowsy and he set the photo album to the side. His eyes grew heavy and he drifted off to sleep for the night, Duke doing the same, his ears constantly shifting as he listened for signs of danger.

As Jake fell into a deep sleep, visions of the past flooded his mind; images of what had happened to Jess and Cara and what had occurred at the rescue camp.

He began to toss and turn as he relived the horrific scenes of death.

Chapter 8

The Past (July 4, 2009)

"Hey, Cara, Jake's finally waking up," Jess called while she watched over him.

Jake was still sprawled on the floor near the couch, exactly where he fell after passing out. Cara came back into the room, returning from the kitchen, wanting to greet Jake with her sister.

Jake slowly opened his eyes and looked around the room. It took a few moments, but then images of what happened flooded back to him and he sat up with a start.

"Dammit, what happened? How long was I out for?" he asked, clearing his head while trying to get a handle on the situation.

"You've been unconscious for hours. You hit your head on the radiator in the hallway and got a nice cut on your head. I cleaned and bandaged it," Jess said, proud of her work.

"I helped, too," Cara added.

Jake breathed deeply through his nose to clear his sinuses, and got a big whiff of decayed bodies and vomit, all of it mixed with an overwhelming scent of Lysol.

"What's that smell?" he asked, scrunching his nose in disgust.

"It's the bodies in the living room and your puke," Jess said. "So me and Cara sprayed a full can of Lysol around. Thanks for throwing up in my house by the way; it really makes the place look and smell better. Anyway, we left you on the floor. We couldn't get you on the couch, you were too heavy for us to lift," she finished, explaining everything the best she could. "Are you feeling any better? Are you thirsty or hungry?"

Jake gave it some thought. "Yeah, actually I'm starving," he said upon realizing he hadn't eaten for quite some time.

"Good, 'cause Cara's making sandwiches. You want something to drink? A beer?"

"Love one, thanks. Where're my katanas?"

"They're in the corner. They're all washed and they look brand new," Jess said, happy to see him up and around, doing better with each passing second.

Jess went and retrieved a beer for Jake with Cara right behind her.

A minute later, Cara returned and placed a plate full of potato chips and sandwiches down on the dining room table, before three chairs, where they were each going to sit. When Jake had his beer, he opened it and nearly drank half in one gulp.

"Whoa, take it easy, Jake. There's more in the fridge, and since me and Cara can't drink, then I guess the beer's all yours," Jess said, concerned he might choke.

"Listen, I haven't eaten for what seems like forever and I'm starving. If we run out of food, I have a backpack full of items that don't need to be refrigerated," he said while shoving a handful of chips in his mouth.

"About that, uhm, are you enjoying your chips? They're from your backpack," Cara said, worried about what he would say.

Jake was chewing on a mouthful of sandwich and now he paused, his chewing slowing so he resembled a cow masticating its cud.

"Are you saying you went outside to get my bag? Are you two nuts? You could've gotten..." He stopped when he saw the fear in their eyes.

"You know what? It's okay. You didn't get hurt so there's no use talking about it. But don't go outside again unless you're with me. You hear me?"

They both nodded in agreement.

"Don't you guys have any food in the house? Why'd you need to see if I had anything in my car?"

"Don't you remember?" Cara asked. "We were going on that vacation in a few days so Mom and Dad said we needed to eat most of the stuff so it wouldn't go bad."

Jake nodded, remembering Melissa telling him how the family was going to go on a camping trip or something. He felt guilty now for not listening to her better. After taking a couple more bites of his sandwich, he began contemplating on what he was going to do next.

"We have to figure out what we're going to do tomorrow because we can't stay here if there's no food," he told the girls.

"Why can't we stay here?" Cara asked. "There's some food, cans and such, but my mom never stored a lot of that stuff."

"Yeah," Jess agreed, "it could work, and we could clean this place up and it'd be fine."

He shook his head no. "For starters, I don't want to clean up the mess in the living room, and second, it's not safe here in the suburbs. But I'm open to any ideas you might have."

"How about we go into Boston?" Jess suggested. "I heard on the news there were shelters spread out all over the place. In fact, I think one's at Logan Airport. But all the roads are getting blocked by accidents." She smiled wanly, hoping she'd offered a good idea.

Jake stood up and walked to one of the front windows looking out onto the street, thinking about Jess's idea about going to Boston. His eyes went to his katanas leaning against the couch, the sheaths covered in droplets of dried blood.

Crossing the room, he picked them up and slid each one from its sheath. They were shiny and clean, just like Jess had said.

He held them in his hands with such a tight grip his knuckles turned white.

"The trains," he said, turning on his heels to look at the girls at the dining room table. "We can take the blue line train; it goes right past the airport. It's perfect." He grinned widely, proud of himself.

"Oh, that's so brilliant, Sherlock. How're we going to take the train? They're not running due to whatever's happening in the city," Cara said sarcastically.

"Well, if they're not running then we'll use the tracks, you know, walk on them," Jake said. "It's fenced in so there shouldn't be too many of those things to deal with. Or better yet, if the power's still on then we could try and steal one. I heard they're like driving a car."

Jess frowned. "And which station should we try for?"

He shrugged. "Probably Wonderland station. It's the closest."

"Great! When do we leave?" Cara asked, deciding the plan was as good as they could hope for.

"We go tomorrow morning, right when it starts to get light out, that way we can rest up tonight. As for your parents, we have to leave them here," he explained. "I'm sorry, guys, we can't try to bury them. If we go outside we could attract more of those things to us."

Both girls took on a look of grief as they glanced at the bodies in the next room, which were now covered under sheets. Jess had performed the task while Jake was unconscious. The two girls had cried for what seemed like forever, their eyes bloated and red, but they were strong, and though it hurt terribly, they knew their parents would want them to survive.

"Yeah, Jake, it's okay, I understand, we both do. Right, sis?" Jess asked Cara.

Cara nodded. "Yeah, it's okay, we don't have a choice. Mom and Dad would understand."

"Okay, good," he said. "So here's what we'll do and how we'll do it." He quickly filled them in on what he thought was the best course of action, the two girls listening attentively.

After Jake laid out his plan, there was nothing else to do so they returned to their sandwiches, each of them lost in their private thoughts of what the future would hold.

The rest of the day was uneventful, except for talking and discussing about how they were going to do everything the next morning. When they were finished talking about everything worth discussing, Jake brought up the fact that his clothes were filthy. They were covered in dried blood and gore, and he really wanted to change into something new. Jess had already thought of this and had prepared new clothes for him.

"There's new clothes on the bed in my parents' bedroom. They belonged to my dad, so I hope they fit," Jess said.

"Thanks, Jess," Jake smiled. "You and Cara should pack a bag, too. We don't know what'll happen once we leave here, so we should try to prepare for everything and anything."

Jess nodded, and as the two talked through the door while Jake went to the bathroom to change, a loud roar filtered in from outside, sounding like a convoy of vehicles had arrived.

"What the hell is that?" Jake asked. He exited the bathroom and went to the closest window facing the street, not believing his eyes.

Night had fallen, and in the gloom of the moonlight and the headlights of the approaching vehicles, he saw two Army-grade Humvees coming down the street, destroying everything in their path.

The vehicles were plowing over shambling zombies like they were tenpins, a few soldiers jogging alongside, knocking any that got too close with the butts of their rifles.

"Ah, Jess, you're not gonna believe this, but the Army's out there and I'll bet anything they're not friendly. Maybe I've watched too many movies in my day, but..." He was worried what the soldiers might do if they found him and the girls inside the house.

"What the hell are you talking about?" Jess asked. "That's the Army, they're here to protect us. They're what we've been hoping and waiting for." But just as Jess finished her sentence, a loud *bang* sounded from outside.

By now Cara had joined him and Jess, the young girls nervous and excited at the same time, as they looked out the window.

By Jake's side, they saw clearly that the soldiers didn't appear to be friendly.

There were six of them, but where they should have been wearing regulation uniforms, instead they wore their shirts with the sleeves torn off. A few held beer cans in one hand and M-16s in the other. The loud *bang* Jake heard was a grenade tossed out of one of the Humvee's windows. When Jake got a good look at one of the soldiers carefully, he realized he only had one arm.

When a spotlight turned towards the window he was looking out of, Jake quickly reacted.

"Shit, get down," he whispered, taking both of the girls under his arms and pulling them to the floor with him. After the spotlight went by the window, he peered out and saw the two Humvees were now parked out front.

The soldiers were stepping out of the vehicles, hollering and yelling, happy to be alive and seeming to be having a grand ole time. A few of the soldiers spread out, heading off to the closer homes on the street, kicking in doors to see what was inside.

Jake saw the homes' windows light up as the soldiers shot whatever people they found. Whether they were living or undead, Jake had no idea.

When two of the men approached the front door of Jake's house, ready to kick it in, the lead man was distracted when a horde of zombies began pouring out of the nearby homes, attracted to all the noise.

The house Jake and the girls were in was forgotten for the moment, the men now having to protect themselves from the attacking ghouls.

With the soldiers focusing their attention on the attacking zombies, Jake was able to peer out the window again and watch their guns blazing. In the headlights of the Humvees, he saw blood, guts, and gore splashing onto the street. Against M-16s, the zombies never had a chance and were quickly mowed down like wheat to a scythe.

When all of the ghouls were destroyed, the soldiers completely forgot about ransacking the house Jake was in and returned to their Humvees and continued onward, yelling and whooping it up, a few men shooting into the shadows lining the road.

When the Humvees were lost from sight, Jake and the girls stood up, relieved that the zombies had caused enough of a distraction to make the men forget about their house.

It very well might have saved their lives, or the girls might have suffered a fate worse than death. Who knows what the soldiers might have done to Cara and Jess if given the chance.

"Okay, that was too close," Jake said. "Hopefully they'll keep right on going and not come back."

"You think they might?" Cara asked, the fear on her face apparent.

Jake moved next to her and placed a reassuring hand on her shoulder. "They're not coming back, I promise, now let's get ready for bed, it's gonna be a long day tomorrow." He moved away from the window, making sure to close the curtains. "You guys just relax. Well, as much as you can, anyway. I'll be keeping watch for the entire night while you both sleep."

"Okay, Jake, goodnight. I'm going to bed," Cara said and left to go to her bedroom. She was sniffling slightly, but wanted to hold her tears of fear and loss back until she was alone in her room.

Jess walked over to Jake and gave him a kiss on the cheek.

"What was that for?" he asked.

"For saving me and Cara," she said. "Melissa's a lucky girl to have you in her life."

"Nah," he said bashfully. "It's me that's the lucky one."

She grinned. "Maybe, but I'll stick with what I said. Goodnight."

"Goodnight," he replied, feeling happy and sad at the same time. Jess was sweet and now that she'd brought up Melissa, he felt that worry in his gut again. Was she still alive out there somewhere? Or was she dead like so many others.

With both of the girls going to bed, he went to the window and placed a chair in front of it, wanting to watch the street for signs of trouble.

He knew it was going to be a long night for all of them. He only hoped that the incident with the soldiers was a one time thing and prayed they didn't return in the middle of the night.

It was as he relaxed in the chair and stared at the prone, bullet-riddled corpses scattered in the street and front yards of the neighboring homes, that he knew if the soldiers did come back, there wasn't a damn thing he could do about it.

Chapter 9

The Past

The next morning, Jake found himself looking down at Jess while she slept. He was admiring her curves and he was thinking how she was turning into a beautiful young lady. He noticed she was starting to look a lot like Melissa. From her personality to how she reacted to a situation, she was like a smaller version of her older sister.

Jake had no idea Jess had a crush on him. When he saw her stirring in bed, ready to get up, he quickly turned away to look out the window. He'd entered her room for a purely innocent reason.

With the sun coming up, he had wanted to check out all sides of the house and her room had the best view of the north side, so he'd crept into her room to peer out the window.

Jess woke up with a heavy sigh, followed by a slight groan as she stretched. Sitting up, she brushed sleep from her eyes to see Jake still keeping watch as he gazed out her window.

"Good morning, Jake. How're you feeling?"

"Tired. After staying up for the last twelve hours or so, I'm tired as hell and it's only five," he said.

"Oh, that's not good. Okay, so how about you sleep for a few hours and I'll keep watch over us. I'll wake you at seven," Jess said, concerned that if he was sleep deprived, he could become a problem to them all later.

"No, thanks," he replied. "I got plenty of rest when I got knocked out yesterday, even if I was unconscious. I'll be fine, really."

"All right, it's up to you. Look, I'm just going to run to the bathroom, then I'll go wake up Cara."

"You know there's no water, right?" he asked, wondering where she was going to go.

"I know. I'll just go in the bathtub and spray Lysol around if it smells. It's not pretty but what are you gonna do, right?"

"Yeah, guess so," he said.

He thought it was a little weird, but if it worked, who cares? So, with Jess waking up Cara and using the bathroom, he decided to go downstairs and get something to eat. He left his katanas behind in the bedroom, figuring that with all the doors locked downstairs, he was safe.

It was still dark in the house, the sun just kissing the horizon. He moved through the living room, the fetid stench from the decayed remains of Melissa's dead parents and other corpses came to him.

God, there'd been so much death in the last day and a half. He wondered if he could keep managing to hold it together.

Despite the smell he was starving, so after covering his nose with his arm and entering the kitchen, he opened the freezer to find a box of chocolate ice cream.

With the power having gone off in the middle of the night, the ice cream was gooey and melted, only the freezer door staying closed allowing the food to be edible as it slowly thawed out.

He didn't really care, however, because ice cream was ice cream, even if it resembled a milkshake. So he grabbed a spoon from the drawer and dug in.

It tasted like a frappe that had been laid out in the sun for too long, but he didn't mind. When he was halfway through his melted breakfast of ice cream, he heard a noise coming from the basement, which seemed odd.

There was no one else in the house other than him and the girls. The door had always been locked so the zombies had never managed to get down there, but now that he thought about it, maybe he was wrong.

Nah, it had to be Jess or Cara.

Believing it was one of the girls, he decided to call out.

"Hey, Cara, Jess, is that you? If you guys are playing a game, I'm not in the mood. We need to get our stuff together and get going," he said annoyed. Imagine, their parents were dead in the living room and they wanted to fool around and scare him or something similar.

When there was no reply to his challenge, he set the ice cream carton down on the counter and retrieved a flashlight from one of the drawers, remembering where Melissa's father kept it from when he had visited before and a fuse had gone out, dousing the lights and TV on movie night.

With flashlight in hand, he walked over to the basement door and opened it very slowly. Then he heard a crash that was even louder than the first noise to drift up from below.

He opened the door some more and pointed the flashlight beam down the stairs, but there was nothing out of place on the walls or on the small staircase.

Deciding to go down the stairs, he left the door wide open to leave himself an escape route. Halfway down, he heard something drop to the cement floor; it sounded like a cardboard box.

Stepping onto the last step, a creak of wood making him wince, he looked around the basement to see nothing was in view where ever he pointed the light. He went to where he thought the box had fallen, and chuckled to see it was a lawn gnome that had slid off the top shelf of a steel cabinet.

After putting it back on the shelf, he turned around to find himself staring into the dark visage of a newly rotting ghoul, with a missing left eye and maggots already crawling inside the empty eye socket. Part of the ghoul's right cheek was missing and the tongue could be seen flopping inside the mouth like a spasming eel.

Before Jake could do anything to stop the zombie, it lunged for him, knocking him into the shelf behind him and knocking the lawn gnome to the floor yet again. They both fell to the floor with the ghoul landing on top of him.

The ghoul's teeth were only centimeters away from Jake's face and he could smell the rotting breath of spoiled meat coming from the open mouth as the dead lungs continued to exhale. The man had only been dead for a little more than a day, but the human body began to decay and rot almost immediately upon expiring.

With his left hand holding the ghoul's head at bay and his right hand feeling around for something to use as a weapon, Jake's fingers found the lawn gnome. With one quick movement, he picked up the gnome and smashed it over the zombie's head with a loud *thwack*.

The ghoul shuddered for a second and then collapsed on top of him, half its skull now caved in as pulped brains leaked out of the jagged hole. Pushing the ghoul away from him, he quickly grabbed the flashlight, and without looking back, ran upstairs.

He took the stairs two at a time, wanting to tell the girls it was time to leave. If there was a zombie in the basement then who knows where else they could be, hiding and waiting for one of them to find it. While the girls had slept, who knows what could have happened, and Jake cursed himself for not realizing the danger they were all in.

Moments later, Jake was standing upstairs in Cara's bedroom with both sisters, Cara still blurry eyed as she'd woken only a few minutes ago. When the girls saw him, they were shocked to see blood covering his face and chest.

"Oh my God, what happened? Are you hurt?" Jess asked, looking to see if he had any new cuts or if the bandage on his head had come loose.

"I'm fine, but we have to leave now," he said. "Collect everything you can fit in a backpack with food and necessities and we'll meet downstairs in the hallway in five minutes." He gently pushed Jess away from him when she tried to inspect him for fresh wounds. He also took off the bandage on his head, realizing his cut had stopped bleeding sometime in the middle of the night.

Jess and Cara looked at each other and then at Jake. When Jake picked up his katanas, he turned around to see both of them staring at him.

"What, do I have something on my face?" he asked.

"We're not moving from this spot till you tell us what happened downstairs," Cara said, looking at Jake with *the look* all women give to men when they want to be told something.

With a weary sigh, he relented, figuring it would be easier to just tell them so they could get moving.

"Fine, I got attacked by one of those zombies in the basement. Satisfied? So can you stop giving me the third degree and get packed, please?" He was angry they'd made him say something he didn't want to speak of.

"Okay fine, that's all we wanted to know. It's dead now, right?" Jess asked, picking up her bag and packing up the things she thought as *essentials*.

"Yeah it's dead; it was dead before, that's our whole problem in the first place! They're all dead! Now stop talking and get packing."

He was getting frustrated that it was taking them such a long time to get moving.

Ten minutes later, they were packed, ready to leave, and gathered in the first floor hallway.

"Do we have everything we need because once we get in the car, we're not coming back for anything, not even to use the bathroom," Jake said, making sure they understood what he was saying and being a little sarcastic at the same time.

He couldn't help it. Lack of sleep was making him grouchy.

"Yes, Jake, we have as much stuff as we can carry and we both used the bathroom," Cara replied in the same sarcastic tone. "We're not children you know."

"Okay, okay, I just wanted to know for sure," he said with a grin.

Turning, he moved to the front door, and with a brief glimpse to each of them to make sure they were ready, he turned the doorknob. With car keys in one hand, a katana in the other, and the other sword secured to his backpack, he stepped outside into the morning sun.

After giving the girls the all clear sign after looking around the street, the three of them ran to the Cadillac. For the moment there were no signs of zombies anywhere. Jake unlocked the car doors and they jumped inside.

No sooner were doors thumping closed then Jake turned on the ignition, starting the engine and preparing to leave. He idly noticed there were a few bullet holes in the windshield, and a few on the hood from where the soldiers had shot rounds without care.

"This is a nice car. What kind is it?" Jess asked.

"It's a Cadillac, but I don't know the model off the top of my head," Jake said. "I do know it's my..." He stopped talking in mid-sentence when he gazed out the front windshield to see a horde of zombies coming towards them from behind a nearby house, with others appearing to the right. The closing of the car doors was enough to attract them, the street otherwise preternaturally silent. Not even so much as a bird chirped in a tree.

"I'll have to answer that question later," Jake said, putting the car in drive and stepping on the gas pedal, not wanting to deal with the undead horde if he had a choice.

As the zombies swarmed into the street, Jake took off from along the curb. There were loud thumping sounds as the front bumper and grille plowed into bloated bodies, knocking them to the road, more than one becoming road kill in an instant.

Gore shot up into the tire wells, viscera splashing the undercarriage, dark blood painting the ground in a kaleidoscope of colors.

The Cadillac was down the street and gone from sight in seconds. Before Jake took the turn off the street, Cara looked through the rear window to see the crowd of zombies trying to chase after the Cadillac, and she wondered if what was happening to her, Jake and Jess would ever end.

Chapter 10

The Past

Jake, Cara, and Jess were just a few miles away from Wonderland. They were making great time, the roads clear of traffic.

Almost the entire city was either evacuated or the people were hiding out in their homes, as they waited for order to be restored.

Unfortunately the Cadillac was low on gas and Cara was the first to spot this when she glanced at the dashboard.

"Jake, the car's going to run out of gas. It's on E," Cara said from the back seat as she leaned back from peering over Jake's shoulder.

"No it's not. **E** stands for *extra five miles,* and since we're only a few miles away from the train station, we should be fine," Jake replied, feeling he knew what he was talking about.

But a quarter mile later, the car was sputtering and chugging. Then the engine cut out and the car stopped suddenly in the middle of the road.

The three of them looked at each other and Jess was the first one to speak up. "Wow, that five miles sure went by fast, huh?" she said sarcastically.

Jake turned his head to look at her with a devilish gaze and Jess slid over more in her seat, wondering if she'd overstepped herself.

"We passed a gas station about a half mile back. I'll take the gas can from the trunk and go fill it up," he said while opening the door and getting out of the car, ignoring Jess' comment. "You two don't move. If any of them show up, they won't be able to get you if you stay in the car."

Jake went to the trunk and opened it. He grabbed the gas can he knew was inside from previous trips with his father, who used it mostly when he needed fuel for their lawnmower. He strapped his katanas to his back, and got going.

Hopefully, there wouldn't be any trouble on his way to the gas station. Once there, he knew he would have to figure out how to get the gas from the underground tanks if the pumps weren't working, but one thing at a time, he figured.

With one last look at the Cadillac, Jess and Cara now watching him through the rear window like lost waifs, he moved off, the gas can slapping his right thigh with each plodding step.

Jake reached the gas station about ten minutes later, his feet hurting from the walk. As he approached the cement entry leading to the small building from the street, he saw that the power was off here, too.

Oh, well, so much for getting gas from the underground tanks, he thought. With the fuel pumps being electric, it would be next to impossible unless he had a long hose to suck it out, and even then he doubted it would actually work.

He noticed there were a couple of cars parked in front of the station, looking like their owners had run inside for a pack of smokes. He wondered if that could mean there were people inside, either trapped or hiding.

This particular gas station was also a convenience store, where people could get cigarettes, milk and lottery tickets. There were worse places to hole up, he figured.

When he reached the main double glass doors to the building, he saw that one of them was shattered, with pieces of glass shards littering the ground. Realizing it must have been people who wanted to get in or out and didn't feel like waiting for the power to come back on, he continued through the door. The first thing he saw was a rack of brand new tires on his right. He breathed in the new tire smell, enjoying the scent. It reminded him of being with his father when they would go to the tire store to get new ones for the Camaro.

In the next aisle there were plastic cases thrown about and what looked like boxes for handy knifes, similar to box cutters. There were different size boxes, some long, some skinny, others wider, and others still filled with knives with different color handles.

"What a mess this place is," Jake muttered to himself.

The next aisle was the one he wanted. There was motor oil, carburetor and fuel injection additives and cleaners, as well as dry gas and other additives put into gas to clean the engine and carburetors.

He wasn't sure, but he figured in a pinch these additives might be used as a substitute for gas. After all, they went into the tank and were burned with the fuel, so they should work.

When he chose the ones he wanted, he began opening the containers and filling the gas can one bottle at a time.

For the next few minutes, he continually opened and poured the additives into the gas can, and at first he didn't hear what sounded like wheels squeaking, like on a shopping carriage.

But after more than thirty seconds of hearing the odd sound, he finally noticed it and stopped working. He was hidden from view where he was and so was the rest of the store from him.

"Hello? Is anyone there?"

No one answered.

Deciding he should investigate further, he stood up and moved to the end of the aisle, but as he reached the end, the sound moved away. Frowning, he began to see if he could follow it, and soon it seemed he was in a game of hide and seek with the noise.

When he turned right, the sound went left, and when he turned left, the noise went right. He was beginning to wonder if there was more than one origin for the noise, but as he'd been searching for over five minutes and nothing had appeared, he decided if the noise left him alone then he would do the same.

Besides, he wanted to get back to the girls.

Not wanting to waste any more time, he went back to work filling the gas can, this time working faster, wanting to leave as soon as possible. Now as he worked, he made sure to keep an eye out on each end of the aisle, his katanas ready by his side if he needed them. Something was in the store with him and he didn't want to be caught unawares.

That was when the figure showed itself at the front of the aisle, near the cash register.

He appeared to be a middle-aged man, Caucasian, wearing a one piece mechanic's outfit. He also had a couple of white streaks in his hair and a worn face with a few smudges of grease on his forehead.

On his left, breast pocket was stitched the name **Greg**. He was the manager and the mechanic of the small gas station, and Jake knew this immediately by the matching picture on the wall behind the man, the words *manager* and *mechanic* under the photo.

"What the hell are you doing in here?" the man demanded in a low, menacing tone.

Jake quickly stood up to face him.

So this is the origination of the squeaking noise I heard, he thought. The first thing he noticed was the shopping carriage in front of the man. The front of the carriage was covered in knives, so that if the carriage ran into someone, they would be pierced horribly.

In the carriage there was also a shotgun, and to top off the bizarre picture, there was a young woman sitting in the carriage as well, her knees wrapped under her so she could fit. She looked to be in her mid-twenties, with long dark hair and a body that any man would want; she looked unconscious.

All this Jake took in at a glance and he realized he better say something to defend himself, after all, he *was* stealing the fuel additives.

"Listen, uhm, I just came in here to fill up my gas can because my car stalled about a half mile up the road. So, if you want, I have money, I could pay you and I'll be on my way," Jake said, acting calm so the manager wouldn't be rash and use the shotgun. Plus, if the man called Jake's bluff about having money, he was screwed.

He had none.

"You're shoplifting. I hate shoplifters," the mechanic said, getting worked up a little more than Jake would have preferred.

"No, no, no. I'm not shoplifting. I have money," Jake said, trying to calm him down.

"Well, that was what this bitch said when she tried to shoplift in my store," the man said while grabbing the girl's hair and showing her face to Jake.

"Now just wait a second. I'm not here to shoplift, I swear. I'm just here to get gas and go back to my car," Jake said, getting more concerned about the situation. The man seemed to be growing unstable with each passing second. "Look, don't you know what's going on out there in the city? It's nuts, man."

That was when the man snapped and started to look like the Hulk, except he wasn't turning green and didn't have huge muscles.

"I don't like anyone shoplifting in...my...stooooooorrrreee!" he screamed, and then was charging full speed down the aisle at Jake, the knives of the shopping cart looking even more sinister now that they were coming for him.

It took Jake a second for the information to go from his eyes to his brain, then to his feet, that it was time to leave the gas station. Picking up the gas can, he ran full speed down the aisle, the opposite way, of course, with the man closing in on his tail.

When Jake reached the end of the aisle, he quickly made a right into another one, but the man also took the right turn. Then he stopped, perhaps realizing how silly it was for him to chase Jake around the inside of the store.

Suddenly, he took out his shotgun and started firing like a madman. Only Jake was too fast for him and he jumped over the counter, knocking the cash register over, managing to miss being hit just in time, the blasts going over him.

The man ejected the spent shells and began walking down the aisle towards Jake, tiptoeing, hoping Jake wouldn't hear him.

"You're not gonna make this easy for me, are ya," the man said, getting closer and closer to the cash register.

Behind the counter, Jake was breathing heavily, trying to figure out what he could do to get out of his present situation. His heart was going a mile a minute and he fought to control his growing panic.

Jake peeked over the cash register and saw a chain holding the tires on the rack a few feet away. That gave him an idea.

Moving closer to the cash register, the man was nearly upon his prey. When he reached the counter, he lowered the shotgun and fired both barrels behind the cash register, wanting to hear a blood-curdling scream, but when there wasn't one, he looked over to see there was no one there.

"Where the fuck are you!" the man yelled at the top of his lungs.

"I'm right over here, dumbass," Jake snapped, coming from the first aisle where the tires were. It had been tricky crawling around on the floor and remaining hidden, but he had managed it just in time.

The man spun the shopping carriage in a circle, and like a bull, began running down the aisle towards Jake. Evidently, he didn't want to shoot Jake now, but wanted to skewer him on the knives.

"You're not getting away from me!" the man screamed, charging down the aisle, the knives glistening in the sunlight filtering through the dirty windows.

With a wide grin, Jake responded by cutting the thin chain holding the tires in place with a pair of bolt cutters he'd found in one of the closest aisles.

With the chain broken, the tires rolled off the rack to land on the man and the girl in the shopping carriage. When Jake went to see if the man was dead, he was surprised to see that the girl was gone.

That was fast. Where'd she run off to? he wondered.

Deciding the mystery wasn't worth thinking about, he went to check on the fallen man, who seemed to be having a heart attack. He was mumbling something, a saying or a lyric, but Jake couldn't make it out.

Then Jake had to jump back from him, waving his katana in front of him, when the man sat straight up and said, "Clean up in aisle one."

That was when he spasmed and his eyes flicked open and closed, his mouth curling up into a rictus of a grin as he suffered a major heart attack. His eyes closed and he slumped forward, never to see the light of day again.

Breathing a sigh of relief that he was still alive and unhurt, Jake retrieved the mostly filled gas can and hurried back to the Cadillac.

He'd been away for almost an hour and figured the girls must be worried sick about him.

He was only a few minutes away from the Cadillac, knowing all he had to do was turn the next corner, when he began to hear screaming coming from the same direction of the car and the girls.

Putting on a burst of speed, he began running, the fuel sloshing around in the can causing him to become off balance.

When he finally reached the car, there were five zombies surrounding it, trying desperately to get inside. Calling out to get the ghouls' attention, Jake charged at them, and when he was almost upon them, he threw the plastic gas can at the first one, the weight of the can knocking it to the ground.

He knew the fuel would be fine, the thick plastic container easily able to take a hard landing on the ground.

With his hands free, he pulled his katanas from his back, and as the second ghoul approached him, he cut both its hands clean off. Dust and dirt came off the limbs from the filthy clothing, and dark blood squirted out to splatter the road.

Jake took his katanas and rested them on the ghoul's shoulders, so that the head was in-between the two blades. Pressing them together, he sliced the head off.

With the head rolling on the ground, he swung his right foot out and kicked it away, the oblong ball with matted hair rolling into the gutter.

There were only four zombies left, so he slashed low and took out one of them at the knees, which left the zombie legless, and with the edge of the katana facing downward, he brought it down onto the head, slicing sideways.

As the first ghoul tried to get up after being knocked over by the heavy gas can, Jake danced in and sliced its head in half at a slant, the half-skull sloughing off the shoulders to drop onto the road.

The last two came at him and he used a blade on each of them, jamming the tip into their chests. With a yell of rage, he dragged the blades across their sternums, the razor-sharp edge slicing through their spines, the two bodies collapsing.

The top halves were still active, but the lower extremities were useless. Jake ignored them, knowing they could be dealt with later if need be, but wanting to check on the girls.

When he was finished with the zombies, he called out to Cara and Jess, letting them know it was safe to leave the car.

"Wow, Jake, that was great. How'd you know how to fight like that?" Jess asked, opening the car door. "I never knew you could use a sword."

"Yeah, me neither, it just came naturally to me when this whole thing started," he replied. "I mean, I used to mess around in the backyard with a fake wooden sword, but then I gave it up after about a year. Guess it's like riding a bike, huh?"

"So you never had any formal training?" Cara asked from the backseat as she peeked out the open driver's door. She'd already decided she wanted to stay inside the car.

"Nope, never."

"Cool," Jess said, sighing heavily, her crush on Jake growing just a little more.

Jake was oblivious to her batting eyes as she dreamed of her and him getting married.

"Okay, Jess, you keep an eye out and I'll fill the gas tank," he said, as he picked up the gas can. The container was none the worse for wear after being tossed like a bludgeon.

It didn't take long to drain the makeshift gas into the Cadillac, and when Jake was finished, he screwed on the cap and tossed it back into the trunk.

Jess and Jake hopped into the Cadillac and he started the engine. At first it didn't seem like it was going to start and he was getting nervous that his idea about the additives was wrong, but then the engine roared to life, running rough but running just the same.

He let the engine idle for a few seconds to make sure it was going to keep running, and Cara leaned forward from the backseat.

"So, Jake," Cara said, "did anything interesting happen at the gas station?"

Jake glanced at the rearview mirror to see Cara's face looking back at him.

"Do me a favor, will ya?" he sighed. "Don't ask."

Before she could reply, he stepped on the gas pedal and the car surged forward, Cara falling back into her seat with a squeak of surprise from the motion.

Behind the Cadillac, a few more ghouls were slowly approaching, but they were quickly left behind.

While Jake maneuvered through the streets on his way to Wonderland train station, he couldn't help but wonder just who the woman was at the gas station and how she'd gotten there, knocked out and a prisoner of that crazy mechanic.

She must have a story to tell, he figured.

But then, so did everyone.

Chapter 11

The Past

Jake and his tired passengers all breathed a sigh of relief upon reaching Wonderland station.

The ride there hadn't gone as smooth as they would have hoped for, but they managed it nonetheless. As Jake drove through the streets, the undead had come out of houses and alleyways, trying to reach the Cadillac, but each time Jake floored the gas pedal and left the zombies in the dust. The engine fought the menagerie of fuel constantly, but it continued to run, though shaking like it had the worst case of the knocks ever recorded.

"Well, we're finally here," Jake said as he drove into the parking lot of the train station.

"Yeah, and all we have to do is steal a train, that shouldn't be too hard," Cara said sarcastically.

"Well, there's no question about it, the trains aren't running," Jess said as she studied the tracks and the nearby platform. From where they were parked, it was obvious the trains hadn't been running for at least a day.

Jake only grunted as he drove closer to the main doors that would lead to the inbound and outbound platforms. Seems there was no one around, and definitely no transit cops, and he knew he wasn't going to be using the Cadillac anymore, he decided there was no reason to put the car in a parking space.

Swinging the Cadillac around, he parked in front, blocking the entrance like he was a selfish driver, and if anyone did want to enter or leave, they would now have to walk around the front of the Cadillac.

"Nice park job," Jess grinned as she admired the front fender now blocking the entrance.

"So call a cop," Jake quipped. He opened his door and climbed out, the engine still knocking, as if it refused to turn off, knowing it was probably the last time it would ever be used.

Jake pocketed the car keys and then realized there was no point in it, so he tossed them on the front seat. If someone else could use the car, more power to them.

While the three survivors collected their belongings, they saw things were definitely too quiet.

"This is the first time I ever saw Wonderland so empty like this," Jess said, and when she turned, she saw Jake patting the car like it was a pet.

"I'm sorry, baby, but we can't take you. I know we've only been together for a little bit, but you were my favorite car ever," he said. "I know my dad loved you a lot, too, and at least you gave it your all."

"Come on, Jake, I just saw a butt load of those things coming our way," Cara said, rolling her eyes at his silliness and dragging him a little bit by the arm.

"I'll be back...maybe...call me!" he screamed at the Cadillac, while being dragged through the front door of the train station.

"Come on, we have to get to a train and get out of here, dammit!" Jess said, slapping him across the face.

"I'm sorry, you're right. Let's go," he said, snapping back to reality. "God, I know things are bad but lighten up."

Jess ignored him, jealous how the man could brush off everything that had happened to them thus far. Some people were like that, no matter how bad things were they just took it all in stride.

As they made their way through the lobby, a small crowd of zombies, the same ones Cara had seen, were hot on their trail, and if the three survivors didn't move fast enough, they were going to end up as zombie food.

When they reached the turnstiles, where trolley cards would be swiped to enter, the trio realized that with no electricity, they were stuck, but only for a second.

"I didn't bring my card," Jess said, ruefully.

"Doesn't matter," Jake said, throwing his bag to the other side and jumping over. "They don't have any power, so we're going to jump over them. I doubt there're any transit cops around to stop us anyway." He waved the girls to follow him. "Here, throw the bags this way, then you guys can jump over, too. There's more of 'em coming. I can see them through the windows."

Looking over their shoulders at the approaching zombies, both Jess and Cara saw what he was talking about and threw their backpacks to him. Once their packs were over, they too, jumped the turnstiles to land alongside Jake, who was now holding their backpacks and waiting for them.

"Ladies, your bags," he said, like a doorman who was holding their bags for them at a fancy hotel.

"Thank you," and, "Thanks," were said from both girls while they accepted their backpacks from Jake.

With the three of them now on the other side, they ran down the stairs in the direction of the first platform that would have a train going to Boston. But they soon realized they were on the wrong side.

The first wave of ghouls following them found out how to climb over the turnstiles, and though clumsy, they managed just fine. One broke an arm when it landed the wrong way, the bone now protruding like a bent tree branch on an old tree.

Despite the undead being stupid, they were still adapting quickly.

"Hurry up, they're coming. Let's jump down on the rails," he said, ready to jump.

"Jake, there's stairs on both sides," Cara stated, trying to knock some sense into him. "We can cross to the other side that way."

"Fine, if you want to take the easy way down we can do that," he said, stepping away from the edge and going to the stairs. He felt a little embarrassed he hadn't spotted the stairs before her.

They ran down the stairs, taking the steps two at a time, and soon they were on the opposite side of the platform.

Then a second wave of walking corpses, a group of fifteen, began filling the lobby as more climbed over the turnstiles. When the first of these ghouls approached the turnstiles, they couldn't figure out how to pass them. But with so many of them pushing the ones in front, the bodies were merely knocked over to fall like top-heavy grocery bags. They toppled over to land on the other side, then picked themselves up and followed the others before them.

Sadly, for the last couple of zombies, they didn't make it over because there were no more bodies behind them to help them along. They stayed at the turnstiles, like weary commuters waiting to be allowed entry.

"Now what? There's only one train here, and it probably doesn't run," Jess said while looking around.

Jake glanced over his shoulder to see the zombies coming down the stairs as they prepared to cross the rails, and then onto the platform he and the girls were on.

"Well, that's gonna have to do 'cause here they come," he said as he bolted to the train.

Jess and Cara turned when they heard the moans of the dead. Cara screamed, but Jess kept her head and dragged Cara after her as she followed Jake. The zombies crossed the rails and began walking onto the platform.

In seconds, the three survivors were at the front of the train.

"Okay, get that door open and see if you can start it. I'll make sure we're on the right track. We need to be on the *main* track," he said while handing Jess his backpack.

He ran to the handle that moved the tracks that connected the side railway to the main one. The handle wouldn't budge, and he thought he was about to pull something or break his back, when he saw the ghouls falling down onto the rails between the two platforms. Some had seen him and were now heading his way.

Deciding the handle wouldn't move, he used one of his katanas, putting the tip in the gears as he pulled at the handle, using the sword for leverage. After a few seconds of struggling, the handle began to loosen and the side tracks finally connected to the main tracks.

Just when he finished, he heard screams coming from the train.

It was Jess and Cara!

Turning, he ran across the tracks, careful not trip and go head first onto the rails. As he ran, he imagined himself stumbling and falling, his nose connecting heavily with the steel rail while cartilage was pulverized in his face. It was even possible he could kill himself, sending bone fragments into his brain.

Now that would be an embarrassing way to die, he thought as he charged up the cement stairs, one of his katanas held out in front of him.

When he reached the train, Jess was defending Cara against a zombie that looked like it may have been the driver of the train. There was the classic 'T' on the zombie's blue sleeve, which was the uniform for the transit authority.

"Jake, help me, for the love of God!" Jess yelled, just as the ghoul fell on top of her while Cara was kicking at the dead driver to get off her. They were both at the door, and Jake just ran at them, ready to pierce his katana through the ghoul's forehead.

"Jess, push the head up!" he ordered her.

Jess did what he said, raising the head so it was away from her, and the next thing she saw was a sword shooting out of the ghoul's left eye, the impaled eyeball now stuck on the tip of the sword like an appetizer at a dinner party.

As the dead T driver spasmed on top of Jess, Jake reached over and grabbed the body, forcing it to the ground. The odiferous stench of decay was amazing and he had to wonder how this zombie could smell so bad so fast.

"Cara, help me get the door closed!" he called to her as he tried to close the door to the subway car. Cara ran to his aid as did Jess, who knew there was no time for drama. She was freaked out by being attacked, but she was a strong girl and knew their only chance of surviving was to remain calm and stay focused on escaping.

With the three of them working together, they were able to leverage the door closed, just as the first zombies on the platform reached them. Their dead hands began pounding on the doors, but the glass was safety glass and withheld the onslaught.

Jake, breathing heavily, leaned against the doors, the vibration of pummeling dead hands almost feeling like a massage. He knew they were far from safe.

"Come on, we need to get to the front of the train," he said.

They were in the third one down and had to go through the sliding doors that connected each car.

When he moved to the front of the car and opened the inside door, he found five ghouls where the passengers would sit.

"I'll handle these guys," he said to the girls. "Jess, when you can, get to the front of the train and see if you can figure out how to start it while I take care of these bastards!"

"But, there's no p..." Jess stammered. She was going to say *power*.

"Just do it!" he yelled, and then was charging at the zombies, not waiting for her reply.

With one katana strapped to his back, he went in with both hands on the hilt of his remaining sword. He knew the confines were tight and one blade would be all he could manage to use. The first ghoul lost its head in an instant, a dark brown ichor shooting from the jagged neck wound to spray the ceiling and windows of the subway car.

The next zombie wasn't interested in its brother's plight and charged in, a low moan escaping its mouth. He chopped at the eyes, slicing the bridge of the nose and parting the eyes into two halves. Blind, the ghoul stumbled around the car, out of the fight.

Jake sliced the next one in the neck, the carotid and jugular parting in a flash, blood seeping out to lather the floor a dark red, with a generous portion of maroon thrown in. It was a kaleidoscope of reds and browns, all sticky and congealing, making the floor slippery, the footing as treacherous as ice.

When Jess had an opening, she ran through the car, past the ghouls and to the front, where the controls were. As she ran, one zombie reached out and grabbed her arm. She screamed, but when she looked down at the limb, she saw it was no longer attached to a body, now only a stump.

"Go, now!" Jake screamed.

Cara stayed behind Jake, watching as he took down body after body. Jess didn't need to be told twice and she ran forward when told to.

While Jess was trying to figure out the controls and start the train, Jake continued to fight the zombies. One tried to go after Jess and Jake stepped in front of it, slicing its ear off and causing the ghoul to turn its attention back to him.

There were two zombies on either side of him, so he pulled his other katana from its sheath on his back and sliced both ghouls in their foreheads, the blades sinking deep enough to penetrate their brains.

When the zombies slumped over the seats, there was one big slice mark on each of their temples. Dealing with the last one, he pulled his other sword and stabbed his katanas through both of its eyes.

With the last ghoul twitching as its brain shut down, he pulled the blades free and sliced its head into three parts, so that the left and right halves fell down with the middle staying up for a few seconds. Then that part, too, keeled over to the side as the body pitched forward to the blood-stained floor.

After he was done taking care of business, he heard the train start and felt the vibration beneath his feet. Moving to the front of the car, he saw Cara waiting for him. After waving for her to follow, he made his way to the front of the train, where Jess was busy with the controls.

"Wow, you did it, you got it started, that's great," he said, excited.

"Yeah, but I didn't know if it would start, 'cause trains run on electricity," Jess said. "If I had to guess, I'd say the supply wire above us that the train's attached to must be on a separate circuit and that one still has power, though that could change at any moment."

"Who cares why it's happening, I'm just glad it works," Jake said as he looked out the side window to the platform. The train was moving slowly and the ghouls on the platform were still slapping the side of the train facing them. Then one got lucky and managed to break a window, the safety glass shattering, black glass spilling onto the floor of the car.

"Shit, we need to go faster or they might get inside here with us," Jake said as he watched a ghoul trying to climb through the open window. The zombie was halfway in and its legs were now off the platform, kicking up and down like a clown stuck in a circus cannon.

"Then let's go faster," Jess said, pushing the handle forward that controlled the speed of the train.

The train began to move faster, inches first, then feet, then yards.

"Yeah, it's working. Maybe the supply wire is running on a back-up generator or something," he mused as the train picked up speed.

As the train reached the end of the platform, there was a small wall on the edge of it. The ghoul still hanging out the window was cut in half, the wall ripping the lower half off to splat onto the platform. The upper half spilled into the car, the intestines trailing out behind it. For now the ghoul was lying on one of the seats, like a weary traveler after a hard day at work.

Then the train was moving at a good clip, the *click-clack* of the metal wheels echoing off the floor, almost soothing.

There were a few zombies on the tracks as the train left the station and they were plowed over, the bodies crushed under the massive steel wheels. A burning smell of skin as metal melted the flesh off the ghouls filtered up through the floor and all three survivors wrinkled their noses in disgust.

Another zombie—already inside the train—tried to get at the control room just before the train left the station, and Cara was the first to act. As the face snarled at them from the door, she grabbed a small fire extinguisher from the wall and used the bottom of it like a hammer, smashing the ghoul in the face and flattening its features.

Dazed, the zombie fell away to drop heavily to the floor.

"Sorry, no more passengers," she said, while she smashed the face to mush, letting all her aggression and grief out on this one lone ghoul.

Behind the train, more zombies wailed, knowing their meal was escaping, while inside the car, the three survivors breathed a long sigh of relief.

They were free for the moment and on their way to what they hoped was safety. The rescue camps set up over the past two days should be just what they needed to remain safe from the undead.

At least, that was what they hoped for.

Chapter 12

The train rolled down the tracks for another eight minutes, then Jess had to hit the brakes, or else rear end another train sitting like a beached whale on the tracks.

"Shit, I didn't think of this happening," Jake said as he stared at the train now blocking the tracks.

The train squealed to a halt a few feet from the other one and Cara and Jake looked out the front windshield, stumped as to what to do next.

"Looks like we have to walk now," Cara said.

Jake didn't reply. Damn, his plan had been great, but this he hadn't thought about. Then, as he stared at the rear windows of the train in front of him, he spotted movement.

"Hey, guys, I think there's someone in that train," he said.

Jess and Cara both turned to look with him, and when they did, a face slammed against the dirty glass. The second they spotted the face they knew the man was dead. As the zombie rubbed his mouth and nose across the glass inside the other train, blood and saliva was left behind.

"Oh, that's so gross. He's one of them," Jess said as she watched the ghoul.

"Don't look at it, Jess," Jake said.

"He's stuck inside the train, he can't get you," Cara added.

Jake frowned as he stared at the train blocking their path, realizing Cara was right. They had no choice but to get out and walk.

"Come on, we might as well get moving," he said as he turned and left the small control room. Small was an understatement. With the three of them inside it, there was no elbow room at all.

The girls followed and in five minutes they were ready to go. Opening the door connecting two of the cars, Jake was able to climb out and drop down to the tracks. Looking around, he saw the tracks were fenced in so there shouldn't be any zombies to deal with. The girls followed and soon they were all on the ground, heads swiveling as they took in their new surroundings.

"Shall we?" Jake suggested, ushering the girls onward.

Jess giggled and Cara smiled as they began walking down the tracks.

As they passed the train that was blocking their journey, they each glanced up to the tinted windows of the subway cars and their jaws fell open at the sight before them.

The windows were full of people, but these people were definitely dead. Their faces were missing in places and sides of torsos were devoured, more than one zombie holding a leg or an arm against the glass as it chewed happily on its prize.

Dead hands slapped the glass, seeing the three survivors walking outside, and they wanted them badly.

"Oh my God, Jake, will you look at that?" Jess gasped in shock. "It's horrible."

Cara was looking away, one glimpse more than enough for her.

"Don't look, guys, just keep walking, we'll be past them in a sec', they're trapped in there," Jake said. But he couldn't stop looking, and while they walked, he turned his head so he was almost facing backwards.

There was a mother and small child inside the train, but the child was now food, the mother holding the small torso in her arms as she dove in with blood-red teeth. It was a sight he had a feeling he would never forget, no matter how hard he tried.

As they walked further from the train, the slapping and moans of the trapped ghouls followed them, but in time the wind carried it away and they were free of the visceral images and sounds of death.

None of them spoke after that, each too horrified by what they'd seen, so with eyes pointing down at the tracks, they placed one foot in front of the other and moved on.

Twenty minutes later, the three survivors were approaching the Logan Airport train station. Jake was the first to see the two soldiers standing on the platform.

"Hey, guys, looks like we got company," he said as both Jess and Cara looked where he was pointing. Both men wore the standard green uniforms of the Army or National Guard and carried rifles. Jake didn't know it at the time but they were standard M-16s.

Unbeknownst to Jake, these two men had orders to bring any civilians they found back to the temporary rescue camp set up at Logan Airport, at gunpoint if necessary, and any zombies seen too close to the perimeter of the airport were to be shot on sight.

Jake and the girls were almost upon the platform when one of the soldiers spotted them. Without considering whether he was shooting at people or zombies, the man leveled his rifle, prepared to shoot Jake and the girls.

Jake raised his hands into the air, waving them back and forth, calling out, "Wait, we're friendly, don't shoot!"

For a tense-filled heartbeat, he thought the soldier was going to shoot anyway, but then the man lowered his weapon and waited as Jake and the girls walked closer.

"Whew, that was close," Jake said as he let out a massive sigh of relief. "I really thought he was gonna shoot us."

"What do you mean?" Cara asked. "Surely the second he realized we weren't like those others he wouldn't have shot us. He's here to protect us, they all are."

Jake chuckled. "Well, first thing, Cara, don't call me Shirley," he joked, "and the second thing is, I've watched way too many zombie movies in my life, and in those films the soldiers are never kind to civilians," he explained.

"Oh, please, Jake, that's just in the movies. They're here to protect our country and us, like Cara said before," Jess said, trying to make some sense out of what he was saying.

Cara and Jess were assuming that like so many other civilians, when something bad happened in the country, the armed forces would be there to help, only wanting to assist in getting things back the way they were. But those soldiers were people too, with families and flaws, and many would either desert their posts or see what they could get out of a bad situation. And it never hurt that the soldiers were already armed thanks to the government.

If things got really bad, the soldiers would kill and fight anyone to survive, being no different from the people they were supposed to protect. The same went for police and fire services, too.

Upon reaching the platform, Jake and the girls looked up at the barrels of two rifles

"Who the fuck are you people and what're you doing on the tracks?" one of the soldiers asked.

"Please," Jess said in a low voice. "We came for help. I saw on the news there were rescue stations set up by the Army, so we decided to try for one."

"What're your names and where are you coming from exactly?" the second soldier asked, the barrel of the M-16 never wavering.

"Well, my name's Jake Roberts, the one on my right is Jessica Jacobs and the one on my left is Cara, Jess' sister. We came from Melrose; it's about four towns away."

"I know where the fuck Melrose is, asshole," the first soldier snapped.

"Are any of you carrying guns or weapons I can't see?" the second soldier asked, gesturing to the katanas on Jake's back.

They shook their heads that they didn't.

"Nope," Jake said. "All I have are these." He reached up and touched the hilts of the swords strapped to his shoulders.

"Do you know how to use them?" the second soldier asked.

"Yeah, I guess so, haven't gotten any complaints from anyone yet," Jake smirked.

"Don't be a wiseass, it could get you shot around here," the second soldier threatened.

"You three, don't move, we'll be watching you," the first soldier said. The two men moved a few feet away from the edge of the platform to speak privately.

Jake watched them intently, seeing how the second soldier kept casting glances at Cara and Jess. He was getting a bad feeling and he knew against two rifles he would be helpless to protect the girls if the soldiers had any funny ideas.

After what seemed like a heated discussion, the two soldiers stopped arguing and turned, both moving back to the edge of the platform.

"You three can come inside with us when we get relieved from watch; a part of the airport's been set up as a rescue station like you heard on the news." He waved them onto the platform. "Come on, let's go, we'll fill you in on the way. Our relief's should be here any minute and then we'll go together."

After climbing onto the platform, Jake and the girls were told to have a seat on one of the metal benches set up for weary commuters. If Jake had expected to hear more about what was going to happen next, he was sorely disappointed. The two soldiers moved away to talk together and left him and the girls alone, but the men always had an eye on them in case Jake tried something.

A two-way radio crackled on one of the soldier's belts and the man spoke into it. Jake could hear the voice on the radio also. It was a man's voice saying their replacements were on the way. The soldier talked to someone else, as well, but Jake couldn't hear what was being said, though he did hear a few tidbits relating to him and the girls, as in *found more civilians* and *two girls and a guy.*

Finally, two more soldiers arrived from the far edge of the platform and Jake was told to get moving, along with the girls.

They were ushered out of the train station and down a long flight of metal stairs that was really an escalator. But with no power they were merely stairs now.

The set of stairs led to the outside and large glass doors, which they exited from. There was an airport shuttle bus once used by one of the rent-a-car companies, the yellow and black colors a sharp contrast to the gray surroundings. Now the bus was upgraded into a military style vehicle with metal plates along the sides and barbed wire along the top of the roof and the bottom of the bus. Jake was impressed that someone had cobbled this war machine together in only a few days, thinking it was cool, like something out of *Mad Max.*

The soldiers and the three survivors boarded the bus and the first soldier to talk to them earlier got behind the wheel.

The second soldier took a seat in front while Jake and the girls were told to pick a seat in the middle of the twenty-five passenger bus.

With the doors closing, the shuttle bus drove away, leaving the platform behind.

"Okay, so I'll fill you in on what's what around here," the first soldier said. "The camp is run by Sergeant Wilson. I'm Private Ricky and this is Private Johnson. So, Jake, since you have some skills with those swords, you're welcome to join us, with both of your friends of course—hell, especially your friends." He leered at the two girls lecherously.

While they rode to the main part of the airport-turned-rescue-station, Jake used the time to study the two soldiers. Private Johnson looked to be a few years older than Jake. He was a skinny fellow, probably with no muscle mass and that was probably why he was such a jerk. Then he looked at Private Ricky, who looked to be in his early-thirties. Jake had a feeling without the soldier aiming his rifle at him, he could kick the man's ass easily, or at least put up a good fight.

Private Ricky was the exact opposite of Johnson. Ricky's standard issue green shirt had the sleeves torn off at the biceps and Jake could clearly see a tattoo of a cross with a snake twined around it etched on the right bicep. He was a fit man that probably benched two-sixty easy. When Ricky turned back to check on him, Jake quickly looked away. Both Jake and the girls noticed the bodies lying on the road as the shuttle bus made its way to the main terminal. Most of the time Private Johnson drove around the corpses, but sometimes he just rolled right over them, flattening the carcasses to the consistency of road kill.

A few minutes later, the shuttle pulled up to Terminal C, which was where the camp had been set up. There were five other soldiers standing at the barricade on each side of the entrance to the large circular cutout to the terminal, the entire entrance barricaded. One of the soldiers guarding the entrance moved the small barricade to let the bus in.

After the bus rolled past, the soldier moved back the barricade securing the area once more. As the bus came to a stop, Ricky and Johnson exited the vehicle, leading the three survivors into the main terminal.

"Now, if you'll follow me, we can bring you to meet the sergeant," Private Ricky said. As they followed the two soldiers, Private Ricky filled them in a little more. "The guy who let us past the barricade is Corporal Jayden and the one guarding the exit is Private Jolens. Jake, you'll be out here a couple of nights with them to guard the barricade. So far it hasn't been so bad around here; the pusbags have to go a long way to reach us here. The highway is more than half a mile and four lanes wide, so it's been pretty easy to pick them off so far, but if this gets worse, things might change fast," Ricky added, leading the survivors inside the terminal.

Upon entering the terminal, all three of them were awe-struck by how empty the place was. Normally there would be hundreds of people moving to and fro, rushing to catch their flights, but now there was no one, only a few soldiers and civilians scattered about.

Private Ricky slowed as they approached the group of soldiers and civilians, each of them armed with a rifle or sidearm.

"Jake, meet some of the guys," Ricky said. "This is Bill Monroe." He pointed to a man in street clothes. The man was in his fifties with graying hair.

"Hi, son, good to see you again," Bill said as he looked at Jake.

Jake shrugged. "Yeah, Bill, good to see you're in one piece, too."

Bill nodded and with a polite smile to the girls, moved away on some errand.

Private Ricky gestured to another man in street clothes. "This is Hank Truman, he was a cop before all the shit hit the fan and this guy here..." Ricky motioned to another man, "...is Mark Smitherly and his son, Seth. And this little lady is..." Ricky began but Jake cut him off.

"Yeah, we've met, but she wasn't conscious at the time," Jake said as he looked at the woman he'd seen in the shopping cart at the gas station. The same woman he'd saved from the crazy mechanic.

The woman stepped forward with her hand out. "Sorry I didn't stick around to say thanks. I'm Rosa," she said with a slight smile.

"I'm Jake," he said, "and these are my friends Jess and Cara." The girls said hello and Rosa reciprocated, the three immediately chatting while Ricky continued to introduce a few more of the soldiers standing around.

"How'd you end up here?" Jake asked her.

Rosa shrugged. "The soldiers found me and took me back here with them, end of story."

"Okay, that's enough of the introductions for now, let's go," Private Ricky told Jake. The girls were about to follow and Ricky held up a hand, stopping them. "Uh-uh, not you two, just him," Ricky said.

"I'll be fine, Jess, you stay here with Rosa and the others," he said calmly, but inside he couldn't help but feel a little nervous.

With a last glance at Jess and Cara, Jake was ushered away to meet the leader of the little refugee camp.

He just hoped it would go better than it did in those zombie movies he used to watch.

Jake was led down a long hallway off the main terminal. Neither soldier spoke, making him feel even more uneasy. Eventually they reached the end of the hallway where there was only one door, and on that door about head height, was a piece of masking tape, with the words, **_Sergeant Wilson_**, scrawled in black marker.

"All right, Jake, go on in, but leave your backpack and swords out here with me and Johnson. Once you're done here, we'll bring you to the food court where everyone else will be," Ricky said, pointing with his M-16.

"Let me correct you, they're _katanas,_ not swords," Jake said, correcting Private Ricky.

"I don't give a fuck if they're King Arthur's goddamn swords; now get the fuck in there before I shoot your ass." As Ricky was speaking, Johnson opened the door with the name on it and Ricky placed the sole of his boot on Jake's butt, sending him tumbling into the room.

Jake fell to the floor, which was carpeted with a low commercial weave, and came up in a crouch. There was a single desk in the room with another soldier sitting behind it. To the man's left was another man, who looked like he'd been through a war and lost. The man was missing many parts of his anatomy, including an arm, and looked like a war veteran who'd had one hell of a time.

Before Jake could say or do anything, Private Ricky stepped up behind him and said, "Sarge, this is one of the civilians we found at the train station. Says his name's Jake Roberts."

"Fine, that'll be all for now, Private."

"Yes, Sergeant," Private Ricky said and left the room, closing the door behind him.

A pitbull trotted from behind the only desk in the room and began sniffing Jake. Soon the dog was licking him, Jake chuckling despite his present situation.

"Hey, cut it out. I like you, too," Jake said as he ruffled the dog's ears.

"Hello, Roberts. I'm Sergeant Wilson. This is Private Lucky and it appears you've already met my dog, Duke," Wilson said, introducing himself.

Jake then looked over to the man with the missing arm and realized he was one of the soldiers he'd seen when the Humvees had passed Melissa's house the day before.

"Your name's Lucky, huh? You don't look that lucky with an arm missing, one ear cut off and all those scars," Jake said, jokingly.

"I'm alive aren't I? That's why I'm lucky. Now, don't speak unless you're spoken to," the one-armed man snapped.

"Easy, Lucky, he's new here, he doesn't know the rules yet," Sgt. Wilson said.

Not giving it much thought as to what Lucky told him, Jake decided to speak up anyway.

"Okay, so now that we got the introductions out of the way, what is this place and where are the rest of your men? I didn't see too many out there when I was brought in here," Jake said, wanting some answers. "And why the hell is a sergeant running this place, anyway? Seems to me there should be someone higher up the chain of command, like a captain or something."

"There, was," Wilson, said. "But everyone of higher rank is dead now, or walking around out there as a *pusbag*. So it fell on me to take charge. Think I've done a damn good job of it, too. Right, Lucky?"

"Fuck yeah, Danny. Uh, I mean Sergeant," Lucky replied.

Danny stood up and crossed the room. There was a small mini bar raided from the airport's supplies for the air planes set up and he picked up a paper cup and a single serving bottle of Scotch, emptying the tiny bottle into the cup.

"Okay, Roberts, or Jake, or shithead or whatever the fuck I feel like calling you, I'll give you the 4-1-1 on this place. You see, we were set up in a parking garage in Boston, just off of Mass. Ave, but then someone got inside that was infected. Well, it didn't take long before half the camp was overrun with those damn pusbags. I saw my colonel get ripped to pieces by a mother and her two kids. It was fucking nuts. So I gathered as many men as I could and we got the hell out of there. We left the city and ended up here. The airport was shut down by then so it wasn't hard to take over this terminal. We set up a barricade and I have men walking the perimeter. We're low on soldiers so I've conscripted civilians as well to help out. As long as they can fight they're part of my unit. And if one of those dead fucks gets near here, my men have orders to shoot on sight. Every few hours we send out a patrol to the neighboring towns to see if there's anyone we can save and if we can find more supplies. We've found a few people so far, the rest are either hiding or at other camps across the city."

"Yeah, I think I saw one of your patrols yesterday," Jake said, looking at Lucky. The one armed man grinned widely, his eyes filled with menace.

"You probably did at that," Sgt. Wilson said.

"Why don't you just take a plane and fly out of here, there's got to be someplace better than here," Jake suggested. "And why is the electricity still on here?"

"One thing at a time; just shut the fuck up and let me talk, dammit!" Wilson snapped. "So, as I was saying. We can't take a plane, so far I haven't found a pilot, and as to the electricity, well, we have a couple of high powered generators that are keeping this place running with power." He finished his Scotch and walked over to Jake. The pitbull was still with him and he pushed the dog aside roughly, the dog whining from the force of the shove.

"Okay, listen up, shithead, you've been drafted into my Army and I have a couple of rules if you want to keep breathing. If you break any of my rules, you'll be severely punished." He stopped when he was no more than five inches from Jake, his eyes staring into Jake's like two heat seeking missiles. "Rule one, we never go out alone, you must always have someone with you. Rule two, tell one of my soldiers where you're going at all times. Finally, rule three, I'm the boss around here, and you'll always answer to me. Any questions?"

Jake scowled as he glared back at Wilson, seeing exactly what the man was doing at the airport. The way he spoke, his attitude, it was everything Jake believed was wrong with the military and the government. Give a man some power and he would only want more.

"You're a sick bastard," Jake spit. "You want to stay here and carve out your own little kingdom. Christ, man, you're a soldier, you're supposed to be helping people. You should be ashamed to wear that uniform."

Before Jake could do anything, Wilson snapped out his right hand, knuckles facing outward, and backhanded Jake across the mouth.

"You're not exactly getting off to a good start here, Roberts. If you want to keep breathing, you better know your place and keep your goddamn opinions to yourself," Wilson spit, not liking Jake's attitude.

Wilson turned to Lucky and said, "Take him back to the food court. I don't want to see him unless he fucks up, which I have a feeling won't take too long to happen."

"You got it, Sarge," Lucky said as he moved over to Jake. "Come on, fuckwad, get a move on," he hissed and shoved Jake a little.

Jake said nothing, still rubbing his jaw. Turning, he moved to the door which was now open thanks to Private Ricky, who was wondering what was going on and wanted to get in on it to.

As Jake and Lucky walked through the doorway, and just before it closed, the pitbull woofed softly and trotted after Jake, slipping through before the door clicked shut.

"Duke, Duke! Get your furry ass back here!" Wilson yelled with venom. "Damn dog, fine, go with him if you want," he grumbled as he went and grabbed another tiny bottle of Scotch and sat back down at his desk.

Christ, the guy's here for five minutes and he's already managed to steal my dog, Wilson thought.

He couldn't help thinking that Jake Roberts was going to be a real pain in the ass.

Chapter 13

The Past

At the food court, Bill Monroe was talking to some of the other people there.

"Yeah, I know the guy who was taken to Sergeant Wilson's office. His name's Jake Roberts. I used to work with him at the tomato farm up in Pittsfield. Funny how things happen, you know? I tell ya, it's a small world when you come right down to it."

"Do you know the two girls that were with him, too?" Mark Smitherly asked. Beside him was his son, who was listening intently. Seth was almost sixteen and had immediately taken an interest in Jess, thinking she was hot.

"No, don't know 'em," Bill said while shaking his head.

A few minutes later, Jess and Cara were brought to the food court, with a few other civilians, escorted by Private Ricky and Private Johnson.

After the two soldiers had left the girls alone, Bill decided to go say hello.

"Hey, girls, I'm Bill Monroe. I used to work with Jake. So, what're your names?" he asked.

"I'm Jessica, but everyone calls me Jess, and this is my little sister, Cara," Jess told him.

"Jess and Cara, they sound like great names. Okay, so let me give you a rundown on a few of the fellas around here. Over there is Hank, he's a police officer. At the table in the corner is Rosa, and sitting at the table at the far wall is Mark and his son, Seth."

There were many others in the food court also, but Bill only introduced the people he'd befriended in the short time he'd been there.

"So, how do you two know Jake? And how'd you end up here? I hear it's gettin' pretty bad out there," Bill said.

"He's our sister's fiancé and he saved us when those crazy people attacked our house yesterday," Cara said while shaking her head in disbelief of what happened. "It's still hard to call them what Jake does...*zombies*, it's all so unreal."

"Yes, honey, I know exactly what you mean," Bill said. He changed the subject. "So, he's your sister's fiancé, huh? Yeah, Jake would talk about her all the time. Oh, okay then, that means you two are Melissa's sisters. I think he's mentioned you once or twice. So, you kids hungry? How about we get you something to eat and drink and get you both situated," he suggested, leading them to a deli station that also had a large pot of simmering soup.

"We've got food in our backpacks but a warm meal would be great," Jess said, Cara also nodding in agreement.

Moments later, after the girls had gotten a sandwich and soup, and were sitting at one of the tables with their meals and new friends, Jake was seen being dragged by Lucky.

"Now, you stay here, Roberts," Lucky ordered him.

"Bastard," Jake said under his breath while he rubbed his arm where Lucky had grasped it. "You wouldn't be so tough without that rifle."

"I don't need this M-16 to deal with someone like you, Roberts," Lucky sneered.

Lucky might only have one arm but his grip was fierce. Jake was sure he was going to have a red mark where Lucky's fingers had locked onto his arm.

Then Jake was distracted when both Cara and Jess ran over to him, wrapping their arms around him in a big hug.

"Oh, Jake, we were so worried about you. What happened?" Jess asked for both herself and Cara

"It's okay, I'm fine," Jake told them and was distracted when he looked down to see the pitbull, Duke, at his feet rubbing his legs.

"Who's your friend?" Cara asked while wiping her mouth clean.

"That's Duke, the sergeant's dog. He seems to like me for some reason. How's it going, buddy?" he asked the dog as he rubbed Duke's ears some more. The dog's small tail was moving so fast it looked like it was going to fly off his behind.

Looking around some more, Jake spotted Bill amongst the people in the food court, so he told Jess and Cara he would be back and walked the few feet separating him from Bill.

"Hey, old timer," Jake said, holding out his right hand for Bill to take. Bill did and the two shook like old friends, which they were.

In many ways Bill had been a surrogate father to Jake when they had been on the job, and right now Bill was all he had left of any semblance of family.

"So, how'd you end up here?" Jake asked. "The last time I saw you was when you dropped me off at my house."

Bill moved closer to Jake and lowered his voice. "Listen, son, let's talk where nobody can hear us, all right?"

"Yeah, sure, hold on a second, just let me tell Jess and Cara I'll be right back." Jake ran over to the girls and said, "Hey, guys, I have to go talk to Bill for a minute in private. Why don't you two sit down with Duke and finish eating."

"Sure, Jake, just hurry back," Jess said, Cara nodding also.

"Will do." He spun on his heels and jogged back to Bill, who was waiting for him by the windows overlooking one of the runways.

"Okay, Jake, listen carefully," Bill said. "I think the guy in charge around here, Sergeant Wilson, is a nut job. He's a no good bastard and he's trouble. You need to watch your ass around him, you hear me?"

"Ah, he doesn't seem that bad," Jake said. "Sure, he's an asshole, but I've dealt with assholes before."

"Oh, really, and did those other assholes carry M-16s and could they shoot you if you looked at them funny?"

"Well no, I guess not," Jake replied.

"Exactly, so as I said, you need to watch your ass around here, you *and* the girls. If there was someplace better to be right now, I'd be so gone from here."

"How'd you get here in the first place?"

"There's not much of a story, really. They were looking for survivors after the outbreak, or whatever this thing is, and I ended up with Wilson and his crew. Then, after getting closer to Boston, Wilson picked up some more people and we all came back here; one big happy family."

"Has anyone figured out how this shit happened yet? Was it terrorists or what?" Jake asked.

Bill shook his head. "No one knows for sure, but they think it might have been something in the water. At least that's what they said before the news cut out."

Jake began thinking, and Bill smiled.

"Looks like that brain of yours is working overtime, what're you thinkin' about?" Bill asked.

Jake shrugged. "Nothing, I was just thinking about what you told me about that bacteria or whatever at the plant with my grandfather and the guy who turned into a zombie. Maybe they did something with that shit, you know, tossed it into the water near the farm or something, maybe buried it in the dirt where the tomatoes are grown." He shrugged. "I don't know, it all sounds so crazy."

"You mean crazier than dead people running around trying to eat you? Shit, Jake, sounds like it might make a whole lot of sense. More sense than anything else I've heard so far."

Jake frowned. "Then that could mean we might have helped start this shit. Christ, Bill, the fucking tomatoes, the farm used the water from the reservoir to irrigate them. If that shit got in the tomatoes and other produce grown there and then people ate them..." He trailed off, still too shocked to want to believe his assumption.

"Then that could mean we helped start all of this," Bill finished for him, his face pale with guilt.

"Is it true?" a voice asked from behind and both Jake and Bill turned to see Cara and Jess standing there.

"What, no, no, no. You see, it's not entirely our fault. Well, maybe just a little bit," Jake said, trying to calm her down.

"You bastard, it is your fault," Jess said. "You two are the reason why this whole thing started. You two are the reason why my sister Melissa isn't with me and Cara!"

"Then that means you're the reason why our parents are dead!" Cara yelled. "I hate you!" She turned and ran away with tears filling her eyes.

"Cara, wait!" Jake called, but was stopped by Bill.

With a look of disproval, Jess turned and gave Jake her back, wanting to go find Cara, but she did toss out a, "Jerk," to him as she walked away.

Jake dropped to the floor with Bill resting a hand on his shoulder, trying to console him.

"My parents are dead, everyone else I knew, too, and it's all my fault," Jake sobbed into his arm.

"It's okay, son, just give her time to process, both of them. I'll go talk to them later when they've cooled down some," Bill said as he patted Jake's shoulder. After fifteen minutes passed and Jake was still a mess, Bill decided to leave him alone, to let the young man work it out on his own.

As for Jake, he just sat there for the next few hours, not moving, lost in guilt and grief for his dead family.

*   *   *

Later that night, Rosa walked over to Jake, who was still sitting by the window overlooking the runway, watching a small crowd of zombies walking around. When Wilson had used the word *pusbags* to describe the infected, Jake decided he also liked the name, so had made up his mind not to call them *zombies* anymore. Besides, the word *zombie* was childish and ridiculous.

"Hey there again, my name's Rosa Garcia if you don't remember," she said, sitting down next to him.

"Yeah, I remember. Nice to see you got away from that gas station in one piece. I looked for you but you were gone so..." he trailed off.

"That was you, huh? Thanks, I was out of it if you didn't know. That asshole knocked me out, whacked me over the head. I still have the lump to prove it," she said while rubbing the back of her head. "I was with another woman who was trying to make it home, too, but she took off when she saw that guy knock me out. She just ran away and didn't look back, not that I can really blame her, though. I didn't know that guy was behind me till he hit me over the head with something, and then the lights went out. The next thing I knew I was under those tires."

"Yeah, sorry 'bout that, that was only meant for the guy, not you, too," Jake said ruefully.

"It's okay," she smiled. "So anyway, when the tires fell on top of us, I came to and I decided to run for it. I hotwired a car, my brothers taught me how, ya know, and then got the hell out of there. Then I ended up here. So, what's your story?"

"I'm searching for my fiancée, Melissa, and her two sisters, Cara and Jess wanted to come along for the ride."

"Melissa? Does she have long brown hair?"

Jake nodded, hope filling him anew that his fiancée was still alive.

"Yeah, that was the woman who left me at the gas station," she said, remembering her ordeal. "One second we were together and the next she was running like a scared little girl, but it's not like there was anything she could have done to help me, that guy was twice her size and she didn't have a gun. Shit, I would have left her ass, too, come to think of it."

"Well, hold on now, how do you know it was my Melissa? There's plenty of people with that name with brown hair," he said, trying to stay calm.

Rosa frowned at the accusation she was wrong. "She looked like one of those girls you were with only older. Oh, yeah, she was definitely your woman."

"Okay, if you're right, then where'd she go after she left you? You have to tell me!"

"Shit, calm down, man, I'll tell you. I owe you for helping me back at the gas station. She said she was going to a cabin in New Hampshire or someplace up north."

Just as Rosa finished her sentence, they both looked up to see Sgt. Danny Wilson and Lucky crossing the food court, heading directly towards the two of them.

"How's it going, Roberts?" Wilson spit. "You're going on patrol tonight. I don't care if this is your first night here. I'm sending you out with Hank; he's the cop," he said, then turned to walk away without waiting for Jake to reply.

But then he paused and looked back at Jake. "And one more thing, asshole, I'm gonna need my dog back, too, and when I do, I'm gonna give that mutt a beating of a lifetime for leaving me." He began laughing as he strolled away with Lucky by his side.

"What a jerk," Jake said. "I can see what Bill meant about him. He wants me and everyone to follow the rules but he doesn't follow them himself. Someone needs to take that guy down a peg," he mused and then stood up, smiling slightly at Rosa. "Look, I gotta go, but we'll talk later." As he walked away from her, he gave her a small wave. "Thanks for the info, you don't know what it means to me."

"Glad to help," she said while waving goodbye. She stood at the window for a few seconds, watching the ghouls moving across the runway and it caused her to shiver in fear.

With nothing else to do, she moved away herself, soon blending into the shadows of the food court.

An hour later, Jake was outside with Hank and Private Jayden. Jake's job at the moment was to relieve each man on guard duty so they could take a break to use the bathroom.

Jayden and another soldier went first, which left Jake and Hank alone. With nothing else to do, Jake decided to break the silence between Hank and himself.

"So, Hank, how'd you end up here?" he inquired, hoping it wasn't a sore subject with the man. Many of the civilians at the camp had lost loved ones and didn't want to talk about how they'd arrived at the airport.

"I was at the Boston Medical Center when the shit hit the fan on the Fourth of July," Hank replied. "At first I tried to help, you know, to protect and serve, but it didn't take me long to figure out things were too far out of control for me to do anything. So I jumped in my squad car and took off. I heard on the scanner there was an encampment set up here, so I drove here, hoping maybe I could do some good once I arrived. When the roads were too blocked to pass, I left the squad car and walked the rest of the way. Nearly used up all my ammo on the way here, too, shooting those bastards out there." He was happy to share his tale as he looked off at the surrounding rooftops of East Boston a half mile away.

While Hank continued talking, one lone zombie was sneaking up to the barricade. Jake and Hank didn't notice the stumbling form, the ghoul sticking to the shadows. Whether this was on purpose or completely by accident, either way it was working in the ghoul's favor, as the figure snuck up on Hank from the right side.

If either man had been more observant, the zombie would have never made it so far, but Hank wasn't paying attention and Jake was new to the whole *on guard* thing.

Before Jake realized there was danger, the zombie appeared next to Hank and bit down on his right shoulder, blood squirting out of the wound as the ghoul came away with a piece of torn shirt and a chunk of raw flesh.

Hank screamed in agony as the zombie pulled away from him, chewing merrily on the bloody meat in its mouth.

Jake, reacting almost immediately after the initial attack, pulled out one of his katanas, but Hank beat him to it and drew his 9mm Glock from the holster on his hip, shooting the zombie between the eyes. The back of the ghoul's skull exploded, brains and gore spraying the ground behind it. Hank screamed in pain and fell to the ground, shock beginning to set in as blood seeped from his wound.

The bullet hole in the zombie's head smoked just a little, and the body pitched forward to sprawl unmoving.

Private Jayden had been returning from his break and he dashed to the disturbance, his rifle in his hands. "What the hell just happened?" he asked, his M-16 at waist height, ready to shoot any threat.

"One of those bastards came out of nowhere and attacked Hank," Jake said as he searched the shadows for more potential threats, but the darkness was still, the area empty.

"Shit," Jayden said. "Now we have to kill him and Sergeant Wilson isn't gonna be happy about that. We're low on men as it is. Jake, you should've watched his back better. Christ, how the fuck did the pusbag manage to sneak up on you like that?" Jayden asked accusingly, his index finger tapping Jake's chest while he spoke.

"Don't touch me. I *was* watching his back. I was talking to him, but that damn pusbag came out of nowhere," Jake said defensively.

As both bickered about whose fault it was, Hank decided to do the honorable thing, not wanting to either turn into a ghoul or suffer the indignity of being put down like a rabid dog. With tears in his eyes, he stuck the muzzle of the Glock in his mouth and pulled the trigger.

The loud report filled the area and both Jayden and Jake spun around, Jayden bringing up his M-16.

Unfortunately, it was too late to help Hank. The man's brains were splattered all over the pavement.

The other soldier, who went by the name of Private Shane, returned from his break to find Hank slumped on the ground with half his head blown off, and Jake and Jayden standing over him.

"What the fuck happened here? I was only gone for ten minutes," Shane gasped, looking down at Hank's corpse.

"A pusbag snuck up on him and he got bit," Jayden told the man. "Hank took the easy way out and ate his gun, poor bastard." Jayden turned to look at Jake, his eyes wide. "This is your fuckup so you deal with it. Take his body to the side of the barricade about fifty feet from the end, and dump it in the ditch over there."

"Where is it exactly? Shit, it's dark out here. How the hell am I supposed to find it?" Jake protested.

Shane and Jayden grinned at Jake's question. "Don't worry, you'll find it easy enough," Shane said. "Just follow the stench of rotting bodies."

Jake frowned but did as he was told. As the new man, he knew it wouldn't be smart to argue. Reaching down, he picked Hank up under the armpits and began to drag the body across the asphalt, while Jayden and Shane talked and made wisecracks.

Dragging Hank's corpse into the night, the voices of Jayden and Shane were soon muffled from distance, and Jake had never felt so exposed. Anything could be out here with him and he wouldn't know it was upon him until it was too late.

He couldn't help but feel guilty over Hank's death, after all, this was his first night here and someone had just died partly because of him.

With each yard he dragged the body, his shoulders began to ache a little more, and he was almost glad when the redolence of death filled his sinuses, telling him he was close to the ditch.

The moon appeared from behind a few clouds and bathed the ditch in a pallid glow. There were at least ten bodies in the sunken ditch, all with different wounds on them. Some looked like gunshots while others had to be from bite marks.

Flies filled the air and maggots covered every square inch of exposed flesh, and it looked like a few of the bodies seemed to be moving. As he peered closer, he saw a rat poke its bloody nose out of an exposed cavity.

"Oh, God, that's so gross," he gasped, realizing rats were inside the bodies, burrowing through the entrails like tunnels, causing the flesh to ebb and flow like there were air bladders under the skin being filled and drained repeatedly.

"Sorry, Hank, I really am," he said and rolled Hank to the edge of the ditch, then let him slide down the incline to join the other corpses.

Making the sign of the cross, he turned and walked away, but then he decided to run, wanting to get away from the stink of the rotting corpses as soon as possible.

After seeing all the bodies, he knew Sergeant Wilson had something to do with them, and he swore right then the man needed to be taken down.

How he would do it was another matter completely, but he knew it had to be done, and fast, before more people were killed.

Chapter 14

The Past, last week of October 2009

Three months after Jake and the girls arrived at the airport rescue camp, Sgt. Danny Wilson and his second-in-command, Private Lucky, were talking in his office about an upcoming search party for the rest of the airport.

"Okay, Lucky, I want you to take a few people with you to terminal D and see if there's anything there worth taking. There's a few restaurants inside, too, and they should have something we can use. If you find any pusbags while you're looking, blow their goddamn heads off."

"No problem, Danny," Lucky said. When the two were alone, Wilson let Lucky call him by his first name. The two had been friends for more than a year and Danny knew he could trust Lucky implicitly.

"Good, and I want you to take Ricky, Johnson, Mark, Bill, and katana boy—that's Roberts, if you don't know who I mean. Watch your ass out there, man, who knows what's in that terminal," Danny said.

"I got it, Danny, piece of cake," Lucky grinned and moved to the door.

As he was opening it, and about to exit the office, Danny called out to him. "Oh, Lucky, one more thing. I want Roberts and the old man, Bill, to have a little accident while you're over there. Since that asshole arrived, he's managed to get one of my men killed and I hear he's been going off without permission like he owns the place. And I hear the old guy is stirring up trouble, too. I warned Roberts when he arrived what I do to people who don't follow my orders." Danny tone was murderous. "But I hear he's pretty popular with most of the civilians and some of my men, so you need to make it look like an accident. You got me?"

"I know what you mean, Danny, I'll make it happen." Lucky was grinning as he left to go gather the men for the search party. The assignment Danny had given him was so simple. He already knew there were zombies in Terminal D, and when he and his men took them out, it would be quite easy to accidentally have Roberts shot. Friendly fire was nothing new, and even if it didn't look like an accident, what was anyone going to do about it?

Nothing, that's what.

As Lucky strolled down the long corridor, a devious smile came to his lips as he thought about how he was going to put a bullet in Jake Roberts' head.

Jake was sitting at one of the tables in the food court with Bill, talking about how upset Cara and Jess were.

"I don't know if they'll ever forgive me, Bill. It's been nearly three months and they still won't talk to me," Jake said, depressed about the situation.

For the past three months and change, the people in the camp had begun to get to know each other, talking, eating and having a great time given their circumstances. There was only so much cheer when a person was surrounded by a city filled with the walking dead, and everyone they had ever known was now dead or walking around as a zombie.

Over the past few months, the amount of walking dead arriving at the airport had increased by the hundreds, but so far the soldiers and civilians had managed to remain safe within the confines of the airport terminal.

The four lane highway leading into the airport, to wind its way through the terminals, was now filled with rotting corpses, the ghouls left where they'd fallen after being shot. Crows, rodents, dogs and cats feasted on the bodies, the highway resembling a massive battlefield.

Hank's body, three months dead, was nothing but a skeleton, the corpse still lying in the ditch. Since he was dropped into the ditch, many more bodies had been added with his, the mass grave soon needing to be filled and another one excavated.

There were a couple of times when the zombies had almost made it past the guards at the barricade, but the ghouls had been brought down quickly when the rest of the camp rallied together.

Cara and Jess had adapted, too, not really having much choice in the matter. They were usually found hanging out with Duke, the pitbull becoming their best friend.

As for Jake, they still hadn't forgiven him for what he'd said about the tomatoes and the farm. Though deep in their hearts they knew Jake wasn't really at fault, it felt better to have a real person to blame, to focus their anger and despair on something tangible. Instead of the ubiquitous zombies that now arrived like harried travelers afraid they were late for their outgoing flights.

When Duke wasn't with the girls, he would seek out Jake, who would play with him like the girls did. Wilson wasn't pleased about it, but he had better things to do than chase his dog all over the terminal. One of the reasons Duke liked Jake and the girls was they treated him with kindness, unlike Wilson, who would kick Duke whenever he was angry, even if it wasn't the dog he was angry at. Wilson had a mean streak a mile long and beating animals was the least of his crimes.

Bill nodded to what Jake had said about the girls, understanding completely.

"I know, pal," Bill said. "Just give them some more time. They'll come around sooner or later." It was as Bill finished his sentence that Lucky came strolling in with a wide smirk on his face. His M-16 was over his shoulder and he wasn't alone, Private Ricky and Johnson were right behind him.

"Roberts, Monroe, the sergeant has a mission for us, we leave in an hour. Get your shit together and let's go," Lucky ordered, not in the mood for any back talk. "Meet me at the front doors in forty-five minutes."

"We'll be there," Bill said with a wan smile. He didn't like Lucky any more than Jake did, but the man had Wilson's ear so Bill knew to defer to him.

An hour later, the group of men had gathered outside the front doors of the terminal, talking amongst themselves.

Lucky stood in front of them, looking at each man with hard eyes.

"Okay, shut the fuck up and gather round, people. Right now we're gonna take a shuttle bus to Terminal D and infiltrate the premises to see what supplies we can find. That's our main goal, but our second objective is to shoot down any pusbags we come across. Ricky, you take Mark and Monroe and I'll take Johnson and Roberts. You come in a minute after us so we can scope out the situation. We get in, get what we can, and get the fuck out. Then we're done and we come back here to our women." He scanned the men's faces. "Any questions?"

"Yeah, I have one," Jake said. "I didn't see any blind women with a lack of the ability to smell in the terminal. So who exactly is your woman?"

"Fuck off, Roberts, or so help me," Lucky warned. He looked to the other men. "So, like I just said before shithead spoke up, any questions?"

None had any and they loaded onto the shuttle bus with the re-inforced windows and sides.

Private Ricky was the first to get on the bus, as he was driving, and the others boarded behind him, a few of the soldiers joking and making wisecracks about whatever they could think of. No one was worried about the mission. It was a simple grab and shoot, piece of cake.

Bill carried a 9mm Glock pistol that was once Hank's, the dead cop not needing it any more, now that he was rotting in a hole on the side of the terminal.

Mark, who carried a pump-action shotgun, was also part of the team, but his son, Seth, had remained behind, too young to go out just yet, but would soon. He was learning how to shoot with one of the soldiers, and in another week or so would go out on his first patrol. Mark wasn't exactly pleased about it, but at the same time was proud his son was becoming a man.

Lucky and the two other soldiers coming on the mission carried M-16s. Jake was left without a gun, only having his katanas, which could be deadlier than any gun if he used them right, and he had the added advantage of not having to reload.

With the six of them on board, the soldier guarding the barricade moved it to let the shuttle bus out. It took Private Ricky only minutes to reach the next terminal, the bus weaving its way through the bodies sprawled on the pavement.

The first thing the men saw as they approached the next terminal were the stalled cars spread across the road with charred bodies hanging out of the windows. Dried blood splatter covered the front windshields and side glass of some of the cars.

When the bus reached the main doors to Terminal D, they saw there was nothing moving, either living or dead, which was unsettling. Only stray pieces of newspaper caught in the breeze blew about, getting snagged under bumpers and between tires.

"Okay, men," Lucky said. "When we go inside, stick together with your group and watch each other's backs. No one gets left behind. My team, we go down the right side and Ricky's team will go down the left, then we'll meet in the middle at the back by the restaurants. Okay, my team, let's move out!" he yelled as he stepped off the shuttle bus, Jake and Johnson following close behind.

When Jake reached the main glass doors to the terminal, the glass covered in blood splatter as well, he looked inside but saw nothing. It was pitch black with only a few thin rays of light piercing the darkness here and there.

Lucky turned to Private Johnson and Jake, his eyes as cold as ever.

"Johnson, you go first. Roberts, you follow him, and I'll cover the rear," Lucky ordered them.

With both men nodding they understood their orders, they prepared to go inside.

Lucky opened one of the glass doors and Johnson stepped inside the terminal, his rifle held at eye level as he swung the muzzle back and forth in preparation of shooting anything threatening. Jake was next with his katanas in hand, the blades glinting in whatever feeble light managed to penetrate the filthy glass doors. Lucky followed, closing the door behind him.

With Johnson on point, the three man team moved down the right corridor, towards the security gates of the terminal. So far, there was no sign of anything, either living or dead, which was odd. There should have been a couple of ghouls inside, but there wasn't. As they continued onward through the security gates, the metal detectors standing like silent sentries, the terminal remained deathly quiet.

"Where the hell are all the fuckin' pusbags?" Johnson whispered, wanting to get the zombies out of hiding so he could take their faces off with bullets to the head.

"I don't know," Jake hissed softly, "but let's go down a little further...and keep quiet."

Lucky grinned as he watched Jake's back in the shadows. The man was oblivious to his coming death. Lucky had filled Private Johnson and Ricky in on what Sgt. Wilson wanted to happen to Jake and Bill on the shuttle ride over, but Mark was completely in the dark about it.

He would never let it happen, as the man was a close friend of Jake's. All Lucky was waiting for was for them to reach the back of the terminal, where there would be absolutely no chance Mark would witness the deed, then he would go back and tell Wilson it was done, letting the rest of the camp think it was just a terrible accident.

Lucky knew Wilson was smart. The sergeant didn't want to make a martyr out of Jake, only get rid of him.

Upon reaching the rear of the terminal, with Jake now in the lead as he peered into the darkness, he suddenly heard the *click-clack* of safety's coming off, and when Jake turned around, he suddenly found himself staring down the barrels of Johnson and Lucky's M-16s.

"What the fuck's going on here?" Jake asked, not understanding what they were doing.

Lucky grinned malevolently. "Sorry, Roberts, it's nothin' personal, but the sergeant doesn't want you around anymore," he said, getting to the point of why his gun was pointed at Jake's head.

"Why the hell not? What did I do to deserve this?" Jake asked, hoping to stall, not that he had any ideas of how he was supposed to get out of this very bad situation.

Lucky shrugged, the barrel of the rifle moving with the gesture. "Hey, he sees you as a threat to him. That's all I know or care about. He tells me to off you, I off you, simple as that."

"Oh, man, come on, Lucky, how 'bout you just let me go. I'll leave now and keep going. You'll never see me again, I promise," Jake said as sweat rolled down his back. His heart was pumping fast and he was wondering if he had a chance of attacking Lucky. But even if he did, Johnson would just take him down.

No, he was screwed, simple as that.

"Sorry, Roberts," Lucky said while shaking his head. "It's gotta be this way. Tell you what. Get on your knees and beg a little and I'll make sure it's quick. *Pop,* one to the head and you're gone."

Jake was seriously considering doing just that when he spotted movement behind Lucky and Johnson in the shadows. At first he didn't know what was back there but slowly, ever so slowly, more than twenty zombies coalesced out of the darkness, each seeming to almost glide across the floor.

Johnson raised his rifle. "Fuck this shit, Lucky, let me shoot the fucker and be done with it."

Lucky sighed and nodded. "Fine. Go 'head, do it and let's get out of here before one of the others finds out what's happening."

With an evil grin showing no mercy, Johnson prepared to shoot Jake dead. His finger was on the trigger, only a half ounce enough to send Jake to Hell, when the first ghoul in line moved up behind Johnson. Before the man knew he was under attack, the brown teeth of the ghoul sank deep into his upper right arm, tearing a large chunk of flesh and muscle from the limb.

Johnson didn't react at first, he merely stared at the decayed head chewing on his arm like it was a chicken leg, but then he went into action, spinning on his heels and raising his rifle.

"Holy shit, my arm, you dead shit," Johnson stammered, trying to stop the blood from squirting out of the deep gash. But the other ghouls weren't waiting for an invitation and they swarmed over him. Johnson fired off half a clip, riddling three zombies with bullets, but the others went around their destroyed brethren and in less than two seconds, Johnson was overwhelmed and forced to the floor.

Pale, clawed hands tore into his uniform to get at the warm flesh beneath. Sharpened nails slid into his abdomen, searching for the wet and juicy treats hidden within.

Jake and Lucky stood side by side, their earlier altercation forgotten for the moment, but then Lucky spun around to face Jake.

"That's it, damn it, I'm gonna finish this job or die trying," Lucky snarled, pointing his M-16 at Jake's head, ignoring the zombies only a few feet away.

From out of the shadows, a ghoul came at Lucky and the man had to fight for his life, using the butt of his rifle as a bludgeon.

Jake ducked and dashed reaching hands as Lucky pushed the zombie away and shot it in the head. Brains shot out the back of the skull to slap the floor like dropped meat at a barbeque.

Lucky's gunshot was followed by a half dozen more, and he turned to see Mark, Bill, and Private Ricky charging down the long corridor, shooting the limping, shambling ghouls while they ran.

Dark ichor and congealing blood sprayed everywhere, with head shot after head shot, taking out the zombies.

When Bill was close enough so Lucky could hear him, he yelled, "Lucky, just what the fuck do you think you're doing, you bastard? I saw you point your rifle at Jake!" Bill shot another zombie in the face.

Jake wasn't immobile while all this was happening. When a zombie came at him from his left, he raised a katana and pierced the tip of the sword through the ghoul's nose, the edge sliding through the head to come out the back of the rotting skull. When he removed the sword, the nose was concaved, maggots pouring out of the wound to spill onto the floor like living M&M's.

Lucky spun around and pointed his rifle at Bill, as Bill did the same to Lucky, both men not firing in fear the other would do the same. It was a Mexican standoff.

"Roberts has to die, those were my orders!" Lucky screamed as he punched a zombie in the face when it tried to bite him.

"No way, Lucky, it's you that's gonna die!" Bill screamed, and before he could pull the trigger on his Glock, Ricky hit Bill over the head with the butt of his M-16, the older man going to his knees from the force of the blow.

"Bill, no!" Jake yelled, coming to the aid of his fallen friend as all around them the ghouls swarmed in.

Mark had been busy and while the others were arguing, he'd been picking off the troublesome undead, but in seconds even his marksmanship wouldn't be able to protect the others.

With zombies everywhere, and Bill now down and out of action for the moment, Lucky had a better idea than just shooting Jake and Bill in the head and leaving them.

The one armed man went over to Private Ricky, shooting three ghouls as he crossed the distance, and slapped Ricky on the shoulder. "Come on, we can't win here, there's too damn many of them and there's still more coming," he said, trying to get his men to move. Lucky called out, "Hey, Mark, you saw what's happening here so now you need to pick a side. Who're you with, them or me and Wilson?"

Mark chewed his lip and shot two more zombies when they came his way, but in the end it wasn't a hard decision. He had to think of his son back at the camp, and though he liked Jake and Bill, his family came first. "I'm with you guys, Lucky. What do you want to do? Are we going to kill Jake and Bill?" he asked as he shot another ghoul in the head.

"No, Mark," Lucky said, "leave 'em alone. Gettin' eaten by pus-bags is a hell of a lot more painful than getting' shot, now come on, it's time to leave." He began heading to the front of the terminal, with Ricky and Mark following behind.

A few zombies followed them, but most stayed with Bill and Jake. Bill had been protected from attack as he lay sprawled on the floor by Mark, who picked off any ghouls getting too close to the downed man, but now that he was gone, Bill had no such protection.

Jake ran over to Bill, who was slowly regaining his composure, the blow to his head not enough to knock him out completely, only dazing him.

At the moment, Bill was sluggish and unable to defend himself.

Standing over his fallen friend, Jake held the katanas in front of him, his eyes flicking back and forth to the shadows, waiting for the zombies to attack.

There had to be another twenty zombies easy, every ghoul in the terminal now swarming out of the darkness after hearing the gunshots, and Jake gritted his teeth and prepared to go down fighting.

A need for revenge burned in his chest when he thought of Sgt. Wilson orchestrating the entire plot to kill him without anyone knowing, and he wanted vengeance on the man desperately. As for Lucky and the others, they were second on his hit list, but Wilson was first.

As Jake stood with his legs wide and katanas ready to taste undead blood, knowing he would need to fight and protect Bill at the same time, he knew before he could get to Wilson, he needed to survive the impossible odds before him.

When the first walking corpse lunged forward with a low moan, others behind it, Jake yelled and charged them, blades flashing in the gloom, his eyes as cold and lifeless as the zombies he was fighting.

Chapter 15

The Past

It had been months since the contaminated tomatoes and other produce grown at the farm took their first victim, the vegetables being trucked across the eastern seaboard and beyond.

Not only were zombies on the ground, they were also thirty thousand feet in the air, and it didn't take long for the infection to spread out to the neighboring states of Massachusetts and New England.

On an airplane approaching Logan Airport, more than a hundred refugees from New York were hoping Boston would become the safe haven they were desperately searching for. In an attempt to escape New York, hundreds of people had flocked to Kennedy Airport in hopes of escaping the beleaguered city. One frazzled pilot had the same idea, however, and though the plane was low on fuel, he took as many passengers as he could fit onboard before taking off again. He could still hear the screams and pleadings of the people he'd left behind on the runway.

But unknown to the pilot, he'd let someone onboard who was already infected, and as the plane swung around Cape Cod on its way to Boston, the passenger began showing the first signs he was sick.

A frazzled stewardess, who'd been on duty for over fourteen hours straight, was working her way through the throng of people to the rear of the plane when she spotted the man looking ill. No one was sitting down or in a seat belt, but that was the last thing she was worried about at the moment.

"Excuse me, sir, are you feeling all right?" the stewardess inquired as she was moving down the aisle, checking on the other passengers along the way.

"I don't know, I think I have food poisoning," the passenger told the stewardess, but then he began to breathe a little heavier and faster.

"Let me check your forehead," she said. When the man complied, she placed her palm on his sweaty brow. When she did, she found it was ice cold. She was about to comment to the man when she looked down and saw his eyes were closed. Getting nervous, she touched his throat to see if there was a pulse, and to her surprise, she realized the man was dead.

"Oh my God, is there a doctor here?" she cried out, frantic about having a dead body on her flight, but knowing she needed to keep it quiet so as not to cause more panic. She knew what was happening in New York, but she still found it farfetched. When the pilot told her what he was doing she thought he was crazy, but when she saw the chaos at the airport through one of the plane's windows, she'd decided to just stay with the aircraft.

"I'm a registered nurse!" yelled a woman from the back of the plane as she fought her way to the stewardess. The noise was deafening, everyone talking at once while children cried and passengers attempted to get cell phone service. The stewardess was bombarded with questions, all of which she knew none of the answers for.

The nurse finally reached the stewardess and they smiled at one another. As a nurse, the woman knew what the stewardess was going through trying to keep so many people calm in such an uncertain time.

The nurse leaned down, checked the man's eyes and then, she too, touched his neck while searching for a pulse.

"I'm afraid he's dead, though I can't imagine what from. A heart attack maybe?" she mused.

Another man in front of the nurse turned when he heard the nurse say the word *dead,* and his eyes went wide with fear and terror.

"Did you say that man's dead? Oh, God, he's one of them, he's infected!" he screamed, causing panic to flow through the passengers like water down a hill. Immediately people began to scream as everyone tried to get away from the dead man. It was almost comical the way the corpse didn't move and yet people were running in fear, though there was nowhere to go.

"People, please, he's dead, he can't hurt you!" the nurse called out, but no one listened to her. As a trained medical professional, she still found it hard to believe what the news was saying. It was medically impossible for the dead to walk. And though she had come to the airport with her husband, she had yet to see an actual zombie, not that she believed she would of course. The outbreaks had been sporadic and many parts of the east coast were still untouched.

So when the dead man's eyes snapped open and he reached up and grabbed the nurse by her hair, the woman was shocked to say the least, and in the church of the walking dead, she became a believer; for all of three seconds.

In that time, the dead man pulled her close and ripped her throat out, her dark arterial blood shooting out to cover the closest passengers in hot, sticky blood.

And if the screaming was loud before, it grew three times in its intensity. The nurse spasmed in the dead man's hands as the newborn zombie chewed on the woman's throat, swallowing the plasma like it was water to a dehydrated and dying man.

The entire passenger list tried to escape the zombie, an old woman becoming trampled in the middle of the aisle, as dozens of feet stomped on her back and head. She was literally flattened into road kill.

When the dead man had his fill of the nurse, he pushed her away and stood up, people screaming and shrinking away from him in fear. If even one person had had the courage to fight, the dead man could have been taken down easily. But no one fought back, all too terrified of the walking abomination of nature.

The victim the dead man went for next was a seventy-five-year old grandmother sitting to the left of him. With stretched, wrinkled skin hanging from her neck from losing weight in her earlier years, the zombie reached out for her. After wrapping a fist in a handful of loose flesh, he tore the wattle of skin off her like he was peeling the cooked, crispy skin off a roasted chicken.

The nurse, who had gasped her last blood-frothed breath and had fallen into the oblivion of death a moment ago, now opened her eyes. When she turned her head, she saw the stewardess leaning over her, wanting to help, and she sank her pearly white teeth into the stewardess' right arm, coming away with a chunk of flesh.

The stewardess, staring down at the large chunk of meat missing from her right arm, the muscle and tendons showing like an anatomy project, screamed as loud as her lungs would allow.

The first dead man now had some company as he began to rip into the other passengers, all of them trapped with nowhere to go. In time he added more and more zombies to the first few, all of the new ghouls attacking the rest of the passengers. When the dead man was done feasting on the grandmother, the co-pilot of the plane stepped out of the cockpit to see why everybody was screaming bloody murder.

He had a .45 in his hand, now standard issue after 9/11.

When he opened the door from the cockpit, one of the passengers who had died and returned jumped the co-pilot, pushing him to the floor where he was abruptly ripped apart as more than a dozen zombies fed on his screaming body.

The first dead man put his now bright red teeth on the co-pilot's nose and chewed it off, the man's nasal cavity immediately filling with blood, choking him. After the dead man was finished with the first co-pilot, he stood up, and with other ghouls with him, they all swarmed into the cockpit, to the stunned horror of the pilot. The co-pilot's gun fell from his limp hand to be kicked around on the floor like a lost child's toy.

Looking up as the ghouls entered the cockpit, and with nowhere to go, the pilot screamed and tried to escape, but was soon pulled out of his chair and fed on. One female ghoul sank her bleached-white teeth into his neck, blood spraying up and across the controls and windows of the cockpit.

With no one controlling the plane, and the auto pilot not engaged, the aircraft began to descend.

Just before the pilot was killed, he was on approach to Logan Airport. When the pilot had tried to contact the control tower and had received no response, he knew with almost empty fuel tanks that he had no choice but to make an emergency landing, and to hell with the consequences.

But the pilot was dead now, ripped into so many bloody pieces that there was nothing left to reanimate.

While the ghouls fed on the trapped passengers, the plane slowly made its descent, the nose now aimed directly at Logan Airport and its now abandoned terminals—except for one.

* * *

Jake held his katanas in front of him, prepared to defend himself and Bill from the crowd of zombies coming for them. He was unaware of the danger in the sky above; he had more than enough to worry about on the ground.

At his feet, Bill stirred, but the older man was still out of it.

For the moment, Jake knew it was up to him to keep them safe, as bad as the odds were for their continued survival. He'd already told himself only an act of God could see him and Bill through this, and allow them to live through the next five minutes.

Three zombies came at him and Jake swung the katanas left and right, severing heads and hands from bodies as gore spewed in all directions. Looking down, he saw a ghoul about to take a bite out of his fallen friend, so he kicked the pale face in the nose, hearing cartilage crack, which sent bone fragments into the ghoul's brain, killing it instantly.

"Dammit, Bill, come on, wake up! For Christ's sake, wake up, please!" Jake screamed while he deftly avoided another zombie's grip. With all his might, he forced his katana into the spinal column of the ghoul to then twist the blade, severing the brain from the body as the twitching corpse flopped to the floor like a marionette with its strings cut.

Bill was finally stirring from the blow he'd suffered to the head, and when he opened his eyes, he was staring up into the dead white orbs of a zombie. With a yell of surprise, he pushed the pale face away.

"What the hell happened?" Bill said, looking around him, his eyes going wide when he realized he and Jake were surrounded by ghouls.

Dancing out of the grasp of another zombie, Jake's left foot kicked something on the floor. When he glanced down, he saw Johnson's M-16. Using the toe of his foot, he slid it under the weapon. Calling out to Bill, he used his foot to push the weapon across the few feet between him and Bill.

"Bill! Heads up!" he yelled as the rifle slid across the tiles to stop beside Bill.

When Bill picked it up, he saw four zombies that were getting too close for his liking, so he shot them right between the eyes, the bullets exploding heads and eyeballs like they were made of plastic stuffed with meatloaf, instead of bone and brains.

A zombie came at him from his left and Bill reached down and picked up his Glock, but when he went to fire it, all he heard was a soft click. So, the weapon had been empty when Lucky had given it to him, after saying he wanted to check it to make sure the gun was okay. Somehow Lucky had managed to switch the full clip for an empty one. Even if Bill had tried to shoot Lucky, the gun wasn't loaded. It made sense, too. With no bullets, Bill would have been easy fodder for the ghouls.

Dropping the Glock, Bill swung the M-16 around in a circular arc, the stock striking the zombie in the jaw, shattering it to pieces. Then he spun the rifle around, jammed the muzzle under the sagging chin, and blew the top of the zombie's skull clean off. The scalp flipped up and danced in the air before falling back onto the blown-off portion of the head. The hair was now upside down, the meat and gristle of the inner scalp facing up on the head like a macabre wig made from a butcher's leftovers or road kill.

Bill thought he'd seen too much that resembled road kill in the past few months. He looked to his left to see Jake valiantly fighting for his life.

When the next three ghouls came at Jake, he was ready, and with all his strength behind the blows, he sliced their heads from sagging shoulders.

When the decapitated heads fell to the floor, black ichor poured out of the jagged neck stumps. Jake was jumping around, so far managing to keep out of reach of the rotting, bloody hands when he saw the next zombie looked familiar. The visage belonged to Johnson, now part of the undead army, and with a snarl of hate for

Johnson—for being a soldier who tried to kill him and now a zombie who wanted to eat him—Jake rammed the tip of both swords through each of Johnson's eyes, impaling the head like a piece of bite-sized ham on two toothpicks.

With a throaty yell, he pulled back and to the sides, the swords slicing through bone and brains and flying out to the left and right, ripping the head apart in a spray of blood. Brain chunks flew everywhere, some splattering the closest zombies, and Johnson wobbled like a drunk for a few seconds before falling forward. The rest of his brains slid out to splatter on the floor, where undead feet soon squashed them to mush.

Killing nearly fifteen ghouls, Jake's eyes scanned the terminal, searching for a way he and Bill could escape the certain death they were in. Then his eyes spotted something on the far wall, just past the zombies. Though uncertain of the outcome, he was confident he'd found an escape route for Bill and himself.

"Bill, we've got to get out of here and I think I know how!" he called out as he took down another ghoul.

"So don't tell me, show me, and do it now, dammit! I'm almost out of ammo!" Bill screamed as he sprayed lead into the torsos of five more zombies, their chests becoming pockmarked with bullet holes. He knew he and Jake were actually very lucky, for the ghouls came at them in small numbers. So despite the overwhelming odds against the two men, the zombies still remained separate from one another, which was the only reason Jake and Bill had managed to survive for so long.

"Fine, follow me!" Jake yelled and took off at a run, slashing two more zombies into pieces as he ran.

Bill watched Jake turn and run, so he did the only thing he could, he began to retreat, shooting down bodies as they came for him, though the undead faces seemed endless.

Bill was just waiting to feel the bite of yellow and brown teeth when a ghoul finally managed to slide past his guard. Just before teeth sank into his arm, he spun and used the butt of the rifle to whack the face away. Now with a crushed visage, the zombie toppled over, its nose and lips now mush.

There was an air duct grate on the back wall near the ceiling of the terminal, with the metal grating hanging wide open. Jake, seeing his chance, slid his gore-covered katanas back into their sheaths, then ran like he was a marathon runner, passing the rotting ghouls as they reached for him, Bill right behind him.

Rotting hands clawed for him, but they were slow, way too slow to catch him, and he charged through them like a linebacker. The limbs of the zombies were stiff, and their treacle-like movements were so slow it was like they were walking underwater.

Managing to reach the metal grate by the skin of his ass, Jake jumped for the opening to the air duct with arms outstretched and hands open wide in anticipation of reaching the edge. With a little luck and a lot of determination, his palms slapped the metal ductwork, and with pale, dead hands trying to pull him back down, he kicked off a zombie's shoulder for leverage and pulled himself into the vent. He didn't know where the air duct led, but it had to be better than where he was now.

There was room inside the vent for him to turn around and he did so, then stuck his head back out into the terminal to see where Bill was.

The older man was working his way to Jake, shooting any ghouls foolish enough to try for him.

"Bill, give me your hands!" Jake yelled as he reached for him.

Bill shot four more zombies in the face, blowing their skulls apart like paper Piñatas, then he slung the M-16 over his shoulder and reached for Jake, needing his hands to climb.

A ghoul came at him and blocked his way, so Bill punched it in the face, pulping the nose and flattening the pale, wrinkled features. As the ghoul stumbled away, Bill shoved it to the floor and then ran at Jake, using the zombie's torso as a springboard.

The top half of the body sat up when Bill slammed his boots onto the zombie's chest, but that little bit of extra lift and bounce was what he needed to reach the vent with Jake in it.

He jumped as high as he could and came very close to missing Jake's outstretched hands, but at the last instant, Jake reached down another inch and managed to grasp his hands.

Bill was now dangling from the vent, his legs only an inch or so from the dead fingers trying to reach him.

"Pull me up, for Christ's sake, pull me up!" Bill screamed as he felt fingers caressing the soles of his boots.

"I'm trying! Jesus, you weigh a ton, why don't you lay off the cheese sandwiches!" Jake snapped back as he struggled to pull him into the vent.

Then a zombie taller than the others moved closer to Bill's dangling boots. It reached up, locking a hand with a massive wound around Bill's left heel. Bill felt himself tugged back down and he screamed, knowing what would happen if he fell.

"Don't let go, Jake! For the love of God, don't let go! Pull me up!"

"What the hell do you think I'm tryin' to do!" Jake yelled back while sweat poured down his forehead to slide into his eyes, blurring his vision. The moans, yells, and stench of death were an assault to his senses, and he shook his head to clear it, then renewed his struggle to pull Bill to safety.

Finally, Bill managed to get some purchase on the wall with the tip of his boots, and it was enough of a respite for Jake to yank back, pulling him up.

Bill's head shot upward to almost crack his head on the ceiling, but then he was bending forward and sliding into the vent.

His kicking legs were now sticking out of the duct like he was a baby being born from the womb, only he was coming out of it feet first.

Breathing heavily, Bill scooted deeper into the duct, and when he was in far enough, his feet hit the metal that was now his floor and he let out a loud sigh of relief.

"Good God, that was close," Bill gasped as he sucked in the dusty air. Little dust particles swam around in the gloom, and he could barely see Jake in front of him. "We should be dead now, you know that, right?"

Jake smiled, Bill barely able to discern it in the shadows. "Well, we're not, so let's go. We still need to find a way out of here."

Without waiting for Bill to reply, Jake spun on his butt and began crawling further into the ductwork, his katanas scraping the overhead metal while he moved. It was already becoming a tighter fit with each yard traversed, and there was a worry it could become so small neither man would be able to fit.

After almost ten minutes of crawling on hands and knees, and sucking in clouds of dust and whatever else was floating in the air inside the ductwork, Jake and Bill found an opening leading to the front of the terminal, not too far away from the main glass doors. These were the same doors they had used to enter the terminal. Jake used the soles of his boots to pummel the grating off, and it flew off the wall to crash on the floor below. If there were any zombies in the area, they would now know Jake and Bill were around.

Sticking his head out to inspect the terminal, Jake was pleased to see it looked empty.

"Holy shit, that sucked, but it looks clear out here. Looks like we made it," Jake said, chuckling as he thought about the very tight spaces they'd crawled through to get where they were now.

Then he focused on what was important to him, and that was to get some payback by killing Private Ricky, Lucky and Sgt. Wilson.

"Yeah, I couldn't agree more, but could you get your ass out of my face, please?" Bill asked, shoving to get him to climb out of the duct.

"Sure, Bill, hold on, let me spin around first," Jake said, and as he prepared to drop down, he slipped on the edge of the duct and fell out of it, hitting the polished concrete floor with a loud *thump*. That was soon followed by a clatter when his katanas struck the floor a second later.

Bill had an easier time. After turning around and sliding out, he landed easily on the floor with his boots slapping the polished cement.

"Let's go, it's time for some payback," Bill said with a snarl as he moved to the glass doors.

Climbing to his feet with a sore back from the fall, Jake winced, then took off after Bill.

"I was just thinking the same thing," Jake said as he caught up to Bill.

The two men stepped into the light of day and blinked, not used to the glare after being in the dark and gloom of the terminal. As their eyes adjusted to the light, they began walking, their destination now Terminal C, which was about three city blocks away.

As they moved through the cars and refuse scattered about the wide, four lane highway that connected all four terminals to one another, Bill began to hear a whining sound that appeared to be growing louder with each passing second.

"Hey, Jake, you hear that?" Bill asked as he looked around the deserted highway.

Jake didn't understand what Bill meant at first, but then he too, picked up the whine and cocked his head as he looked around.

When he looked up and behind him, his mouth dropped open.

"Bill, look up there, does that plane look like it's all right?" he asked.

Bill spun and saw where Jake was pointing, his eyes creasing as he studied the aircraft. It was listing terribly to the right, the landing gear still up, and there was no way the plane looked like it was about to land. But from the way it was fast approaching the airport, there was no doubt it was coming down.

"What the hell is that pilot doing?" Bill asked. "This airport is closed, has been for months."

"Where do you think they came from?" Jake inquired as he raised his hand to his forehead, blocking the glare of the sun so he could watch the airplane's approach.

"Don't know, but I'll tell you this, if it keeps going like that, it's gonna crash."

The two men stood in the road and stared at the plane, and after another minute, both men realized Bill's assumption was devastatingly correct.

"Shit, Bill, you're right, that plane's gonna crash and by the look of it, it's gonna hit..."

Bill cut him off, realizing what was about to happen. "Yeah, it's gonna hit Terminal C with Jess, Cara, Mark, Seth and everyone else still inside!"

"So what do we do?" Jake yelled as the whining grew louder. "What the fuck do we do?"

Bill wasn't listening as he stared at the plane heading almost directly towards the two men. He didn't have the strength to tell Jake what he knew in his heart. There was nothing they could do. When the plane crashed, its fuel tanks would erupt and everything in a quarter mile radius would be enveloped in a blazing fireball.

There was nothing left to do but pray.

Chapter 16

The Past

Twenty minutes before the plane crashed, Lucky, Private Ricky and Mark were returning from their mission at Terminal D.

Inside the food court, Sgt. Wilson was talking with one of his soldiers, Seth was sitting alone playing with a Game Boy Advance, and Cara, Jess, Rosa and Duke were all sitting at a corner table, talking together.

Forty-two other refugees were scattered about the building, either in the food court or other parts of the terminal, some working or others resting in the places now set aside for living quarters.

When Sgt. Wilson saw Lucky and the others enter, he told the soldier he was talking with to get lost and waved Lucky over to him, with Private Ricky and Mark following.

"So, how'd it go? Where's Johnson? Did you get rid of Roberts?" Danny asked, keeping his voice low so no one would hear him. When he said Jake's last name, his tone was cold.

Lucky shook his head. "We got surrounded by a shitload of pusbags. There had to be a hundred of 'em, Sarge," Lucky said, embellishing the numbers so Wilson wouldn't be angry with him. "They got Johnson, he's dead."

"Dammit, he was good man, but I can deal with it if Roberts is dead. So, is he?" Wilson asked again.

Lucky remembered the last glimpse he'd seen of Roberts and Bill. The older man had been lying on the floor with Jake standing over him while they were slowly being surrounded by zombies.

The men had to be dead; there was no way they could have survived.

"Yeah, Danny, Roberts is dead. Saw it myself. He got eaten by a bunch of pusbags," Lucky said with as much confidence as he could portray.

Upon hearing Jake's last name being used, both Cara and Jess walked over to Wilson and the other men, Duke and Rosa following close behind.

Wilson glanced down at Duke and scowled. "Damn mutt, where the fuck have you been? I'm gonna teach you some goddamn manners when I get a chance," he growled.

"Where's Jake?" Cara asked. Both she and Jess had become less and less angry as time passed. They were beginning to realize what happened wasn't Jake's fault. He was a victim as much as anyone else.

"He's dead, sweetie, got eaten," Lucky said with no compassion in breaking the news. "Now go back to what you were doing and let us men talk."

"No, it can't be!" Cara cried out and ran to the windows looking out on the tarmac. She only stayed there for a moment, before dashing into the shadows of a nearby hallway leading deeper into the terminal. Duke wanted to follow her, but Wilson stopped him by grabbing his collar.

"And where the fuck do you think you're going?" he snapped at Duke who whined to be let free. "Shit, what the hell has gotten into you lately?"

"Cara, wait!" Rosa called out, wanting to stop the girl, but she was held back by Jess.

"No, Rosa, I'll do it. She's my sister, after all. I'll go talk to her," Jess said, leaving to go find Cara.

After a few minutes of searching, Jess found Cara crying softly. She was at one of the boarding gates, looking out a window where normally she would have seen the airplanes taking off and landing.

"Are you okay?" Jess asked softly, sitting down next to Cara.

"What do you think? With Jake dead—and he was basically the only family we had left—and Melissa probably dead, too, then there's no one left. We haven't talked to him for almost three months and now I feel guilty. I should've talked to him," Cara cried. "I know it wasn't his fault now!"

"I know, I should've talked to him, too. Now he'll never know how we feel," Jess sighed, holding on to Cara and looking out the window with her.

After five minutes of complete silence mixed with crying, both Cara and Jess began to hear the whining of an engine, similar to the sound of an airplane landing or taking off.

Then, seconds later, the floor and walls began to vibrate, not like an earthquake, but more of a gentle throbbing, which seemed to grow with every passing second.

"Where's that coming from?" Cara asked suspiciously, using her sleeve to wipe away her tears.

"I don't know. I think it's coming from outside," Jess said, moving over to the floor to ceiling glass windows.

Behind the glass wall, there was nothing except the empty tarmac. Any aircraft had long ago taken off, before the airport was closed down.

Jess was still focusing her attention on ground level, and if she had looked up, she would have seen the approaching, distressed airplane heading straight for the runway in front of her.

The vibration began to grow worse and the whining rose in pitch, making her wince. It was then she looked skyward and her mouth dropped open. She saw the plane coming in sideways, the right wing pointing straight down to the earth.

She quickly realized if she and Cara didn't move fast, they would both become bloody, mangled hood ornaments on the front of the plane.

"It sounds like an airplane. Almost like its falling from the sky or..." Cara began, and then she saw the look of abject fear on Jess' face and knew she was right. Then she gasped in shock when she also looked out the window to see the plane.

"Run! Run, now, Cara!" Jess screamed, pulling her sister with her as she turned and ran away.

Both girls turned and dashed back to the food court, knowing they needed to warn the others about what was about to happen.

As their feet slapped the commercial carpeting, the whining grew so loud it blocked out all other sounds, and the entire building began shaking like an earthquake was befalling the airport.

Jess and Cara had just reached the food court, and both were screaming madly as they tried to warn the others to run, when the airplane connected with the runway.

The plane landed sideways and rolled tail over cockpit as the fuselage cartwheeled into Terminal C.

Pieces of the wings, and one of the engines, flew off in all directions as what was left of the main fuselage crashed into the terminal. The only saving grace in such a terrible accident was that with the plane's fuel tanks empty, there was no explosion, only mass destruction.

Inside the food court, all eyes turned to face the large windows as the light was blocked from the rolling plane crashing through the glass, sending thousands of glass shards in all directions. Ten people were reduced to bloody chunks in an instant as glass daggers sliced them apart without mercy.

Mark, Seth and Rosa were still sitting at a table, talking, when the entire ceiling fell in, crushing them into a bloody pulp in the blink of an eye.

The fuselage plowed deeper into the terminal and finally rolled to a stop, concrete and steel wrapping around the plane like an anxious lover. Nothing moved but falling debris for more than five minutes, until the rear emergency door of the plane, which was already dislodged from the crash, began to shift.

For a few minutes the door shook as something behind it tried to break free.

Then the weakened metal gave way and the door fell off to crash below, sending up yet more concrete dust into the air.

The doorway remained empty for a second, then the first undead, pale face popped up, white eyes looking around. The ghoul wasn't there for long, as the zombie was pushed out of the door by others behind it.

Falling to the floor below, the ghoul landed hard, but not so hard that the zombie didn't get up and stumble away, albeit with bones protruding from its body in odd angles.

More zombies exited the plane, each falling out of the hatch as others pushed from behind.

The first ghoul in line was the original suffering man on the plane, and he now led the charge into the rest of the terminal. If anyone was still alive, the zombies would find them.

It had been a long flight and they were hungry.

Sgt. Wilson, Lucky, Duke, and Private Ricky had already left the food court, and were on the opposite side of the terminal, when the plane plowed into the building.

One second Wilson was yelling at Ricky and Lucky about something, and the next second there was a loud whining and the world was turned upside down, as the entire structure shook like the earth was opening up to swallow it whole.

The ceiling gave way, acoustic tiles and ductwork falling on the three terrified men, as the world was thrown into darkness and each man was knocked unconscious.

Slowly, they came awake and now, covered in dust, wood, and pieces of concrete, Wilson and Lucky dug themselves out of the rubble and made their way to the first opening they found in the debris.

"What the fuck just happened?" Wilson gasped, trying to break free from rubble blocking his way. "Duke! Duke, where are ya, boy?" he called, trying desperately to find his dog. He didn't know how long he was unconscious, and when he checked his wristwatch, the face of it was shattered. If he had to guess, it was at least fifteen minutes, maybe more. Though for all he knew he'd been out for hours.

"He's over here with me, Danny," Lucky said, carrying Duke in his arms. He now had another small cut on his face to go with the other scars already there.

"If we're both here and Duke is all right, too, then where's Ricky?" Wilson asked, looking around for any movement that might tell him where Ricky was buried.

"I got no idea, but look behind us," Lucky stammered, pointing behind Wilson. When he turned, his jaw fell open when he saw more than thirty zombies coming from God knew where.

These were the phalanx of the ghouls from the plane, now moving through the rubble as they searched the destroyed terminal for fresh meat. A few had severed limbs in their hands and they chowed down merrily while they walked.

"Shit, we have to get out of here!" Wilson yelled. "Let's get as many weapons, and whatever else we can carry, and get to the truck I've got parked out in the back lot for emergencies. That is, if it's still there and hasn't been destroyed." He turned and dashed to his office, hoping his military grade weapons were still intact. Hell, he hoped the office was still intact

Lucky put Duke down and ran after Wilson, the dog also following close behind.

"But, Danny, what about Ricky? He's back there somewhere," Lucky called.

"Fuck him, there's no time to look for him now. It's every man for himself. If you want to stay and die trying to find him, that's your business."

Wilson ran faster, leaving Lucky behind.

Lucky did actually slow down and glance over his shoulder. Ricky was probably in the rubble where Wilson had been, but then he saw the zombies and changed his mind.

"Fuck that shit," he whispered and took off after Wilson, leaving the shambling ghouls behind.

By the time Lucky reached Wilson's office, he was already packing his guns and ammo. Upon stepping inside the room, Lucky saw the office wasn't too badly damaged and the guns were fine, if a little dusty.

"Don't just stand there, you idiot, get packing!" Wilson snapped at him.

"Oh, shit, sorry, Sarge, okay," Lucky replied and began grabbing anything of value they might need.

"Forget that 'Sarge' shit, man, as of now we're out of the Army," Danny snapped as he finished packing another bag.

As soon as they were done collecting as much as they could carry for survival and protection, they ran out of the office to the main lobby of the terminal. It was in a bad state, the ceiling having collapsed, and even now the sounds of stressed metal could be heard. It wouldn't be long before the entire terminal collapsed like a house of cards.

"What about food?" Lucky asked.

"No time, we have to go. We'll stop somewhere later and see what we can find. Duke, come on, boy, heel," Danny said, glancing at the approaching ghouls while he ordered Duke to follow him.

Lucky and Danny, with Duke, disappeared around a corner of a relatively still intact corridor, as they headed for the northwest parking lot and a waiting Dodge truck.

While Danny was running to the truck, he still wondered what had happened to Private Ricky.

Private Ricky was still buried under debris and was just waking up as Danny and Lucky took off down the collapsed hallway to Wilson's office.

Pulling himself out of the rubble, Ricky spit dust and dirt as he climbed to his feet. It was dark, the choking smoke and dust clouds blocking any sunlight, and he wiped his face and hair to clear it of dust.

Mentally, he did a quick assessment of his body and was relieved to find he was in one piece, though his right elbow pained him and his left knee was sore. Still, he would live to fight another day.

With the generators still running in another part of the terminal, flickering arcs of electrical wires could be seen in the smoke, and his hearing was still muffled from the collapsing ceiling.

As the seconds went by, the ringing in his ears was replaced by muffled sounds, and soon he thought he could actually hear again.

Coughing from the dust he inhaled, he reached down and was lucky enough to find his M-16. He'd fallen on it, protecting it when the ceiling had dropped on him, and the weapon looked fine.

A low moan came to his ears, and though the sound wasn't as clear as he would have liked, he turned to look behind him...and promptly screamed when he saw the dark corridor was filled with the walking dead, no more than five feet from him.

Shaking the cobwebs out of his head, he saw the passengers from the crashed plane were now coming for him, and it was painfully obvious they were all the living dead.

Some had heads at unnatural angles while others had bones sticking out where there should be none. Blood was the attire of the day, coating each animated corpse as they shambled over the fallen rubble towards him.

Bringing up his rifle, Ricky desperately tried to shoot his M-16, but there was nothing but a dry click.

The safety!

Flicking it off, he began firing at the ghouls, but they were already too close. His bullets ripped apart the first two bodies, but as they absorbed the hail of lead, others squeezed around the jerking forms. Still screaming, Ricky felt a dead hand grab the barrel of the rifle, and as he yelled in terror and held the trigger down, the rifle finally cycled dry.

Before he could turn and run, more clawed hands grabbed him by the arms and legs, pulling him to the rubble-strewn floor. When the first sharpened fingernails dug into his warm flesh, Private Ricky's screams turned into shrieks of unbearable agony.

He screamed for a lot longer than anyone would have given him credit for if someone was listening, and his yells only stopped when his throat was torn out, followed by his head becoming separated from his shoulders.

After that his screams were silenced forever.

At least he could take solace in the fact there would be nothing left to come back. Private James Ricky was truly dead forever.

Fifteen minutes before Jake and Bill arrived in the demolished lobby of Terminal C, they were still running across the highway, the loud whine of the plane now gone as it crashed into the side of the terminal, filling the air with the sound of rending metal and steel.

Both men had to dive for cover when pieces of the airplane flew in all directions. Bill was almost flattened by a seven foot hatch piece that landed not more than two feet from where he was.

For more than a minute it seemed to be raining airplane parts and then, just as fast as it began, it ceased and the air was clear once more.

Now the only sound was the collapsing terminal and the fading whine of the now defunct jet engines.

Jake's heart was in his throat as he imagined what it must be like inside the terminal. He kept waiting for a fireball to bloom, but mercifully one did not.

His thoughts were only for Cara and Jess, who he knew were in the devastated building...somewhere.

Jake knew there was something else to worry about as well.

When the plane crashed, the blast wave would have alerted zombies everywhere to come to the airport, from the nearby train station, through East Boston, and probably Revere and Chelsea, too.

He started to think that the zombies seemed more attracted to noise than anything else, and not as much from smelling their food from miles away.

If he didn't hurry and find the girls fast, and then find a car to escape, there was a chance this would be the end of him and Bill when the entire airport filled with every walking corpse in a five mile radius.

Getting to his feet, Jake began to run, Bill right behind him.

Upon arriving in front of the terminal and peering inside, Jake and Bill couldn't see anything. Bill opened one of the cracked glass doors, and the two men stepped inside.

As the door slammed closed, the glass shattered, the small fractures from the crash causing the pane to give out.

With the electricity now knocked out, the lines to the generators destroyed or the generators themselves destroyed, the only thing giving off light were the skylights in the roof and the light through the front doors. The lobby was wreathed in shadows, only thin slices of light here and there.

The dust and smoke didn't help either, and the two men picked their way over the debris of the falling ceiling.

The crash radius hadn't reached this far. The food court was on the opposite side of the terminal and seemed to be where most of the damage was. Jake was optimistic that maybe Cara and Jess hadn't been in the crash zone. Maybe they had been outside or at the far end of the terminal, and were even now safe and searching for him while he did the same for them.

He still had hope they were alive.

"Jesus Christ, Jake, this is bad, real bad," Bill coughed as he stepped over a fallen I-beam. The closer they got to the epicenter of the crash, the worse the damage became.

Bill was beginning to wonder if there would come a time when the entire massive hallway was blocked entirely.

This happened once as they made their way deeper into the terminal. To continue, they had to climb over the concrete and steel rubble, and soon found themselves so high they were even with the roof. They scurried over the debris until they saw an opening and climbed back down. Both men were covered in dirt and dust, sweat pouring off their faces and necks as the exertion of climbing took its toll.

Bill had a bad feeling there was no way anyone would be left alive, but when he saw the look of determination on Jake's face, he knew he had to let the young man find out for himself. There would be no way Jake would leave without knowing for sure.

When they finally reached the food court, there was no one there that was breathing, except for the twenty-one ghouls who were walking straight for them. Jake tried to reason with himself that no one in the food court was left alive because perhaps every-one had gotten out fast enough before the crash, but his hopes were dashed when he caught a glimpse of the dented nose cone of the demolished airplane.

Though there were shadows everywhere and his attention was distracted by the approaching zombies, he spotted Jess's shirt hanging from the torn and collapsed metal of the cone. He remem-bered that particular shirt for two reasons. The first was he'd seen her wearing it earlier that morning and the second was it had flowers on it. It wasn't her shirt actually, but had been taken from the lost and found. It was a Hawaiian shirt that tourists always wore. Cara had teased Jess about it and Jake had laughed when she'd first gotten it, but when the girls heard chuckling, they had walked away from him, still not talking to him.

Now the shirt was ripped and bloody, and it seemed to move by itself in the light breeze filtering through the wreckage.

The shirt could mean only one thing, but he pushed the thought back down, not wanting to face what he knew was fact.

"Come on, Jake, let's get the hell out of here before it's too late for us, too," Bill said, pulling on Jake's arm. He nodded and they both turned and traversed the way they had used a minute ago. Once the two men climbed the rubble, the following ghouls were left behind. Their stiff arms and legs weren't very good at climbing. One adventurous zombie did try, and the dead man made it halfway up before losing his footing and toppling back to the floor. His head cracked on a cement chunk and his brains seeped out, the body twitching as whatever had reanimated it in the first place went back into the dark abyss forever.

Twenty minutes later, with both men breathing hard and exhausted, they finally made it free of the destroyed terminal.

There was a long-term parking lot two hundred feet away and it wasn't hard for the men to steal a car, Bill telling Jake how he'd acquired some unsavory skills from a misspent youth.

With Bill driving, he floored the gas pedal on the small hatchback he'd picked for its easiness to hotwire, and the two men left the airport behind.

As Bill drove away from the airport, avoiding the ghouls shambling down the highway on their way to the plane crash, Jake glanced back to the wrecked terminal, and his heart broke at the thought of Jess and Cara being dead.

It was as they were driving away that something in the terminal caught fire. One second there was silence, then there was a thunderous boom that filled the air and rattled the brains inside a person's head.

Bill slammed on the brakes, both he and Jake jumping out of the car to look back at the terminal. It was now burning brightly, the flames a hundred feet high and growing.

"The crash must've ruptured the gas main underground," Bill, said. "Shit, that could be us in there right now if we'd stayed any longer."

"Cara and Jess are dead, Bill, they have to be. They were in the food court when we left and there was no reason for them to leave there," Jake whispered just loud enough for Bill to hear. When he turned to look at Bill, tears were in his eyes. "They were Melissa's sisters. They were all I had left of her."

"Hey, now, wait a second. You said she might still be alive, that she went to that cabin up in the mountains, right?"

"Yeah, the White Mountains in New Hampshire."

"Exactly, so all we have to do is get there." He turned and climbed back into the car, leaving Jake to watch the flames alone.

Fifteen zombies were closing on the car as they stumbled down the highway, and after Jake checked to see how far away from him they were, he turned back to the massive fire.

He stared at the flames for another minute, then nodded, wiped his eyes, and climbed back into the car, the zombies only twenty feet away and closing.

"You must think I'm a pussy for crying," he sniffed as Bill put the car in drive and drove onward.

"Nah, I think you're human, that's all," Bill smiled in return.

Bill swerved around some of the zombies and struck others with the front bumper, then the car was free and rolling onward, the flames of the fire rising higher into the sky, a giant funeral pyre for all the people who were at the rescue camp.

Bill only managed to make it a quarter mile after leaving the airport, the highway becoming thick with the walking dead. They were coming from all over, attracted to the noise, smoke, and flames of the plane crash.

At first Bill just weaved in and out of the bodies, managing just fine, but when the highway became blocked, he had no choice but to take an exit down to the rural roads of the city.

It was as he was turning a corner, his foot too heavy on the gas pedal, that he realized his speed was excessive and it was going to get them killed.

"Look out!" Jake screamed as Bill drove straight for an abandoned and stalled eighteen wheeler in the middle of the road.

Bill hit the brakes, but the tires skidded on sand and glass covering the pavement, then there was a loud pop as the two front tires blew, thanks to the sharp glass and debris littering the road.

The hatchback spun and crashed into the right rear corner of the trailer, both men tossed around but not hurt.

"You okay?" Bill asked.

"Nice driving, old timer, you almost got us killed," Jake snapped in reply as he rubbed his chest. One of his katanas had whacked him on the back of the head and now he had a small lump there.

The crunching of glass caused both men to look around to see they had picked a very bad spot to park.

"Shit, look at 'em all," Jake said as he shifted his katanas to a better position.

"Come on, we need to get out of here," Bill said as he pushed his door open, almost falling out when it popped open.

The two men climbed out of the car, shook off their fatigue, and darted down the street in what they hoped was a way through the approaching zombies.

There was a warehouse with no doors or windows visible to their left and nothing but an empty street filled with the walking dead to their right. A telephone pole with a platform at its top was in front of them.

Both Jake and Bill had to stop running and hold their ground when they realized they were surrounded on all sides.

Jake shook his head, sweat dripping down his dust-covered face as he turned to look at Bill. "Dammit, we're surrounded!" he yelled in anger.

Unbeknownst to Jake and Bill, the odyssey of the two men had come full circle.

Chapter 17

The Present

Jake's eyes snapped open and he looked around the bedroom, for a moment not knowing where he was. Then reality flooded back to him; so did Duke's wet tongue as the dog licked his cheek, wanting Jake to get up and feed him.

Jake was in Melissa's bedroom, in her house, ending up here after escaping the horde of zombies at the airport, then Wilson had shown up at his house by pure dumb luck and he'd killed the man, getting his revenge. Then he and Bill had driven off, but Jake had wanted to come here, to see Melissa's house one last time. He hadn't been here since the first days of the outbreak, when he'd found Jess and Cara hiding in a closet.

Duke licked his cheek again, wanting some attention now that he was finally awake.

"Quit it, Duke, I know what you lick with that mouth," Jake groaned as he wiped the slobber off his face and rubbed the sleep from his eyes.

There was a wind-up alarm clock on the nightstand, and when he checked it, he was surprised to see he'd been asleep for almost ten hours. Not that it was very surprising, mind you. What with the day he had yesterday, trying to escape the airport and also getting revenge on Wilson, the day had sucked the life out of him both emotionally and physically.

With the memories and loss of Jess and Cara still fresh in his mind, he pushed the feelings down and got out of bed; he really needed to pee.

Pushing Duke away from him, he stood up and headed for the bathroom. He knew the water wasn't working, but he had to use the bathroom badly. He wouldn't be staying in the house for much longer, anyway, and decided *what the hell*, before urinating into the already full toilet, his steady stream stirring up the foul slurry and making him wince from the stench.

He thought of Jess telling him how she had urinated in the bathtub, and the memory made him wince, the emotional turmoil threatening to rise once again as he thought of her, now dead and gone like so many others.

Above the toilet was a window about chest height, and as he finished up, he looked out onto the deserted street, seeing only a few corpses rotting in the morning sun near the sidewalk. There were a few wrecked cars to mar the once ordinary view, as well. He thought it was funny how the human mind could adapt to almost anything if given enough time.

It was while he was gazing outside that he heard the distinct sound of what could only be motorcycles coming down the street. After zipping up his pants, he ran back into the bedroom, then changed into something a little cleaner than what he was wearing.

Fortunately, Melissa had a few items of clothing that were really for men, and he was able to fit into them and not look silly, not that a zombie would care what his fashion sense was when it tried to eat him.

Once he was dressed in fresh clothes, he dashed down the stairs to the front of the house, Duke following him happily like they were playing a game of tag.

He ignored the decayed corpses still on the floor, Melissa's parents still covered with a sheet out of respect.

More memories to haunt him.

When he reached a front window, he discovered Bill was already there, also in new clothes taken from Melissa's father's closet. His hair was combed, and he looked better than he had in days.

"Hey, Bill, guess you heard it, too, huh?" Jake asked as he reached Bill and peered out the window.

"Yup, I was in the kitchen," he said as he pushed back the curtain so he could get a better view of the street. With the noise the motorcycles were making, soon every ghoul in the area would be arriving, attracted by the sound.

Then the bikers appeared, their chrome motorcycles reflecting the sun like polished mirrors. Jake's eyes went wide when he saw the Camaro parked in front of the house against the curb.

He spun on Bill and said, "What the hell is my car doing out front? I thought you parked it a street over."

Bill nodded. "Yeah, I did, but I went to get it this morning seems we'd be leaving in a bit," he replied.

"Yeah, but now those guys are gonna see it and know we're in here," Jake stated as he pointed to the perfectly preserved 1969 Camaro.

"Shit, I didn't plan on that," Bill said. "Come on, who would've thought anyone would show up an hour before we were gonna leave?" he reasoned.

"Forget it, Bill, it's too late now, let's just get ready in case they figure out we're in here. Who knows, they may just drive by and not even notice." Without waiting for a reply, he spun and took off, heading up the stairs to the second floor.

"Where're you going?" Bill asked.

"I'm going to get my stuff, 'cause if those bikers do wanna check this place out, and they're dangerous, then I don't want to be here. I've done enough fighting to last me a lifetime already," he said as he took the steps two at a time. "Get your shit together, we need to go now!"

Moments later, the two men had gathered their things and were prepared to leave out the back door of the house, to then cut through the backyards, when at the last second Jake paused.

"What's wrong?" Bill asked, knowing they should be going. The throaty roar of the motorcycle engines had settled to a rough idle outside the house; the bikers had definitely noticed the Camaro.

Jake shook his head defiantly. "What's wrong is I've lost everything I've ever cared about, and goddamn it, I'm not gonna lose that Camaro, too. It's all I have left of my family, my father."

"So, what're you planning on doing?" Bill asked.

Jake's jaw was taut as he spun on his heels and walked to the front door. "I'm gonna tell them to fuck off and leave my car alone." As he pulled his katanas from their sheaths, he opened the front door and stepped outside, praying the bikers weren't well armed and would simply gun him down the instant they saw him.

Bill shook his head in frustration but he raised his rifle, flicking off the safety. He knew Jake might need the firepower of the M-16 for protection in case things got hairy.

With a few choice imprecations muttered under his breath, he followed Jake, Duke padding right behind him, the dog just happy to go outside again.

Duke ran past Jake and out into the front yard, immediately taking a dump on the lawn. While Duke did his business, Jake looked at the bikers.

The first thing he saw upon stepping through the front doorway, were three people, two men and a woman.

They were talking to each other, and when he stepped out onto the small landing with Duke dashing past him, and Bill right behind him, no one making a sound, at first the three bikers didn't notice they weren't alone.

"Hey, Butch, take a look at this," the woman said while getting off her bike to inspect the Camaro. "This car is mint." She went to the hood and touched it with her hand. "Hood's still warm, this was driven recently."

Butch climbed off his motorcycle, a new Harley Davidson with saddle bags and chrome rims. "Yeah, I see it, Carol, but who does it belong to?" he asked as he approached the car.

"Maybe it belongs to those two guys," the other man said, pointing to Jake, and Bill who had his M-16 aimed directly at the three bikers. Both Jake and Bill stood on the front porch, waiting to see what was going to happen next.

When Jake saw the man gesture to him, he thought, *Shit, they're pointing at us, better introduce ourselves and hope for the best.*

"Uh, hi there, we're friendly. That's my car. I'm Jake Roberts and this is Bill Monroe," he said, hoping they wouldn't do anything rash. If the three bikers looked concerned Bill was aiming a rifle at them, none of them showed it.

"How's it going, guys? We don't want any trouble," Bill added, hoping to avoid a shootout. From the amount of space separating him from the bikers, it would be bloody, that was for sure. He felt good seeing that none of the three bikers were holding a gun.

Bill tensed when one of the bikers reached into his jacket pocket, thinking the man was pulling out a handgun, and was relieved to see it was a handkerchief.

Butch sneezed into it and put it back in his pocket, then with a glance to Carol and the other man, who nodded back, he strolled up the cement walkway to meet Jake and Bill.

"How the heck are ya? I'm Butch, this is Carol and that's Brock," Butch said with a wide smile, sticking out his hand and introducing everyone. He was a burly man with muscular arms, thick chest hair, strong jaw, jet black hair and a matching beard. In many ways he resembled a grizzly bear, only friendlier.

Jake eyed the man for almost a full thirty seconds, but Butch's arm never wavered, his smile never faltered, and Jake decided the man looked genuine.

Jake cast a glance to Bill who shrugged, his M-16 also never wavering in case it was some kind of subterfuge. Jake took the proffered hand, shaking it quickly.

Bill gestured to Butch that it was okay, and Butch turned and called the other two bikers over to him, each quickly introducing themselves.

Jake got an even better look at Butch and the other two bikers as they talked. Butch seemed to be in his early forties, wearing a dirty t-shirt, a leather jacket, cowboy boots, and dark blue jeans. Jake thought he looked like Larry the Cable Guy, that is if the man lost the beard and didn't have so much hair everywhere else.

Carol looked like any old biker chick with a worn leather jacket, a tank top, and clean white jeans. She was pretty and looked to be in her mid-forties, with large breasts and long, curly brown hair. She didn't' have the figure of a runway model, but her body was slim with curves in all the right places.

Brock also looked to be in his early forties. He wore a muscle shirt with a denim jacket, the American flag embroidered on the back. A pair of cowboy boots rounded off his outfit. He also had a big, bushy beard similar to Butch's, and long unruly black hair to match his facial hair.

With all the introductions out of the way, the bikers began to ask questions.

"What're you two doing here in this ghost town? You're the first living people we've seen for hours," Butch said, who seemed to be the leader of the trio of bikers.

Bill frowned when he thought about where he and Jake had been only a day ago. "We were at a rescue camp set up at Logan Airport, but it got wiped out when a plane crashed into the terminal." He turned and pointed to the south, the smoke still rising into the sky from more than five miles away. "You can still see some of the smoke if you look closely. We almost didn't make it out of there alive."

"Oh, wow," Carol said. "We saw all that smoke and wondered about it, but figured we'd just stay away. All that smoke had to mean a big fire and that was a scene we didn't need."

"So why are you here? Is this your house or somethin'?" Brock asked as he looked past Jake and gazed at the house.

"This is my fiancée's house," Jake said. "I figured it was as good a place to stay as anywhere else. Plus, she's missing and it was just nice to come here and see the place, you know, so I could think of her. With her gone, and my parents dead, all I have left in this world is my new dog, Duke, and Bill of course." Jake scratched Duke's head and the dog woofed with pleasure, Bill also smiling at Jake's sentiment. "Actually, we were about to get going."

"Oh, yeah? Can I ask where you're headin'?" Butch asked. "Look, I know we ride bikes, but we're harmless, really. Besides, it's better to travel in numbers, right? Me, Brock and Carol have survived this shit 'cause we stay on the move and the bikes let us get through places we would've gotten stuck in if we were in a car. We can help you guys, too. We have a few guns on our bikes so we can defend ourselves." He glanced at the M-16. "Though it looks like you guys are set pretty well for guns."

"A few more never hurt anyone," Bill said with a grin.

"Yeah, except the pusbags," Jake added.

Bill and Jake chuckled at that but Butch didn't get it, not knowing the name for the ghouls.

After the chuckle had passed, Jake continued. "We're going to New Hampshire. My fiancée's family has a summer house, and I got lucky and found out it's possible she went there when all *this* happened." He waved his right hand around in the air, signifying the neighborhood and the zombie uprising in general. "I've been trying to find her for the past three and a half months and this is the only lead I have," he said, starting to feel dejected about the subject, but not wanting to let it show. "Then it wasn't the right time to go, I had others to watch over and..." He trailed off, thinking of Cara and Jess again.

"Oh, baby, I'm so sorry for you," Carol consoled, moving up to Jake and rubbing his arm. "We've all lost people we loved in this shit. I lost my husband and his family, and my mother. It's terrible, but we all have to carry on, it's our duty. We can't let what's happening win, we just can't."

Brock spoke up then. "You know, Jake, me and Carol were just talking the other day about trying for New Hampshire, too. Figured with all the mountains and shit it might be safer there."

Butch turned on both Carol and Brock. "I never heard anything about this. Were you two planning on saying something to me?"

"Sure we were," Carol said, "but it was just talk so there was no need to yet. 'Sides, you were sleeping when we brought it up."

Butch waved her reply away. "Forget it, doesn't matter anyway." He turned to Jake and Bill. "So, guys, what do ya say, can we come with you or should we get on our bikes and go our own way?"

Brock interrupted yet again. "Uhm, guys, I think we need to make up our mind what the hell we're gonna do, 'cause we have company." He gestured to both ends of the street.

More than two dozen zombies had appeared, coming out of open doorways of homes and from around driveways, where they had been hiding in backyards and in shrubbery, seeking the coolness, wanting to avoid the hot sun.

But with the sounds of the motorcycle engines filling the street, it was like a dinner bell to their befuddled and dead brains.

So they came, shambling out into the light, their teeth clacking as dead hands opened and closed into gnarled claws. Drool and blood slid from slack jaws and glazed, white eyes searched for the humans, and once seen, they moved out, slowly, one plodding step at a time.

"Shit!" Jake spit. "More damn pusbags. I knew it was too good to last," he growled, referring to the fact it had been very quiet on the street up till now.

Bill glanced to Jake. "Well, son, we can either go back inside and board the place up with us in it, or we can get the hell out of here right now. Your call." He hefted the M-16 as he finished his statement.

"I'll do whatever you want to do, Bill," Jake replied as he gripped his katanas tighter.

Bill let his eyes roam over Brock, Carol, and Butch, each of the bikers looking back with open eyes and honest faces. He had less than three seconds to decide what they were going to do, as the ghouls were very close to reaching their position. The bikers were already becoming nervous, knowing their time to escape on the motorcycles was dwindling.

Finally, Bill grinned slightly and said, "Sure, what the hell, why not. The more the merrier, right? It'll be good to have others around besides Jake to talk to." Bill loved Jake like a son, but the younger man could be a real pain in the ass, though in a good way.

"Well, whatever we're gonna do, fellas," Butch said as he gestured to the zombies, "we need to do it now or we're gonna have to deal with *them*."

Carol nodded. "Butch is right, if we don't go now we're gonna have to deal with those *things*."

Jake grinned as he looked at the zombies slowly approaching and then at Butch and Carol. "So why can't we do both?" he said, and before anyone could ask him what he meant, Jake was running down the cement walkway towards the zombies, his katanas already flashing in the morning sun.

Brock watched Jake running away and he turned to Bill. "What the hell is he doing?"

Bill shrugged slightly, knowing the answer would take too long to explain to the biker. With everything he and Jake had been through in the past few months, he had an idea he knew exactly what Jake was doing.

"I think he's gonna blow off some steam," Bill said simply, and as he hefted his M-16, he strode down the steps and followed Jake down the walkway towards the ghouls.

Butch looked to Carol and Brock and shook his head. "These two are crazy, maybe we should just get on our bikes and ride the hell outta here."

Carol shook her head, reached around her back with her right hand, and took out a .45 pistol. The gun had been in easy reach, and if Bill or Jake had appeared hostile, she would have shot both men dead before they knew what was happening.

"Ah, lighten' up, Butch, let's have a little fun before we head out," she said with a grin. Before she received an answer, she too, spun on her heels and strode down the walkway, then shot the first zombie she spotted. The ghoul was fifteen feet away and her first shot was a little high. It took off the top of the zombie's head, but the brain was still intact.

Cursing her poor marksmanship, she fired again, and this time the head snapped back and the body dropped to the ground. With the top of its skull already missing, the brains flopped onto the road like spilled, Chinese sweet and sour pork.

"Damn, she's hardcore," Brock said as he turned and followed her down the walkway.

Butch shrugged, deciding if they were going to have some fun then so was he. As he reached the end of the walkway, he saw a lead pipe lying in the gutter, having fallen off some unknown passing truck months ago.

Picking it up, he slapped the tip into his other palm, liking the feel and weight of the pipe. The weight was more than adequate to bust a few rotting heads in, and a second later he got the chance when a dead housewife came at him, still wearing the apron she'd died in.

Butch swung the pipe as hard as his muscular arm would allow, the pipe connecting with the left side of the dead woman's head like it was made of plastic. The dead housewife wobbled on her feet for a moment, but Butch yanked the pipe back and swung it again, this time the tip going in so far it was hidden from view inside the skull.

When he pulled it away from the destroyed head, dark brain matter covered the tip and was now stuck inside the circular opening of the hollow pipe.

Shaking it clean, he kicked the housewife away from him. She fell heavily to the street and didn't move again.

Carol was having a great time, shooting one zombie after another. When her area was clear, she put her free hand on her hip and watched Jake take out three ghouls with dexterity, the blades of the katanas flashing in the sun as blood and heads went flying.

Bill was to Jake's left, and he shot three zombies consecutively. They weren't close enough for straight head shots, so he shot each one in the torso and then walked the bullets up until they found the face. The last bullet found the pale visage of a dead salesman and the head exploded, bone and brain matter dancing in the air until gravity took hold and it fell back to the ground with a dull *splat*.

Bill spun in a circle, looking for more targets, but there were none available. Jake did the same thing, his katanas now covered in gore. They were still thirsty for undead blood, but there were no more zombies to take down.

Both men turned and watched Brock pick a zombie up, and with the body now raised to chest height, he slammed the ghoul over his knee like a wrestler, the sound of the zombie's back snapping carrying on the wind. But he wasn't finished. Dropping the paralyzed ghoul to the ground, he then raised his right boot and stomped it down on the face like an anvil, the skull collapsing from the blow like it was made of Styrofoam coated with pale flesh.

Brock looked up to see everyone was watching him while he dealt with the last ghoul. "What?" he asked as he scraped the sole of his boot on the corpse's chest.

"Nothing," Carol said. "Just watching you work."

Wiping the swords clean on the back of another corpse, Jake slapped Bill on the back and headed for the Camaro. When he reached Carol and Butch, he nodded politely. "Okay, now we can go," he said casually.

Bill chuckled and shook his head, then went to grab their stuff from the house as Carol and the two bikers climbed on their motorcycles.

"You need any help, Bill?" Jake called from the driver's seat of the Camaro.

"Nah, I got it," Bill replied as he carried their stuff from inside the house and tossed it into the car. Duke was there, running around everyone's legs, and Jake scooted him into the car.

While they had been fighting the zombies, Duke had been running around, barking at the zombies and causing a general distraction that had made it easier to take them down.

With their backpacks in his hands, Bill took an extra second to close the front door behind him. When he reached Jake, Bill saw he was grinning slightly.

"What's that look for?" Bill asked.

Jake gestured to the house with his chin. "You closed the door. That was a nice thing to do, thanks."

Bill had shown deference to the house that meant something to Jake and the younger man knew it.

The odds they would ever return were slim, but by closing the door after he'd exited it, Bill still showed the home respect, even if it might be construed as wasted effort by someone else.

"No problem, son, happy to do it," Bill said. He tossed the gear into the back seat with Duke, who woofed his displeasure of having to share his area with the packs and gear.

Bill climbed into the passenger's seat, closed the door, glanced at Jake and said, "We ready to go or what?"

Jake didn't reply, he just nodded, put the transmission in drive, and stepped on the gas. He waved out the window so the bikers knew he was leaving.

With the throaty roar of the Camaro's exhaust, plus the three motorcycles, the five survivors and a dog moved out, leaving behind a street filled with mangled corpses, a cloud of flies already descending on the putrid feast of rotting meat.

Fifteen minutes later, the Camaro and the three motorcycles were parked on the onramp for the interstate heading north.

Before they moved on, Jake and Bill wanted to ask a few more questions of the bikers, so as to be absolutely sure they knew who they were traveling with. But after the battle with the zombies to escape the neighborhood, both Jake and Bill were satisfied they had found three good people.

"So, Brock, where're you guys from originally?" Jake asked as he rubbed Duke's ears, the dog staying close to his new master.

"We're all from Providence. When the shit hit the fan and everything began to fall apart, we decided to head north, to just pack it up and leave," Brock said while taking his black half helmet off his bike seat and rubbing a few specks of dried blood off it.

"And how do you three know each other?" Bill inquired.

"We're all family. Carol's my sister and Brock is my cousin," Butch said happily.

Jake heard what sounded like a soda can being kicked. He turned slightly, glancing over his shoulder, to see a dozen zombies walking slowly towards his location.

They were a motley bunch, with wounds on their arms and faces, and their torsos ripped open to expose their glistening insides. The ghouls' sluggish gait was taking them closer and closer with each plodding step.

"Shit, get on your bikes, here comes another group of pusbags," Jake said, shoving Duke into the Camaro and getting into the car himself, Bill doing the same thing.

"Don't worry, boys, we can take 'em," Carol said, pulling out her .45 from the left saddle bag on her bike. Butch and Brock pulled out their guns, too, Brock holding a shotgun and Butch holding a .50 Desert Eagle. The shotgun had been strapped to the side of the motorcycle.

"Take 'em out, guys!" Butch yelled, and a half second later, the zombies were being riddled with bullets. Some of the ghouls received a bullet right between the eyes, and a few more had their heads blown clean off, all thanks to Brock's shotgun.

After a minute or two of guns going off, the firing ceased, all the zombies down for the count.

"Why the hell did you do that?" Jake yelled from inside the Camaro. "You could've saved your bullets and we could've just driven away!"

"Don't worry, hon, we got enough bullets to last us a lifetime," Carol said as she patted one of her saddle bags, which was bulging with boxes of ammo. Getting on her motorcycle, she popped out her empty clip and slapped in a new one, all with practiced ease.

When all three bikers were all on their motorcycles, they started the engines, the heavy rumble filling the air, calling out to any more zombies in the area.

Knowing it was time to leave, Bill, now driving, started the engine on the Camaro.

"Do you guys have bullets for an M-16?" Bill yelled, trying to be heard over the sound of the motorcycle engines.

"No, sorry, we don't have that caliber!" Butch called back.

Ready to go, they drove up the on ramp for the interstate, the Camaro rolling over a few rotting carcasses strewn on the pavement like discarded trash.

With his new friends traveling by his side, Jake now had a clear path to New Hampshire, and hopefully, Melissa.

He'd been planning the trip for months and now he was finally doing it.

After only a few minutes of driving down the interstate, the steady drone of the 350 engine calming him, images of what happened at the airport flashed back into Jake's mind.

Visions came of when the airplane had crashed into Terminal C, where his friends had been, Jess and Cara among them, all jumbling together to haunt him.

He shook it off, knowing it was time to leave the past where it belonged, behind him.

He pushed the memories down deep, only wanting to focus on the future, and for the first time in months, it appeared he might actually have one.

Chapter 18

The journey to New Hampshire wasn't as easy as Jake would have hoped.

A tractor trailer had jack-knifed on Interstate 93 months ago, when the outbreak first began, and it had caused a giant mess. More than thirty cars and trucks had crashed after the initial trailer had wrecked, and with the outlying police and fire services already busy containing the outbreak, there was no one to deal with the dead or help the wounded in the pile up.

Traffic had backed up for miles, this part of I-93 only two lanes wide, with just the small shoulder open on the right. The vehicles behind the accident had no choice but to wait for whatever was happening to clear up.

Of course, that never happened.

Jake imagined everyone sitting in their cars, wondering why they were stopped, and too afraid to use the shoulder of the road in fear of getting a ticket.

Which was now working fine for Jake and the bikers, as there was always just enough room for the Camaro to get by. A few times a car had blocked the shoulder, and they all got behind the abandoned vehicle and pushed it out of the way so the Camaro could pass. Even now, as they drove by the tractor trailer, with only an inch on both sides of the Camaro for clearance, Jake wondered if there would be a time when he would have to leave the car behind.

He could see why Carol, Butch and Brock favored their motorcycles. The two wheeled machines were much more maneuverable than a car, but if they found themselves surrounded by a horde of ghouls, the car would definitely be the better place to be.

Maneuverability over safety, that was the choice the driver had to make.

Once they made it through the trailer crash, the highway opened up some more.

Though there were a lot of cars and trucks still scattered on the highway, the spaces were big enough for the Camaro to get through easily.

They drove for another ten miles, and then a green sign for a gas station appeared, letting travelers know that a mile ahead were restrooms and fuel.

Butch pointed to the sign with his right hand, signaling that the bikers needed a rest. Bill waved back, letting the man know he understood.

"Looks like our new friends want to take a break," Bill said to Jake, who shifted his position in the passenger seat to get more comfortable.

"Fine," he nodded, then glanced into the back seat, where Duke was sleeping. His nose and ears would twitch now and then, signifying the dog was dreaming.

Jake had been taciturn for the past hour or so, his silence due to knowing he was getting close to the end of his quest to find Melissa. Only a few more hours and he would be at the cabin, and if she wasn't there, then he knew he would never see her again.

A few minutes later the gas station came into view, and Carol signaled she was going to the right with her hand, everyone following her.

Upon pulling into the gas station, Jake wondered if there would be anyone around. There had been no sign of human life for miles, only a few squirrels and birds to mar the emptiness of just the forest lining both sides of the highway.

The three bikers got off their motorcycles, while Jake and Bill got out of the car. Jake let Duke out to do his business, the dog now looking refreshed after his nap. Duke began to sniff around, found a pole to mark, then dropped a steamer on the ground.

Brock, Carol, and Butch had parked their bikes next to the one fuel pump, the small, one-story building to the right like something out of an old painting. There was a one car garage connected to the building, the windows dusty and dirty, and of course there was the requisite old clunker off to the side, rusting back to the earth a day at a time.

"How long you gonna be?" Jake called out to Butch.

"I don't know, a couple of minutes maybe. How about you and Brock go inside and see if they got anything we can use, while Carol stays with me and Bill. If I can siphon some gas from the underground tank, we can fill your car up, too," Butch explained, taking off the gas cap on his motorcycle.

Jake nodded, knowing the gas tank in his car was low. You didn't own a '69 Camaro if you were worried about fuel efficiency, not with a four barrel carburetor.

Jake followed behind Brock, the larger man carrying his shotgun in his hands. Jake also had one of his katanas with him, just in case.

When they entered the gas station, the electricity was off, the only illumination coming from what little light filtered in through the dirty windows. There were a few aisles of odds and ends, crackers and cereal mostly, and it looked like whoever had owned the gas station had been stocking a few items like a poor man's convenience store for travelers passing by.

There was a shelf that had souvenirs of the area. The *Old Man of the Mountain* shirts and other knick-knacks, plus buttons for *Storyland* and *Clark's Trading Post*, not to mention pamphlets for *Santa's Village* and *Six Gun City*.

It was while they were going up and down the small aisles, collecting what they thought was relevant, that Jake caught the scent of burned meat, a sickly sweet taste that clung to the back of his throat and made him want to gag.

"Hey, Brock, you smell that? It smells like something got burned in here," he said, covering his nose with his shirt sleeve.

"Yeah, yeah I do." Brock looked around, his nose twitching. "I think it's comin' from behind the counter," he said, moving over to the cash register.

When Brock peered over the counter, he saw the most disgusting sight he'd ever seen in his forty plus years, and that said a lot.

Thanks to the charred and oil-covered gray coveralls with the word, **mechanic**, stitched on the breast pocket, it was obvious the burned man had been the mechanic who worked at the gas station.

Only now his upper body, face, and hands, were burned to a crisp, the skin resembling beef jerky.

Though a strong man with a tough constitution, at the sight of the peeling, burnt body, Brock just wanted to throw up right there, but he held it down with all his might. When he turned around to tell Jake what he'd found, the burned corpse suddenly moved slightly, the charred eyelids snapping open.

Oblivious to the burned ghoul getting up, Brock stood in front of the counter with his back to the zombie. Before he knew he was in danger, he suddenly felt blinding pain on his right shoulder, as perfectly white teeth sank into his flesh. The zombie's teeth tore through Brock's jacket, and came back with a mouthful of material and skin.

"Holy shit! Jake, help me!" Brock screamed, trying desperately to get the ghoul away from him, but the charred mechanic had gone back for more, and his teeth were now clamped tight onto Brock's shoulder.

When Jake heard Brock cry out, he ran to the front of the gas station, his katana raised and ready in his right hand. Without hesitation, he reached out and pulled the ghoul off Brock, a new chunk of red, bloody flesh still locked in the burned zombie's mouth.

Brock fell away from the counter, hitting the floor hard, his free hand going to his bleeding shoulder. Meanwhile, Jake sliced the ghoul's head into two separate sections, one swipe slicing the head in half and the other slicing the rest off at the neck. After Jake was finished, the body toppling back behind the counter, he went to Brock's side.

"Oh, Jesus, Brock, that looks bad. Can you stand?" Jake asked, keeping his hands on Brock's arms, trying not to move him, but still wanting to keep the man steady.

"I don't know, man. Am I gonna turn into one of those dead things now?" he asked while blood seeped out of his wound and down under his jacket to pool on the floor. The wound looked bad, and if it wasn't attended to soon, he was in danger of losing too much blood.

"I think so, yeah. That's what happened to everyone I've seen so far. If you get bit, you're screwed," Jake said sadly. "I'm really sorry, Brock. Should I go get Carol or something? Shit, what should I do here? What do you want me to do?"

Brock shook his head. "No, don't get Carol, don't get anyone. There's no point, I'm already dead and that sucks, but fuck, at least I made it to forty, it could've been worse." He gestured to his shotgun on the floor where it had fallen. "I want you to take that and...shoot...me. I don't want to come back as one of them, you hear me? You need to do this for me, man, promise me."

Jake's throat was tight, but he nodded. "Yeah, Brock, I promise. But don't worry about that now, it's just a bite, for now we'll get you fixed up and then you'll..." He stopped talking, realizing that though Brock's eyes were open, the man wasn't seeing anything.

Brock had passed on.

Jake reached out and closed Brock's eyes with the tip of his fingers.

He looked down and saw the large pool of blood, realizing Brock must have been bleeding out worse than he thought. Inside Brock's jacket, the wound's true seriousness had been hidden. The ghoul had snagged an artery, and with each pulse of Brock's heart, he'd been a second closer to death from blood loss.

"Dammit!" Jake yelled, punching the side of the counter in anger. "How the hell am I gonna explain this to Butch and Carol?"

Leaning back on his haunches, he slid his katana back into its sheath after wiping the blade on a rag found on the floor. He looked at Brock's shotgun lying nearby.

Not wanting to grant Brock's last request, but knowing he had no choice, Jake picked up the shotgun and cocked it, then contemplated about what he should do next. Should he shoot Brock now or wait for the man to come back? Or what if Brock was the first one who didn't come back and Jake sat in the gas station waiting forever?

All these conflicting ideas filled his mind, and then the decision was taken from him when Brock's eyes snapped open. The biker's head swiveled back and forth, as if the newly born zombie didn't know where he was or what he should do. Then the dead eyes locked onto Jake and his mouth fell open, a low guttural moan issuing from pale lips.

It was just as Brock was leaning forward, hands outstretched to grasp Jake, that he lowered the business end of the shotgun at Brock's head.

"Sorry, man," he whispered as he pulled the trigger, the report of the shotgun filling the gas station. After cocking it again, he saw that had been the last shell in the weapon. But there was no need for another. Where Brock's head once was, there was nothing left but a mangled mess of blood and skull pieces, all sitting on the stump of a neck.

Jake stood perfectly still for more than a minute, and was about to wonder why none of the others had come in to investigate the shotgun blast, when he heard more gunshots coming from outside. Then Duke began barking and more gunshots, followed by a few curt yells.

Realizing something was happening out by the gas pump, he spun on his heels and took off for the door, hoping that whatever was going on out there, wasn't as bad as what had occurred in the gas station.

A few minutes ago

While Brock and Jake were going into the gas station to search for supplies, Butch was filling up the motorcycles. Carol was sitting on her bike, filing her fingernails, while waiting for her turn, as was Bill, who was checking his rifle.

Though the power was off, Brock had managed to jury-rig a small pump with some spare parts found near the garage. A garden hose and the small hand pump was all he needed to siphon gas from the underground fuel tank into a small plastic bucket. From the bucket, each of the bikes and the Camaro could be topped off.

For a few minutes there was silence, no one speaking as each went about their business.

Then Carol said to Butch, "So, do you like Jake and Bill?"

"They're all right, I guess, but Jake's kind of a wiseass," he remarked, putting the gas cap back on his motorcycle.

She smiled and nodded, agreeing with his assessment. "Yeah, he is, but I think its endearing on him. And Brock likes him."

Butch didn't reply, but waved her over so she could get her fuel tank filled. Not bothering to start the engine, she pushed the bike until it was closer, then set it back on the kickstand.

Butch began filling her bike's tank and the two chatted some more.

Behind them, near the garage, a pair of pale and filthy hands appeared, dragging themselves along the peeling paint of the building. The hands were soon followed by a jaundiced-colored and drawn face, the rest of the body becoming visible a few seconds later.

Stepping out from behind the garage, a zombie with sagging flesh, and maggots squirming in the split skin of its face and arms watched the survivors. Behind this one another stepped out, and another after that until there were six zombies. Slowly, they left the shadows of the side of the garage and walked towards the humans oblivious to their presence.

Carol was still chatting about Jake and she paused in mid-sentence when she saw a shadow fall across her own. Looking up and around, she was shocked to see three ghouls only a foot away, and another three behind those.

Before she could pull her .45, a gunshot cracked across the driveway, and the first ghoul in line pitched forward with half its head missing.

Butch spun on his heels and muttered a few choice imprecations as he reached out and grabbed the next ghoul in line, punching it in the face and sending bone fragments into its brain, the blow disabling the zombie.

Another shot cracked and the third body went down, Bill now lowering his M-16 as he ran towards the disturbance. But there was no need.

Now that she wasn't in danger of being attacked, Carol calmly reached around her back and drew her .45. Standing with feet spread and arms wide, and the .45 leveled, she shot each of the remaining ghouls in the head. Their bodies dropped to the dirt to twitch, while flies circled around the rotting flesh like tiny helicopters waiting to land.

Duke was running around the fallen corpses, barking at them in a defensive tone.

"You guys all right?" Bill asked when he reached the others.

Butch was wiping his fist clean of gore. "Yeah," he nodded, "no problem, there were only a few of them."

Bill nodded and looked to Carol admiringly. "Nice shooting, you took them down clean and quick."

"Thanks, handsome, I've had a lot of practice. But I don't like to do *everything* clean and quick," she said while smiling seductively as she holstered her pistol. With one last glance to Bill, she walked away with a sexy swagger to make sure the ghouls were indeed down for good.

Butch chuckled. "Oh, boy, looks like my sister's got her eye on you, Bill."

"Is that okay?" Bill asked, knowing how brothers could be about their sisters, no matter what their age.

He shrugged. "Hey, whatever, she's a grown woman. I stay out of her love life as much as possible."

Bill smiled, realizing there were now possibilities where a second ago there were none. "Well, all right then," he said cheerfully. He gestured to the bikes and the gas. "You need some help?"

Butch shrugged. "Sure, the sooner we're done we can leave."

Bill walked closer to see what he could do and then Jake's voice was calling out. All three survivors looked up, including Duke.

"It's Brock, you need to come in here," Jake said, his voice low and serious.

"Why, what's wrong?" Carol asked.

With the shooting outside, no one had heard Jake firing the shotgun inside the gas station.

Jake looked at each of them before locking his gaze onto Carol.

"You need to come in here and see for yourself." Then he was gone, stepping back into the gas station, the door creaking thanks to the rusty hinges.

"It sounds serious," Butch said as he dropped the rag he was wiping his hands with, and began walking. "Come on, we should all go."

Bill looked into Carol's eyes as he walked up to her, seeing the concern within. Together, they followed Butch into the gas station, each of them now having a feeling of dread creeping into their stomachs.

Chapter 19

The sun was high in the sky, only a few clouds to mar the otherwise clear blue, as the four survivors stood around the fresh grave of their fallen friend.

Carol and Butch stood side by side, the brother and sister consoling one another, as Jake and Bill waited silently with Duke.

Both Jake and Bill felt awkward, especially as Jake had blown Brock's head clean off with the shotgun. When Carol had entered the gas station and seen the remnants of Brock's head, she almost fainted, but she was a strong woman and managed to keep it together.

Jake explained what happened, and the burnt corpse of the mechanic was all the proof Butch and Carol needed to believe what Jake said was true.

After finding a tarp to wrap the body in, they carried Brock's corpse outside and buried him on the edge of the gas station, where the treeline began.

Jake volunteered to dig the grave and Butch helped, the two soon coated with a layer of dust and dirt.

Carol was crying softly as she looked down at Brock's grave, her tears slowing and a few sniffles coming once in a while.

After a few minutes of standing over the unmarked grave, Butch turned and walked away, followed by Carol.

Jake and Bill were left alone.

Bill turned to Jake, patting the younger man's shoulder. "It's not your fault, Jake. You know that, don't you? Whoever'd been in there with him would've had to do the same thing. It was just you that God picked today."

Jake sighed. "Yeah, Bill, I know, but it still sucks. He was a good guy. I liked him. He shouldn't have died like that, hell, no one should."

"Hey, you two comin' or what?" Carol called from her motorcycle.

"Come on, Jake, let's get going and leave this place behind," Bill said and walked away, taking Duke with him and leaving Jake alone.

Jake glanced down at the fresh grave one last time, shaking his head slightly. "I'm really sorry, Brock, really. Hell, who knows, maybe you're the lucky one now. At least you don't have to live like this anymore, always running and hiding, afraid death is waiting around every corner."

"Jake! Let's go! We're burnin' daylight!" Bill called and Jake waved that he'd heard.

"See ya, Brock, I hope it's better on the other side," he said, then turned and jogged back to the others. When he reached Carol, having to pass her to get to the Camaro, she picked up Brock's shotgun and tossed it to him.

Jake had a quizzical look on his face and Carol nodded.

"It's yours now, hon, treat it with care. Brock loved that damn gun."

"But it's out of shells," he said.

Carol pointed to the saddlebags on Brock's motorcycle. "Nah, he's got a shitload of shells in there, go get 'em."

Jake did as instructed, and upon reaching Brock's bike, he opened the rear saddlebag and saw it was indeed full of shells. Deciding it was easier to unhook the bag, he did so, and carried it back with him. He also noticed the keys to the motorcycle were in the ignition and he commented to Carol on this.

"Leave 'em there, Jake. Maybe some other poor soul will be in trouble and Brock's bike will save them from getting killed. If that happened, then Brock's death wouldn't be for nothing. I know he'd want us to do that." She grinned wanly. "Unless you wanna take the bike and leave the car behind."

Jake shook his head. "No way, Carol, that's my dad's car, I love it. It's all I have left of my family."

"Fair enough, hon." She turned to Butch. "You ready, big brother?"

"Sure am, sis, let's get this show on the road," Butch replied as he started his bike, the roar filling the area. He glanced over to the grave and then looked away. He and Brock had been close their entire lives and now the man was gone. It was going to take some getting used to.

Carol started her bike, too, and the throaty roar joined Butch's engine. Jake turned and walked back to the Camaro. Bill was driving again and Jake didn't mind, not wanting to have to deal with all the obstacles on the road at the moment.

Climbing in, he put the shotgun and saddlebag of ammunition on the back seat with Duke, who woofed happily at his master's arrival.

"Hi, boy, missed you, too," Jake said to Duke as he closed the passenger door.

Carol and Butch drove off onto the highway and Bill swung the car around behind them, the rear tires kicking up dust into a small cloud, which soon dispersed in the wind.

After only a minute, the noise of the engines faded away as the two motorcycles and one car were lost from sight, leaving the gas station to bake in the sun, deserted once more.

As for the corpses of the slain zombies that lay sprawled in the dirt, they too, would rot in the sun, the once human bodies—the once human beings—of people filled with hopes and dreams, now nothing but road kill.

* * *

Two hours later, with Jake now driving the Camaro after a quick break fifteen minutes ago, he turned off the interstate and onto the rural roads of New Hampshire. He knew where he was going, having gone to Melissa's family cabin on numerous occasions.

Jake glanced in the rearview mirror to see Butch and Carol behind him, the two bikers riding side by side.

Carol wasn't wearing a helmet and her hair was fluttering behind her as the bike weaved its way down the road.

When they reached the small town the road cut through on the way to the mountains, Jake noticed the undead were few and far between. It seemed this part of the state hadn't been destroyed too badly. Houses and storefronts, when they were seen, appeared to be intact and in good repair.

A few survivors were spotted, as well, their dirty faces peering out from behind curtains or from around parked vehicles.

The Camaro still had to work its way through stalled cars and trucks sitting in the road, as well as a few rotting corpses here and there, which were lying on the street or on the sidewalk. As to how long the bodies had been there was anyone's guess, but by the look of decomposition, weeks to months was a good guess.

It was as he neared the end of town that Jake had to slow and finally stop the Camaro. There were cars and trucks blocking the road, the vehicles more compacted than other times he'd come upon wrecked vehicles. It looked like there had been a large accident here, and the vehicles had never been cleared.

Putting the car in park, Jake opened the driver's door and got out, Bill doing the same. Duke hopped out also, already sniffing whatever was closest, but the pitbull knew enough not to stray too far from Jake.

The throaty roar of the motorcycle engines cycled down and Butch and Carol stopped fifteen feet behind the Camaro, each of them turning off their bikes and climbing off them.

Carol had dirt on her sun-kissed face from the long drive and Butch's tanned visage was now an even darker brown from the sun beating down on him.

Carol looked around the street, seeing the closed storefronts and the drycleaner on the opposite side. The street was filled with blowing newspaper and other signs of debris, and when she looked behind her and to the right, she saw what was obviously a rotting human arm lying in the gutter.

"Nice place to visit," Carol said sarcastically.

Jake shrugged. "It used to be, yeah. When I would come up to the cabin with Melissa, we'd always stop in this town and grab some supplies. The place has gone downhill since the last time I was through here, though."

"No shit. You think it might have something to do with the dead walking around?" Butch joked.

"Yeah, Butch, I think it might be at that," Jake replied in a joking tone of his own.

Bill wasn't listening to the banter; instead he was inspecting the wrecked vehicles blocking the road. His M-16 was slung over his shoulder, ready if he needed it. He frowned as he studied the wrecked cars. With the exception of a few feet on each side of the street, the metal hulks were solid, and when he looked harder, there was no doubt the vehicles had been placed there intentionally.

Bill turned and called out to the others, "Hey, guys, I think there's something funny going on with these cars." He began to walk back to Jake, but then halted in his tracks, seeing men and women appearing from out of the nearby storefronts, each of them armed with an assortment of handguns and rifles. "Uh, guys," he said, "I think we have company."

Jake, Carol and Butch all turned and looked where Bill was staring, and each of them watched the small group of townspeople coming towards them, their guns aimed at the trio in a definitely non-peaceful manner.

Jake counted five men and two women, all of mixed ages, though most seemed to be in their late thirties or early forties.

A man in a sheriff's uniform led the others. He held a wicked looking assault rifle in his hands.

He didn't wear the standard hat that came with the sheriff's uniform, but the dark glasses were prevalent, as were the polished black boots.

As the sheriff got closer, Jake could see his once spit-shined boots were covered with flaking blood, his uniform filthy.

"No one move and you don't have to die. We just want your supplies, that car, and the motorcycles," the sheriff said as the others of his group spread out around him. The rest of the towns-folk wore a similar look of harried exhaustion and filth.

Before Jake or Bill could do or say anything to the townspeople turned raiders, Carol pulled her .45 from behind her back and shot the sheriff in the chest, while yelling at the same time, "Fuck that! No one takes my bike from me!"

The sheriff went down with a bloody hole in his chest, the exit wound on his back twice the size. The rest of the townspeople stared with dumbstruck looks, shocked to see their leader gunned down before he'd finished speaking.

Then another raider realized they were all in danger of following the sheriff into death, and he fired his gun, the rest doing the same.

As Bill and Jake dove for cover behind a wrecked car half on the sidewalk, all hell broke loose on the street in the once quaint town nestled in the mountains of New Hampshire.

Chapter 20

Jake dropped down low as bullets flew over his head like angry hornets, the townspeople trying to kill him with what seemed like genuine abandonment. Behind him, Duke sat still, his ears twitching at the gunshots.

"Jesus Christ, Jake!" Bill shouted. "We drove right into an ambush!"

"What do we do?" he yelled as a bullet ricocheted six inches from his boot. With a yelp, Jake pulled it back under cover.

"We fight, what else? You need to get that shotgun Carol gave you!"

"What? I'm not goin' out there!"

"Yes, you are, now when I say run, you run!"

Jake bit his lip but knew Bill was right. If they didn't have more firepower, it would be nothing for the raiders to kill them all.

"Now!" Bill yelled and sprayed half a clip at the shooting townspeople. One of his bullets found a home, and a woman with dark red hair fell to the street with half her head missing.

Jake took off like a sprinter, and while bullets were seeking his body, he jumped the last few feet until he was behind the Camaro by the driver's door. The townspeople were on the other side of the car and he was safe for the moment. That is until the passenger window blew out, raining glass onto the seat.

"Son-of-a-bitch!" he yelled, angry at the destroyed window.

Bullets slapped into the metal quarter panels, sounding like tin being slapped, and he cringed, thinking how he was going to have to fix those holes. He was going to need a hell of a lot of Bondo and fiberglass to get the job done.

Reaching into the car, he grabbed the shotgun, the saddlebag of shells, and his katanas—just in case he needed them—then waved to Bill he was ready.

Bill nodded and popped up, spraying the last of the clip, yelling for Jake to leave the fragile cover of the Camaro and get back to him. One of Bill's bullets found another target, but the man only received a flesh wound.

No sooner did Jake run back and fall next to Bill, then a stray bullet found the Camaro's gas tank and the car exploded into a raging fireball, lifting three feet off the ground before crashing back down.

A piece of Jake died then, as he watched his father's car burning, black oily smoke seeping out of the blown windows and from beneath the undercarriage.

"You bastards, you no good bastards! I'll kill you for that!" Jake yelled, now firing at the raiders who had to duck back. Bill popped out his spent clip and slapped in another, his last one.

"Calm down, Jake, it's just a car, it's not worth dying for," Bill snapped at him.

But Jake didn't agree with him at the moment, the anger he felt overriding all thoughts of self preservation. With a scowl of hate on his face, he joined Bill as the two men began firing at the attacking townspeople.

Butch and Carol weren't standing idly by when Jake and Bill ducked for cover. After Carol took out the sheriff, she swung her pistol to the left and fired three times, hitting a man in the neck and shoulder. Bright arterial blood spurted from the wound. The man dropped his rifle and placed his palms to his neck, hoping to staunch the flow of blood, but his knees grew weak and he slumped to the pavement, eyes fluttering as death took hold.

After shooting the man with the rifle, Carol spun and prepared to fire again, but before she could do so, she felt a tug at her left arm. Glancing down, she saw a small blood spot that was quickly spreading, and realized she was shot. Too angry to care, and thoughts of running for cover the farthest thing from her mind, she ignored the wound and fired a round at the shooter, hitting the man in the abdomen. He doubled over in pain and slid to the ground.

That left three more raiders to deal with and Butch was happy to take out two of them. When Carol began shooting, he was already reaching into his saddlebag and coming up with a revolver. Before two of the raiders knew what hit them, they were struck in the chest with numerous bullets, the force of the impacts throwing them backwards.

The man Carol had gut shot wasn't dead yet and he crawled to his knees, firing his gun, the bullet hitting Butch right between the eyes. The large man's head snapped back like it was tugged from behind, and he dropped to the ground, his eyes turning inward, looking cross-eyed, as if he was trying to see the hole above his nose.

Carol saw her brother go down and she spun on her heels. "Butch! Oh, God, no!" She turned and faced the gut shot man, and with a look of rage creasing her face, shot him three times. The body fell backwards, blood spurting out of the man's back to bathe the street a dark red.

Carol glanced around the street, and seeing it was empty of targets, ran to her fallen brother.

But there was one raider left, a rather large, fat, three hundred pound, middle-aged woman with a rifle, who'd been hiding while the battle raged on. Now she popped up, and when Carol ran to Butch, thinking it was safe, the fat woman shot Carol in the back. Like she'd been punched in the back by a giant hand, she was thrown forward, a large exit wound appearing on her shirt, right below her breasts.

Her mouth dropped open and her eyes took on a far away look as she continued running, the momentum of the blast helping her along. While spitting blood, her knees gave out and she crumpled to the pavement, only a few inches from Butch.

Lying on the asphalt, she reached one shaking hand out to him, to touch her brother one last time. Before her hand was halfway there, it dropped limp to the ground, her eyes losing what life remained.

Bill saw the fat woman pop up, and though he didn't have time to stop her from shooting Carol, he did manage to hit her a second later. With no time to aim, Bill sprayed the fat woman and the car she was hiding behind, an old Datsun, one of his rounds finding the gas tank. With the fat woman crouching behind the car, the Datsun went up in a blazing fireball that consumed the woman and threw her ten feet from the blast.

But she wasn't dead, and as the flames licked at her body, she jumped to her feet, screaming and shrieking like a wild banshee.

Her hair became ash almost immediately, and her eyes began to melt in their sockets as her flesh blistered on her bones. The woman began running at Bill and Jake, her feet slapping the pavement. Each time a foot came down, pieces of her sneakers and the skin of her feet were left in her wake.

She was shrieking madly and neither Jake nor Bill understood how this woman was still mobile, let alone alive. She ran like an extra in a fast-moving zombie movie, heading right for the two men.

Bill fired three times, the bullets impacting the fat woman's chest. She merely absorbed the blows and charged forward, the weight and girth of her body able to withstand the impacts.

Fat sizzled in the flames as she took one tortuous step at a time, her face now a rictus of death. The flesh was entirely gone on her face and arms, the smell of burnt bacon filling the air.

Bill fired again, but only grazed her shoulder.

He slapped Jake on the arm. "Shoot her, Jake! Use that damn gun in your hands and shoot her!"

Jake was snapped from his fugue state of watching the walking funeral pyre. He raised the shotgun.

The woman was only a few feet from him and closing fast. Jake aimed the shotgun so it was in line with her head, and when he fired, the head disappeared in flaming chunks of skull and bone matter. The wet brains landed on the road, sizzling, having been cooked inside the skull from the heat of the fire, but the large body still continued forward.

"Jesus Christ, she's still alive!" Jake screamed, but Bill knew that wasn't the case.

As the headless, burning body stepped forward, Bill grabbed Jake by the arm, yanking him back just as the body toppled over like a massive, flaming oak tree in the midst of a forest fire.

When the body hit the ground, it split open, the fire consuming too much flesh and tissue to hold it together. The melted fat and internal organs spread out like the spilled vomit bucket from the aftermath of an 'all you can eat' contest.

Duke padded over to the muck and sniffed, then turned and went back to Jake, the brains unappetizing, even to the pitbull.

Smoke was thick in the air, filling the street as both the Camaro and the Datsun belched flames. Both men moved out from cover to see Carol and Butch prone on the pavement. Bill kept his eyes out for more raiders, but it seemed all had been killed.

Bill shook his head sadly, knowing his group had suffered serious causalities. He took one last look around to make sure it was safe, but he was confident if there were any more townspeople still alive, they would have tried to shoot him and Jake already.

"Looks like we got them all," he said as the two men walked over to the bodies of Carol and Butch.

"Yeah, guess so," Jake added.

Upon reaching the two fallen bikers, Bill knelt down and checked each one for a pulse, but it was very obvious they were dead.

"Shit, both of 'em," Bill sighed.

Jake didn't reply, but he did let out a sigh of his own, his eyes creasing with grief or from the cloying smoke blowing into his face.

"Shit, Bill, what the hell just happened here?" he asked.

Bill shrugged. "Figure the people who still live here must block the road, kill whoever shows up and take their shit. Simple, really, it probably works, too. Guess they didn't expect us to fight back and have weapons as good as theirs."

A low moan filtered to him on the air, overriding the crackling of the burning cars. Jake looked down the street to see more than two dozen zombies heading their way.

"Shit, we got pusbags coming, Bill. What do you wanna do? We can't just leave them here like this." He gestured to the bodies of Carol and Butch.

"I agree with you, son, but there's no time." He glanced back to the zombies. "There's too many of them, we need to go before it's too late."

Bill stood up, looking down at Carol one last time. She was a good woman and he would miss her. He thought the two of them might have gotten together, but it didn't matter now. He hated leaving her, not giving her a proper burial, but with the arrival of the undead, there was no other choice.

Looking past the burning Camaro, Bill saw that Butch and Carol's motorcycles had managed to make it through the exploding Camaro and ensuing gun battle unscathed.

When he gazed beyond the flames, he saw the zombies slowly approaching.

"Guess the people who lived here shared the place with the pus-bags," Bill mused as he stood up. He slapped Jake on the arm. "Come on, we can take the bikes, they look okay. Do you know how to ride one?"

Jake smiled a little. "Me? What about you? Of course I know how to ride. I had a dirt bike when I was a kid; had a blast on the dunes with it, too."

"Yeah," Bill said, "I know how to ride. Us oldies can do lots of stuff. I can cut my own steak, too."

The two men ran to the bikes while Duke scampered behind Jake. The dog sniffed at Carol and Butch one last time, then backed away, the smell of death making him uneasy.

By the time Duke reached Jake, he was on the bike. He patted the back seat and Duke jumped up, understanding what his master wanted.

"Well will ya look at that, he did it," Bill said. He'd been wondering if the dog would be able to balance on the rear of the seat. He knew dogs could do it, but Duke might have been one that wouldn't or couldn't. "You ready?" he asked as he started Carol's bike. The engine purred and the vibration filled his body.

"Let's go, already, they're gettin' closer," Jake said as he glanced over his shoulder. The zombies were only twenty feet away and closing fast.

Bill nodded and put the motorcycle in gear, then rolled it around the flaming Camaro, to the side of the blockade. Only a few feet of clearance was between the blockade and the buildings lining the street, and though it was tight, the motorcycle scraped by.

Bill had to raise his legs into the air as the rear brake pedal, foot peg, and clutch pedal risked catching on a dented bumper. Jake had an easier time and was soon through, Duke sitting behind him with his tongue hanging out. Jake had to be careful while he maneuvered, as any sudden movement could cause the dog to fall off, but Duke seemed to have a good sense of balance. The pitbull was a natural.

Bill didn't slow down after clearing the blockade. He made sure to check his mirror to see that Jake was still behind him, repositioned his rifle, and opened the throttle some more, the motorcycle surging forward.

Jake did the same and soon took the lead, as he knew where the cabin was in the mountains.

The cabin was a little more than an hour away, the roads winding and lonely as they cut through the mountains. He fixed his katanas on his back and made sure the shotgun was secure.

With the wind blowing through his hair, he pointed the front tire of the motorcycle towards the cabin, and hopefully, Melissa.

* * *

The sound of the two motorcycle engines echoed for a few minutes until reaching an incline and fading away.

The fires in town still burned, the noxious smoke filling the site of the gun battle with thick black smoke clouds that coated everything with dark ash.

The first zombie finally reached the blockade, and without hesitation fell on the first corpse it found. Soon, the others arrived, and like a tour bus full of overweight people attacking a free buffet, the ghouls fell onto the corpses and began tearing into the still warm bodies.

The sheriff was first, two zombies digging into his chest, their task easier thanks to the bullet wound. Like the beginnings of a tear on a bed sheet, the ghouls ripped at the wound, peeling the flesh from the sheriff's bones like he was an orange. Soon hands were breaking the ribcage and pulling out the heart and kidneys, fetid teeth biting into the organs as blood and viscous fluid shot out to spray others nearby.

Carol and Butch were soon found by the dead, and each was ripped apart, teeth tearing at their clothing to get at the soft flesh beneath. Carol's breasts were ripped from her chest while a dead hand slid down her throat, pulling out the tender meat within.

Pale white fingers, with sharpened nails from exposure to the elements, scooped out the tender eyes and chomped on them merrily, as pinkish ooze slipped from the corners of their mouths.

If anyone had been watching—anyone alive that is—the zombies' faces seemed to take on a visage of contentment as they fed on the bodies and chewed on severed limbs.

Butch's head was pulled off his shoulders, the ghoul shoving its arm into the skull to scoop out the warm brains within. Like it was tripe, the zombie fed, pink and gray parts of the brain sliding out of its mouth to slap the ground like rotting cottage cheese.

To those ghouls that preferred their meals cooked, the fat woman was set upon, her charred flesh now peeled from the bones by yellow teeth.

The heart and other internal organs were par cooked and the chewy morsels were consumed with what appeared to be gusto.

The street was awash with congealing blood, as more than two dozen walking corpses fed on the flesh of the townspeople they'd wanted for more than three months.

And as the first crows appeared overhead and began circling, waiting for their turn to feed, the banquet of the dead continued.

Chapter 21

The winding road meandered its way deeper into the mountains, Jake and Bill following the dirt road like two monks on a quest.

The asphalt had ended an hour ago, the road becoming just dirt, and there was no sign of human life, living or dead.

Melissa's family cabin was deep in the White Mountains, surrounded on all sides by acres upon acres of woodland. There was a small river a quarter mile from the cabin, and Jake had fond memories of him and Melissa playing in the cold water on warm summer days.

Jake was in the lead once more, Duke sitting behind him. The pitbull would sometimes lean forward and try to rest his head on Jake's back. Bill would chuckle when this happened, teasing Jake that Duke was like his girlfriend. Jake took the ribbing in stride, his mood light now that he was so close to ending his search for Melissa.

The trees were thick overhead and it was a beautiful day. The amount of sunshine under the tree branches was less, due to the thick canopy, and slices of light filtered through where ever the branches were thinner.

All around them were signs of nature, whether it was birds in the trees or squirrels running on the ground. Once, they spotted a deer, before the engines of the motorcycles scared it away.

Eventually Jake slowed his bike, Bill following suit.

Jake turned off the engine, and after setting the kickstand, he climbed off the motorcycle. Duke immediately jumped down to begin investigating his new surroundings.

"What's up? Why'd we stop?" Bill asked as he rubbed his face. A few mosquitoes had found his face and one had flown into his mouth. He still remembered the sensation as he gagged on the small insect.

"We're here," Jake said nervously, and pointed further up the road. "Just around that corner is the driveway that goes to the cabin. I thought it might be better if we walk the rest of the way."

"Why? You think there might be trouble?" Bill asked.

Jake shrugged. "Who knows. I hope not, but after everything we've been through, do you really want to just drive up to the cabin on the bikes and let anyone inside know we're here?"

"No, 'course not, that's a good idea, Jake."

Bill unslung his M-16 from his shoulder. "Just in case, right?"

"Definitely, just in case," Jake replied, and with his new shotgun in hand, and the two katanas secured on his back, the two men and a dog began to walk the rest of the way to the cabin.

What they would find would be anyone's guess.

Twelve minutes later the cabin came into view, but it was slightly different than the last time Jake had seen it. For one thing there was a mish-mash of wood, rocks, small trees, logs, and brush surrounding the cabin's perimeter, the homemade fence as good as any man-made stockade fence.

The fence was about six feet high and the only part that looked like it opened was in the middle of the gravel driveway. A gate made of thin logs had been cobbled together, and it looked like it swung inward or outward.

The middle of the gate was crisscrossed with smaller branches, some as thick as a man's thumb, others smaller and thinner, the size of a newborn baby's pinky. When it was all woven together, it made a mesh fence as strong as metal wire.

"Someone's been busy here," Bill said as they approached the gate. "What do you think?"

Jake shook his head. "Don't know yet." He knew anyone could be holed up there, and Melissa may have never made it here. But he knew there was someone inside the cabin; there was smoke wafting from the small chimney.

"You stay here, Bill, I'm gonna see who's in there," he said, then walked up to the gate. There was a six inch bell hanging from the fence and a stick hanging next to it to ring it. There was a small wooden sign with words carved into it, nailed next to the bell.

IF YOU'RE FRENDLY, RING THE BELL, IF YOU'RE NOT THEN LEAVE BEFORE YOU GET SHOT!

Jake turned to look at Bill who could read the sign from where he was standing. He only shrugged at Jake.

Deciding that if he wanted to know who was in the cabin, he really had no choice, he rang the bell three times and waited. His shotgun was in his hands, and from the cabin the weapon was clearly visible to anyone watching him.

Jake waited for more than a minute and was about to consider doing something else, like hopping the fence, when a gunshot rang out from the left side of the cabin and a bullet went so close to Jake's head he felt its passing.

"What the...!" he yelled as he ducked to the side, picking a thick part of the fence to hide behind. Bill was now running up next to him, and he skidded in the gravel, going to his knees.

Duke galloped into the woods a little to the side and hunkered down. The dog had been around enough gunfights recently to know how to duck and cover.

"Who's shooting at us?" Bill asked as he tried to get a peek over the fence. As he poked his head up, another shot rang out and a piece of wood six inches from his face exploded into splinters, a few hitting his cheek.

"Son-of-a..." he began, then stopped when another shot rang out, causing him to duck lower.

"What the hell?" Jake yelled. "I rang the damn bell. We're friendly! Stop shooting at us for Christ's sake!"

After Jake called out, the gunshots ceased and Jake and Bill exchanged glances.

"Think it's safe?" Bill asked.

"That's a good question. Why don't you stick your head up there and see," Jake suggested.

"Screw that, you do it, this is supposed to be your place, not mine."

Jake didn't reply, but knew Bill had a point. Still, they'd traveled so far and overcome so much, he wasn't about to turn around and leave now.

Taking a leap of faith, he stood up and climbed onto the fence so his head and chest were visible over the top to anyone watching from the cabin.

If someone wanted to shoot him, he was now an easy target.

"Melissa! It's Jake! Melissa, are you in there! Hey, whoever's inside, we're friendly! My girlfriend's family owns this cabin!"

As he said the words, he thought how ridiculous it sounded. If there was some stranger inside who had taken the cabin as his own, he wouldn't care that Jake knew the previous owners.

Now that Jake was on the fence, he could see the cabin had been fortified as well. The windows now had wooden bars made of branches nailed to all the frames and the door was reinforced.

Off to the right of the cabin, there was a small vegetable garden. Near it was a water well that tapped into the underground stream. It looked like it was being used. The wooden cover wasn't on the top to protect the well from falling debris like leaves and bugs, but instead was leaning against the small stone wall of the well, as if someone had dropped it and had taken off back into the cabin after being startled.

As Jake waited for the bullet that would hit his chest and kill him, he saw a curtain flutter at the window to the right of the door. He caught a wisp of brown hair and curls, and he could have sworn it was Melissa, but it might have been his imagination.

With his heart pounding in his chest, the trepidation overwhelming, he waited for what would happen next.

Tense-filled seconds past, then the front door was thrown open, the creaks of the hinges carrying on the wind.

Before Jake could tell who was there, Melissa ran out and onto the driveway, while inside the cabin, a gruff voice called out to her.

"Dammit it, woman, get back in here before you get killed!" the gruff voice snapped.

Melissa turned and looked back inside the cabin, which was wreathed in shadows. "But, Grandpa, it's Jake, it's really him!" Then she was running down the driveway.

Jake felt his heart leap into his throat with happiness. He climbed over the fence and dropped down while Bill waited, peering through a thin crack in the wood.

"Jake? Jake! Oh my God, it is you!" Melissa screamed as she ran to him, her arms pumping and her hair flowing behind her.

Jake dropped the shotgun and ran to her as well, the two meeting in the middle of the driveway. He wrapped his arms around her as she fell into his embrace. The two hugged, Jake never wanting to let go. They kissed once, it was rushed but passionate, then she gazed into his eyes.

"I don't believe this, how did you get here? I thought you were dead," she said in shock. "After the Fourth of July barbeque, everything went crazy. I tried to call you but the phones were out." She stopped and stared deep into his eyes. "Jake, my family. They were supposed to come up here, too, but they never arrived. Are they all right?"

Jake's smiling face sank and grief filled his eyes. Melissa, upon seeing it, understood immediately. "Oh, God, no, not my family. All of them? My sisters, too?"

He nodded, feeling guilty about Jess and Cara. "I'm so sorry. I don't know what to tell you," he said as tears welled up. Not wanting to let loose the emotional turmoil inside him free, he forced it back down.

Melissa didn't feel the same about holding back and she began to cry, finally knowing the fate of her family. Though she had always assumed, she'd still held onto a thread of hope.

Now that hope was gone.

As she fell into his arms, he brushed her hair and consoled her as best he could. "I'm so sorry, honey, I really am," he whispered.

Behind him, Bill was walking towards him after climbing the fence. Duke had found an opening near the bottom that other animals had used for egress, and he squeezed through like a rat through a hole, popping out when his haunches became stuck for a second.

Jake looked up when he saw an old grizzled man step out of the cabin. The man carried a worn, but well kept rifle, and he recognized the grizzled war veteran immediately.

Jake waited for the old man to reach him before holding out a hand in greeting, while Melissa sobbed in his arms.

"Good to see you, Dale," Jake said to the old man.

Dale Jacobs was Melissa's grandfather and had served in WW2. He was almost eighty, but he was still strong and spry. He chocked it up to not smoking, drinking a glass of wine before bed each night, and having lots of sex. He would always grin slyly as he told someone the last bit. In truth, he hadn't been with a woman for almost twenty years, not since his wife passed away. He was through with women. His wife had been the only woman he'd ever loved and he planned on keeping it that way.

Dale shook the proffered hand and scratched his lightly bearded chin. "Sorry about almost shooting you, son. I thought you were from the town."

Bill chose that moment to speak up. "Having trouble with them?" Dale looked to Bill, knowing he was with Jake but nothing more.

"This is Bill Monroe, Dale, he's a good friend," Jake told him. "He's been traveling with me since everything happened."

"Ah-hah, okay, a friend of Jake's is a friend of mine," Dale said and held out his hand, which Bill shook.

"So," Bill continued, "you been having trouble with the people from the town?"

"Yup, sure have, in the past month or so a few of 'em tried to get at us here, but each time I managed to chase 'em away with ole Betsy." He patted his rifle. "But I know sooner or later they're gonna try to get in here in force, but for some reason they were takin' their time. I reckon it was 'cause there was no rush. Why, you know somethin' I don't?"

Bill shrugged. "Maybe. On our way up here, we ran into some of the townsfolk when we went through town. They tried to ambush us. We managed to kill them first, but not before they blew up our car and killed two of our friends."

Jake filled Dale in with more details about what happened to his father's Camaro, Butch and Carol.

Dale nodded. "Ah, so that was the smoke I saw earlier. I was wonderin' about that."

"That was us," Bill replied.

Melissa had regained some of her composure and Jake released her from his embrace, the two still holding hands. Though she was sad at the loss of her family, now finally knowing the truth, she was still elated to have Jake with her again. It was a storm of emotions, both happy and sad, raging inside her at the moment.

The four talked for a few more minutes, Melissa making friends with Duke almost immediately.

Then Dale spoke up. "You two hungry? I got some rabbit stew on the fire, just made it this morning."

Jake looked to Bill who nodded happily. They hadn't eaten for almost a day and both men were ravenous.

"That sounds wonderful, Dale," Bill said. "I could eat a horse."

Dale chuckled at the analogy. "Well, Bill it's not that bad around here yet, but don't count your eggs too soon," he said. "We got a garden and a water well and there's plenty of wildlife to hunt, so we're doin' pretty good for ourselves so far."

"Better than most," Jake agreed. "It's not good out there, you know."

Melissa rubbed his back, placing her head on his shoulders. He breathed in her hair, which smelled crisp and clean. There was no trace of chemicals in her hair, only the scent of wood and the river.

"Dale, we have a couple of motorcycles," Jake informed the old man. "I didn't know who was up here, so I left them parked at the bottom of the driveway and we walked the rest of the way."

Dale nodded. "Uh-huh, that's okay, leave 'em be. They can keep, 'specially if you took care of those townsfolk. Other than them there's no one around for twenty miles, maybe more."

"Seen any of those *things* up here?" Bill asked.

"You mean the walkers? That's what I call 'em anyways. Nah, not really. A few have found their way up here now and then, but it's easy enough to take care of 'em. That's why I built the fence, for protection.

"Amen," Bill said, already liking the old war veteran.

"So let's go and eat," Dale said, and with Bill and Duke by his side, the three headed for the cabin while Jake and Melissa hung back for a moment.

Bill was chatting with Dale about his shooting, complimenting the old man's marksmanship, Dale had already begun telling a story about the war and how he'd learned to shoot so well.

When Bill said he had been in the Army at the end of the Vietnam War, Dale immediately knew he was going to like Bill, the two men now having war stories to share and trade.

"Oh, Jake, I can't believe you're really here," Melissa said. "I thought you were dead for sure."

He smiled at her, looking deep into her eyes. "No way, I never stopped trying to get to you, though I had a few detours along the way. But the entire time, I never gave up hope you were alive."

She leaned forward and kissed him, their tongues mingling together as one, then she pulled away and smiled up at him.

"Tonight, when everyone's asleep, I'm gonna rock your world," she whispered, then turned and walked to the cabin, her backside swinging like a seductress.

Jake's jaw dropped at hearing what she said, and a massive smile grew on his face from ear to ear, so wide he couldn't have wiped it off if his life depended on it.

As he followed her into the cabin, he stopped and looked back over his shoulder, and was surprised to see a wisp of black tendrils of smoke still circling up from where his Camaro and the Datsun were either still burning, or the fire had spread to the some of the neighboring buildings of the town.

The smoke rose high into the clear blue sky, and was then dispersed by the wind to disappear like it never existed.

As Jake watched the smoke clouds, he realized that the smoke was a lot like his past. The visions he'd had of his past were nothing but smoke, to be torn apart and destroyed by the wind if he so chose.

Now, all he had was the present, and as he turned and walked into the cabin, he knew he had a future, too...with Melissa.

And with the world in its new state of decay, that was all he could hope for and more.

Just the beginning...

PLAYING GOD: A ZOMBIE NOVEL
by Jeffery Dye

It was supposed to be a regeneration virus to help soldiers on the battlefield—regrowing limbs and healing wounds— but a simple act of carelessness unleashed it on an unsuspecting world.

For the virus was not perfected, and once exposed, the host quickly dies, only to rise again as one of the undead.

As countries are quickly overrun, scientists and military teams battle to contain the outbreak.

There is no other option.

If the infection continues to spread, soon the entire globe will be consumed. And perhaps that will be a just punishment for a mankind that dared to try to play God.

DEAD HOUSE: A ZOMBIE GHOST STORY
by Keith Adam Luethke

The old mansion on the edge of town, aptly named Dead House, has a history of blood, pain, and death, but what Victor Leeds knows of this past only scratches the surface of the true horrors within.

But when his girlfriend is attacked by a shadowy figure one rainy night, he soon finds himself caught up in a world where the dead walk and ghostly wraiths abound. And to make matters worse, a pair of serial killers are fulfilling carefully made plans, and when they are done, the small town of Stormville, New York will run red. The last ingredient to open the gates of Hell, and plunge this small upstate town into madness, is rain.

And in Stormville, it pours by the gallons.

The Lazarus Culture
by Pasquale J. Morrone

Secret Service Agent Christopher Kearns had no idea what he was up against. Assigned on a temporary basis to the Center for Disease Control, he only knew that somehow it was connected to the lives of those the agency protected...namely, the President of the United States. If there were possible terrorist activities in the making, he could only guess it was at a red alert basis.

When Kearns meets and befriends Doctor Marlene Peterson of the Breezy Point Medical Center in Maryland, he soon finds that science fiction can indeed become a reality. In a solitary room walked a man with no vital signs: dead. The explanation he received came from Doctor Lee Fret, a man assigned to the case from the CDC. Something was attached to the brain stem. Something alive that was quickly spreading rapidly through Maryland and other states.

Kearns and his ragtag army of agents and medical personnel soon find themselves in a world of meaningless slaughter and mayhem. The armies of the walking dead were far more than mere zombies. Some began to change into whatever it was they ate. The government had found a way to reanimate the dead by implanting a parasite found on the tongue of the Red Snapper to the human brain. It looked good on paper, but it was a project straight from Hell. The dead now walked, but it wasn't a mystery. It was The Lazarus Culture.

BOOK OF THE DEAD
A ZOMBIE ANTHOLOGY VOL 1
ISBN 978-1-935458-25-8
Edited by Anthony Giangregorio

This is the most faithful, truest zombie anthology ever written, and we invite you along for the ride. Every single story in this book is filled with slack-jawed, eyes glazed, slow moving, shambling zombies set in a world where the dead have risen and only want to eat the flesh of the living. In these pages, the rules are sacrosanct. There is no deviation from what a zombie should be or how they came about. The Dead Walk.

There is no reason, though rumors and suppositions fill the radio and television stations. But the only thing that is fact is that the walking dead are here and they will not go away. So prepare yourself for the ultimate homage to the master of zombie legend. And remember... Aim for the head!

REVOLUTION OF THE DEAD
by Anthony Giangregorio
THE DEAD SHALL RISE AGAIN!

Five years ago, a deadly plague wiped out 97% of the world's population, America suffering tragically. Bodies were everywhere, far too many to bury or burn. But then, through a miracle of medical science, a way is found to reanimate the dead.

With the manpower of the United States depleted, and the remaining survivors not wanting to give up their internet and fast food restaurants, the undead are conscripted as slave labor.   Now they cut the grass, pick up the trash, and walk the dogs of the surviving humans.   But whether alive or dead, no race wants to be controlled, and sooner or later the dead will fight back, wanting the freedom they enjoyed in life.

The revolution has begun!

And when it's over, the dead will rule the land, and the remaining humans will become the slaves…or worse.

KINGDOM OF THE DEAD
by Anthony Giangregorio
THE DEAD HAVE RISEN!

In the dead city of Pittsburgh, two small enclaves struggle to survive, eking out an existence of hand to mouth.

But instead of working together, both groups battle for the last remaining fuel and supplies of a city filled with the living dead.

Six months after the initial outbreak, a lone helicopter arrives bearing two more survivors and a newborn baby. One enclave welcomes them, while the other schemes to steal their helicopter and escape the decaying city.

With no police, fire, or social services existing, the two will battle for dominance in the steel city of the walking dead. But when the dust settles, the question is: will the remaining humans be the winners, or the losers?

When the dead walk, the line between Heaven and Hell is so twisted and bent there is no line at all.

RISE OF THE DEAD
by Anthony Giangregorio

DEATH IS ONLY THE BEGINNING!

In less than forty-eight hours, more than half the globe was infected.

In another forty-eight, the rest would be enveloped.

The reason?

A science experiment gone horribly wrong which enabled the dead to walk, their flesh rotting on their bones even as they seek human prey.

Jeremy was an ordinary nineteen year old slacker. He partied too much and had done poorly in high school. After a night of drinking and drugs, he awoke to find the world a very different place from the one he'd left the night before.

The dead were walking and feeding on the living, and as Jeremy stepped out into a world gone mad, the dead spotting him alone and unarmed in the middle of the street,
he had to wonder if he would live long enough to see his twentieth birthday.

THE CHRONICLES OF JACK PRIMUS
BOOK ONE
by Michael D. Griffiths

Beneath the world of normalcy we all live in lies another world, one where supernatural beings exist.

These creatures of the night hunt us; want to feed on our very souls, though only a few know of their existence.

One such man is Jack Primus, who accidentally pierces the veil between this world and the next. With no other choice if he wants to live, he finds himself on the run, hunted by beings called the Xemmoni, an ancient race that sees humans as nothing but cattle. They want his soul, to feed on his very essence, and they will kill all who stand in their way. But if they thought Jack would just lie down and accept his fate, they were sorely mistaken. He didn't ask for this battle, but he knew he would fight them with everything at his disposal, for to lose is a fate worse than death.

He would win this war, and he would take down anyone who got in his way.

MONSTER PARTY
Edited by Anthony Giangregorio

Zombies, vampires, werewolves and ghosts are just a few of the monsters in this anthology.

But this isn't any anthology, you see, this is a party.

Or to be more to the point…a *Monster Party*.

Ever wonder what would happen if a werewolf and a zombie squared off? Or perhaps a vampire and a Frankenstein monster? Or better yet, how about a world where every conceivable monster is real and humans are their prey?

If those burning questions have been driving you mad, then look no further than this book.

So go on over to the buffet table, grab yourself a plate (the shrimp looks good) and get yourself a drink, and enjoy the fun ride that is the *Monster Party*.

THE WAR AGAINST THEM: A ZOMBIE NOVEL
by Jose Alfredo Vazquez

Mankind wasn't prepared for the onslaught.

An ancient organism is reanimating the dead bodies of its victims, creating worldwide chaos and panic as the disease spreads to every corner of the globe. As governments struggle to contain the disease, courageous individuals across the planet learn what it truly means to make choices as they struggle to survive.

Geopolitics meet technology in a race to save mankind from the worst threat it has ever faced. Doctors, military and soldiers from all walks of life battle to find a cure. For the dead walk, and if not stopped, they will wipe out all life on Earth. Humanity is fighting a war they cannot win, for who can overcome Death itself? Man versus the walking dead with the winner ruling the planet. Welcome to *The War Against Them*.

DEADTOWN: A DEADWATER STORY
BOOK 8

by Anthony Giangregorio

The world is a very different place now. The dead walk the land and humans hide in small towns with walls of stone and debris for protection, constantly keeping the living dead at bay.

Social law is gone and right and wrong is defined by the size of your gun.

UNWELCOME VISITORS

Henry Watson and his band of warrior survivalists become guests in a fortified town in Michigan. But when the kidnapping of one of the companions goes bad and men die, the group finds themselves on the wrong side of the law, and a town out for blood.

Trapped in a hotel, surrounded on all sides, it will be up to Henry to save the day with a gamble that may not only take his life, but that of his friends as well.

In a dead world, when justice is not enough, there is always vengeance.

END OF DAYS: AN APOCALYPTIC ANTHOLOGY
VOLUMES 1-3

Edited by Anthony Giangregorio

Our world is a fragile place.

Meteors, famine, floods, nuclear war, solar flares, and hundreds of other calamities can plunge our small blue planet into turmoil in an instant.

What would you do if tomorrow the sun went super nova or the world was swallowed by water, submerging the world into the cold darkness of the ocean? This anthology explores some of those scenarios and plunges you into total annihilation.

But remember, it's only a book, and tomorrow will come as it always does.

Or will it?

ETERNAL NIGHT: A VAMPIRE ANTHOLOGY
Edited by Anthony Giangregorio

Blood, fangs, darkness and terror...these are the calling cards of the vampire mythos.

Inside this tome are stories that embrace vampire history but seek to introduce a new literary spin on this longstanding fictional monster. Follow a dark journey through cigarette-smoking creatures hunted by rogue angels, vampires that feed off of thoughts instead of blood, immortals presenting the fantastic in a local rock band, to a legendary monster on the far reaches of town.

Forget what you know about vampires; this anthology will destroy historical mythos and embrace incredible new twists on this celebrated, fictional character.

Welcome to a world of the undead, welcome to the world of *Eternal Night*.

DEAD HISTORY 2
A Zombie Anthology

Edited by Anthony Giangregorio

From the dawn of mankind, the walking dead have been with us.

The greatest moments in history are not what they appear.

Through the ages, the undead have been there, only the proof has been erased, documents destroyed, and witnesses silenced.

The living dead is man's greatest secret.

In this tome, are a few of the stories of what really happened all those years ago.

History isn't alive, it's dead!

INSIDE THE PERIMETER: SCAVENGERS OF THE DEAD
by Alan Spencer

In the middle of nowhere, the vestiges of an abandoned town are surrounded by inescapably high concrete barriers, permitting no trespass or escape. The town is dormant of human life, but rampant with the living dead, who choose not to eat flesh, but to instead continue their survival by cruder means.

Boyd Broman, a detective arrested and falsely imprisoned, has been transferred into the secret town. He is given an ultimatum: recapture Hayden Grubaugh, the cannibal serial killer, who has been banished to the town, in exchange for his freedom.

During Boyd's search, he discovers why the psychotic cannibal must really be captured and the sinister secrets the dead town holds.

With no chance of escape, Broman finds himself trapped among the ravenous, violent dead. With the cannibal feeding on the animated cadavers and the undead searching for Boyd, he must fulfill his end of the deal before the rotting corpses turn him into an unwilling organ donor.

But Boyd wasn't told that no one gets out alive, that the town is a death sentence.

For there is no escape from *Inside the Perimeter*.

KINGDOM OF THE DEAD
by Anthony Giangregorio
THE DEAD HAVE RISEN!

In the dead city of Pittsburgh, two small enclaves struggle to survive, eking out an existence of hand to mouth.

But instead of working together, both groups battle for the last remaining fuel and supplies of a city filled with the living dead.

Six months after the initial outbreak, a lone helicopter arrives bearing two more survivors and a newborn baby. One enclave welcomes them, while the other schemes to steal their helicopter and escape the decaying city.

With no police, fire, or social services existing, the two will battle for dominance in the steel city of the walking dead. But when the dust settles, the question is: will the remaining humans be the winners, or the losers?

When the dead walk, the line between Heaven and Hell is so twisted and bent there is no line at all.

RISE OF THE DEAD
by Anthony Giangregorio
DEATH IS ONLY THE BEGINNING!

In less than forty-eight hours, more than half the globe was infected.

In another forty-eight, the rest would be enveloped.

The reason?

A science experiment gone horribly wrong which enabled the dead to walk, their flesh rotting on their bones even as they seek human prey.

Jeremy was an ordinary nineteen year old slacker. He partied too much and had done poorly in high school. After a night of drinking and drugs, he awoke to find the world a very different place from the one he'd left the night before.

The dead were walking and feeding on the living, and as Jeremy stepped out into a world gone mad, the dead spotting him alone and unarmed in the middle of the street,
he had to wonder if he would live long enough to see his twentieth birthday.

THE CHRONICLES OF JACK PRIMUS
BOOK ONE
by Michael D. Griffiths

Beneath the world of normalcy we all live in lies another world, one where supernatural beings exist.

These creatures of the night hunt us; want to feed on our very souls, though only a few know of their existence.

One such man is Jack Primus, who accidentally pierces the veil between this world and the next. With no other choice if he wants to live, he finds himself on the run, hunted by beings called the Xemmoni, an ancient race that sees humans as nothing but cattle. They want his soul, to feed on his very essence, and they will kill all who stand in their way. But if they thought Jack would just lie down and accept his fate, they were sorely mistaken.   He didn't ask for this battle, but he knew he would fight them with everything at his disposal, for to lose is a fate worse than death.

He would win this war, and he would take down anyone who got in his way.

LIVING DEAD
PRESS
Books to
Die For!